# A FIERCE LIGHTNING FLASH FLOODED THROUGH THE VIEWPORT . . .

A moving dot registered on the television screen. Demetrios increased magnification, and immediately the image of something incredible resolved to crystal clarity.

It was some sort of gigantic ship, a dreadnought hanging in space like a Christmas-tree ornament from hell, bristling with more spines than a sea urchin. Two particularly large pointy spines shot bouts of blue-green fire.

"Look at this," he said to the others.

"What in the world is it?"

"An alien space vessel, and it's engaged in combat with something farther away. Yes, another blip on the scanner. This one is headed our way, though. If it gets too close—"

A tremendous flash lit up the area of space around the spacetime ship.

Inside the ship, the lights flickered and went out. . . .

# DR. DIMENSION

by
John DeChancie
and
David Bischoff

A ROC BOOK

ROC
Published by the Penguin Group
Penguin Books USA Inc., 375 Hudson Street,
New York, New York 10014, U.S.A.
Penguin Books Ltd, 27 Wrights Lane,
London W8 5TZ, England
Penguin Books Australia Ltd, Ringwood,
Victoria, Australia
Penguin Books Canada Ltd, 10 Alcorn Avenue,
Toronto, Ontario, Canada M4V 3B2
Penguin Books (N.Z.) Ltd, 182–190 Wairau Road,
Auckland 10, New Zealand

Penguin Books Ltd, Registered Offices:
Harmondsworth, Middlesex, England

First published by Roc, an imprint of New American Library,
a division of Penguin Books USA Inc.

First Printing, June, 1993
10  9  8  7  6  5  4  3  2  1

This book is dedicated to these immortals:

E. E. Smith, Ph.D.

John W. Campbell, Jr.

Edmund Hamilton

Jack Williamson

September, 1939. . . .

# Chapter One

"Hand me that bastard file!"

"No need to swear, Doc."

Demetrios Demopoulos, Ph.D., pulled his frizzy graying head out of an access hatch and gave his lab assistant a sardonic leer.

"Talbot, you incredible boob. For your information a bastard file is a file of a certain grade of coarseness suitable for use on metal. There's a bit of flange on this thermocouple and I simply must file it down. So if it's not too much trouble—?"

"Oops! Sorry, Doc." Talbot moved his big athletic frame toward the toolbox. He was tall and lanky for a football player but was the best quarterback Flitheimer University had. In fact, he was the only quarterback, the starter and backup both out for the season with mononucleosis and terminal pyorrhea respectively. Troy, the third stringer, was doing fairly well, considering. He could throw a dangerous screen pass (discounting that it was sometimes dangerous for his own team). Nevertheless, Flitheimer had lost every game so far this season. But the season was still young.

"Speaking of incredible boobs," Demetrios said, "where has our pulchritudinous research assistant got to? Miss Derry!"

Diane Derry, tall and blond with cornflower-blue eyes that could melt a glacier at fifty paces, came scurrying out of the control room hugging a clipboard to the ample bosom that her white lab coat tried to hide and her tight red wool sweater voluptuously accentuated.

"Here, Dr. Demopoulos! I've got those resistor calibrations for you. I just worked them out on my slide rule."

"Good," Demetrios said, taking the file from Talbot. "As a rule, I can't resist a good slide. I'll need them in just a second, as soon as I . . . Now, let me see . . ." He passed a tremulous hand through the tangle of salt-and-pepper curls that topped his head, then adjusted his black round-rimmed spectacles, the lenses of which looked very like the bottoms of Coca-Cola bottles.

"You'd better let me handle that, Doc," Talbot warned.

"Nonsense, I'll have it fixed in a jiffy. If I can just get into position here . . ."

"Doc, you're lousy with tools. You know that."

Demetrios steadied himself on the tall ladder. "Don't trouble that handsome and mostly empty head of yours, Talbot. I'm no grease monkey, but I am a member of the order of primates, all of whom have five—count 'em—five prehensile appendages on the end of each arm, making ten fingers in all, and all of which, working together in a complex and coordinated way, are perfectly capable of manipulating tools. Tools, Talbot. Primates are tool users. So I know whereof I speak."

He leaned forward and reached inside the strange contraption, which took up most of the shoddily constructed and supposedly temporary Lab Annex of Flitheimer University's Physical Sciences Building.

"Yeah, Doc, but that doesn't mean—"

"YEEOOWWWW! *Goddammit!*"

"Skinned a knuckle, eh, Doc?"

Demetrios said quietly, "Talbot, you consummate moron, yes, I've skinned a knuckle. Any other brilliant empirical observations you'd care to make?"

Miss Derry winced in sympathy. "Does it hurt, Professor?"

"Don't be thilly," the professor mumbled around the finger he was sucking, "I jutht thcream periodically to equalithe the preththure!" He popped the finger out. "Help me down from this thing."

They eased him down the ladder. Once safely at the bottom, the distinguished physicist took a step back and, arms akimbo, surveyed the complex and sophisticated machine that was the culmination of years of dedicated scientific research and painstaking technological development.

"What a pile of shit," he said.

"Oh, no, Dr. Demopoulos, don't say that!"

"Well, it is." A sneer formed on the professor's thin lips. " 'Time machine,' my ass. This thing couldn't give you the time, much less travel in it."

"But we haven't incorporated all our latest test data yet," the pretty research assistant reminded him. "These last few adjustments might do it, Professor."

The "time machine" was in the main a copper-clad aluminum sphere, constructed of welded sections, sitting on a tripod affair of titanium struts. A few mammalian bulges—housings for various sensing and communications devices—afflicted its smooth surface here and there; its main hatch, a circular lozenge near the circumference of the sphere, hung forlornly open. Otherwise, the device was slickly futuristic in a quasi-art deco/Bauhaus/de Stijl kind of way, and very sexy indeed.

The trouble was, it didn't work.

"Hell, we've been tinkering with it for two years," Demetrios complained. "We've tried everything and it's all come to dog poop."

"It's not, Professor," Diane protested. "It's not dog poop!"

"Hound leavings! Canine fertilizer!"

"No!"

"Doggy detritus! Puppy premiums!"

"No, Doctor, please," Diane pleaded, giving him a consoling, motherly hug. "Don't belittle your tremendous accomplishment!"

"God, I'm depressed," Demetrios said and buried his face between the twin peaks of Diane's mountainous breasts. He was almost a head shorter than she, and it seemed the thing to do.

"There, there," she murmured, patting his back affectionately.

"Here, here," came his muffled reply.

"Hey, Doc, you're gonna smother yourself," Talbot put in as he climbed the ladder, bastard file in hand.

"I'll die happy," Demetrios said. "What do I give a shit."

"Don't you talk like that, Dr. D.," Diane chided gently.

Demetrios finally disengaged his face from Diane's chest. "All these years I've been waiting for the breakthrough, for the day when I could jump up and yell, 'Ευρηκα!' But all I can say to myself is, 'You idiot!' "

Dr. Demopoulos was wont to drop a Greek word now and then, as he was a great believer in ethnic pluralism and multiculturalism. He was quite ahead of his time for 1939.

"Oh, what the heck, Doc," Talbot said as he began filing the recalcitrant thermocouple. "As long as we get that grant from the Flitheimer Foundation, we'll all keep our jobs for another two years."

"Sure," Demetrios said gloomily. "Fat chance of that."

"There's always hope," Diane said reassuringly. "As the poet said, 'Hope springs eternal in the human breast.' "

"Or breasts," Demetrios said, casting a glance at Diane's bosom.

Diane went on, "If you can make a good presentation to the Flitheimers at the department meeting—"

"Old Sam and Sarah," Demetrios said, now staring gloomily at the bare concrete floor. "But it's what Sarah wants that counts. The old battle-ax runs Sam like a pony at Aqueduct. She calls the shots, and she just happens to hate my bloody guts."

"Well, Doc, you shouldn't have gone skinny-dippin' in her swimming pool at that fancy party she threw for the faculty and staff."

Demetrios shrugged. "I was drunk. Besides, the two department secretaries I got drunk with were naked, too. It was the gentlemanly thing to do."

"Mrs. Flitheimer doesn't exactly hate you," Diane said.

"She hates me exactly. It is exactly me she hates more than anyone in the world."

"Professor, that's not true!"

"No, it isn't," the professor admitted. "She hates Hitler more than me. But she hates me more than she hates Hermann Göring."

"But you're a distinguished scientist," Diane said. "She should put personal prejudice aside and award the Flitheimer Sustaining Research Grant on the basis of merit."

"She'll award it to whoever our schmuck of a department chairman says to award it to, and our schmuck of a department chairman is the pliant creature of another woman who'd like to have my gonads stuffed and mounted on a wall."

"That couldn't be Dr. Vivian Vernon, now, could it?" Talbot asked with a chuckle.

"Granted, he's engaged to Dr. Vernon," Diane said, "but I'm sure Dr. Wussman is capable of making an unbiased recommendation."

Dr. Demopoulos snapped, "Dr. Wussman couldn't make poo-poo on a potty chair without having Mother Vivian around to wipe him. She's got the grant, and that's that."

Talbot made short work of the filing and began to

bolt the small access door. "Hey, what about Dr. Cherkinov and Dr. Scheissmuller?"

The physics professor grunted. "Those two clowns. The commie and the Nazi."

Diane shook her head. "They don't have a chance. At least Scheissmuller doesn't."

"Neither do we," Dr. D. said glumly. "Not the chance of a Chinaman throwing snowballs in hell. You people had better start looking for new jobs."

"But there are other sources of grant money," Diane reminded her boss.

"There's a depression on, didn't you know? Besides, the Flitheimers own this podunk college. The trustees even changed the name of the damn place to suit 'em."

"True," Diane admitted, nodding sadly. "I liked 'Cowper College' better."

"Or 'Cowpie College,' " Talbot quipped as he climbed down again, "like the wits used to say down at the frat house."

"Robert Benchleys to a man, those frat boys," Demetrios said.

Diane gripped her mentor's arm and said earnestly, "Dr. Demopoulos, let's give it another try. Another static test run!"

Demetrios heaved his skinny shoulders. "Hey, what the hell. I've got nothing better to do."

"That's the spirit, Doc!" Troy Talbot said, encircling the diminutive physicist in thick sinewy arms and lifting him off his feet.

Demetrios winced. "What do I look like, a tackling dummy? Down, Tarzan, down."

"The department meeting is in forty-five minutes," Diane said, looking at her watch. "If you can give them positive results—"

"Yeah, sure, and pigs will start a major airline. Okay, once more unto the breach, dear friends. Let's

give it the old cow college try. I just hope we don't
soil our breaches.''

"Doctor, that's a terrible pun.''

"Just remember, I'm the brilliant scientist, you're
the beautiful assistant. Let's keep it basic.''

They all filed into the glass-fronted control room,
where Demetrios seated himself at a large console that
bristled with levers and switches. He threw a few of
these latter and watched needles pulsate on luminous
dials. His assistants took their stations at instrument
panels behind him.

"Current on!" Demetrios announced.

"Drawing two thousand volts at twelve amperes!"
Talbot reported.

"Electron multipliers activated!" Diane averred.

"Radium clock reset and running!"

"Coils at full inductance!"

"Super-heterodyne circuits engaged!"

"Rectifiers at maximum voltage!"

Demetrios, frizzy hair standing on end, stared out
through the glass as the copper-hued spherical machine began to emit a low ominous whine. From other
auxiliary equipment in the lab came the buzz of surging energies and the snap of hurtling electrons, and
with these sounds the thin-walled Lab Annex reverberated from gray slab floor to corrugated tin roof.

The whining increased in pitch until it became an
earsplitting yowl.

"Maximum thrust!" Talbot shouted above the din.

Suddenly the coppery globe became the source of
weird ionized discharges that played about its surface
like glowing spidery fingers.

"Now," the professor said, scratching his chin. "Do
I give it negative or positive polarity?" He reached
tentatively toward a switch.

"Negative means the time machine will go into the
past, positive, the future," Diane told him. "At least
that's what our equations say."

"Either that or the thing will levitate," Demetrios said. "I've never really decided whether the contraption's supposed to be a time machine or an antigravity device."

"The field equations can be solved both ways, Doctor!" Diane yelled as the lab whooped and whistled. "We've gone over that a hundred times!"

"Yeah. I wonder what would happen if I left it on positive and inverted the phase delay on the carrier voltage?"

"Dr. Demopoulos, we've never tried that!"

"We've tried everything else." He poised his finger over the push-button phase switch. "Here goes."

"But Dr. D.—!"

Demetrios's finger descended on the switch.

But before he made contact, Troy screamed, "Doc! Overload!"

There came a loud report. A spark leapt from the copper sphere to a nearby tesla coil, and gray mushroom clouds of smoke arose from both. Lightninglike spears of energy shot around the lab, making the tin walls shake and rattle. Sparks cascaded in a dazzling fireworks display.

"Throw the emergency cutoff!" Demetrios shouted.

"Gotcha, Doc!" Talbot lunged and hit the main circuit breaker.

For all his All-American reflexes, though, he was a microsecond late. The Lab Annex blew up quite nicely.

However, a split second before it did, the extremities of the spherical machine's tripod legs began, tentatively and almost imperceptibly, to lift off the concrete floor.

# Chapter Two

A terrific explosion shook the campus.

"What in heaven's name was that?"

Dr. Geoffrey Wussman, a bald, gnomish man in tweeds, whirled around on his morocco leather office chair and nearly toppled over.

Vivian Vernon, Ph.D., was sitting on the window seat with her shapely legs crossed, calmly smoking a Pall Mall in a teak cigarette holder. Diffuse afternoon sun glamorously backlighted her auburn hair.

"Just the Lab Annex blowing up," she told him after a glance out the window.

"What!" Wussman, chairman of the physics department, jumped up and rushed to the window. "That's the second time this year! I'll bet it's Demopoulos!"

"Who else? The man is a complete incompetent." Dr. Vernon blew smoke at the back of Dr. Wussman's bald, light bulb-shaped head. "You're blocking my view, Geoffrey."

"But he continually makes a shambles of that place! If we have to keep dumping money into repairs, we'll never get the permanent lab building."

"Relax," Vivian told him. "Dearest Demmy's grant source has run dry. He's strapped. He'll have to stop his experiments. Then we can clear out all his junk and the department can reclaim the Annex."

"Reclaim a wreck, you mean! That's what he's turned it into!" Dr. Wussman halted a motion of turning from the window, brought up short by an arresting sight: the hiked hemline of Dr. Vernon's tight black dress. Her long and lovely legs were exposed almost to their ultimate juncture, the enticing V of her pelvis.

Wussman felt a sudden lustful pang. "Uh . . . my dear, did I ever tell you what wonderful legs you have?"

"Many times, Geoffrey dear." She took his tie and yanked his head down. "You're sweet." She pecked his shiny bald pate.

Dr. Wussman raised his head and smiled craftily. "And when we finally get married, I'll get to see every inch of them, not just the tantalizing portion you torture me with every day."

She tweaked his nose. "Naughty boy."

He straightened and let out a sigh. "By the way, when *are* we going to get married?"

Vivian's smile was sphinxlike. "Soon, dear, soon."

"But we've been engaged for eight years."

"All good things are worth waiting for, Geoffrey dear." She looked over his sloping shoulder. "Here comes the fire brigade."

Wussman sat down and gazed out the window. "Well, I'll have to have a serious talk with Demetrios very soon. We have enough unscheduled expenses around this place. What with the Depression and the constant budget cuts, we're lucky this university still has a physics department."

"Depression or none, the Flitheimers are looking to dump more money on the university."

"I guess the department-store business must be Depression-proof."

"Perhaps Sam can be persuaded to give us a new lab building."

"Oh, how I wish!"

Vivian shot smoke across the room. "This research grant is peanuts. They have more money than they know what to do with, and all you have to do, Geoffrey dear, is show them what valuable research the department is doing.''

Dr. Wussman nodded, then seemed unsure. ''Uh . . . for instance?''

Vivian frowned. ''Why, my work on the electrodynamics of isotropic crystal formation, for instance.''

''Oh, that. You've been doing that since you were an undergrad.''

''Are you saying it's not valuable work?''

''Oh, no, of course not,'' Wussman hastened to reassure her. ''Of course it's legitimate scientific investigation and all. It's just that . . .''

Vivian frowned. ''What?''

''Well, Vivian, my pretty darling, it's just not box office.''

Scowling, Vivian took a long puff and blew smoke out the open window. ''Whatever do you mean?''

''The Flitheimers don't know anything about science, let alone solid research work in physics. They won't be impressed by something so esoteric. Now, what Demetrios is working on—well, there's something with punch.''

''His time machine?''

''His—?'' Wussman did a take. ''Time machine? He's supposed to be working on splitting the atom.''

''That would be too mundane for Demetrios. My sources tell me it's a time machine.''

''How do you know? He hasn't told anybody what he's working on.''

''Oh, I have my little ways of getting information.''

''No doubt you have, my dear. But still, time machines are a little more glamorous than crystal formations.''

Vivian tapped her cigarette out on the windowsill and rose to her full height, which was considerably more than that of the bald, homuncular Dr. Wussman. In doing so she revealed her full figure. She was a knockout in a slinky black dress, and this was not lost on her department chairman. He got to his feet and looked up into her gray-green eyes—and despaired. He gathered her in and clung to her for dear life.

"Oh, darling, it's been such a long wait," he said breathily. "Couldn't we . . . just once—"

She encircled her thin arms around his neck. "Now, Geoffrey, darling. We've restrained our passions this long. We can put it off just a bit longer." She thrust her pelvis against him. "However . . ."

Wussman's eyes widened. "However?"

She grinned wickedly. "Grant money makes me horny."

"It does?"

"Any kind of money does. And the research grant is just the start, Geoffrey dear. If we can sell the Flitheimers on the importance of pure scientific research, this department will be sitting pretty. Mrs. Flitheimer is active in politics, Geoffrey. She has no end of friends in Washington. One of them is a certain tallish, bucktoothed lady by the name of Eleanor."

"Eleanor? Uh . . . you don't mean Mrs. Roosevelt."

"The same. A war just started in Europe, Geoffrey. The U.S. could be dragged into it."

"Um . . . war?" The contents of Geoffrey's mind had surged to his soft, babylike hands, which at the moment were preoccupied with tracing the flaring convexity of Vivian's pert posterior.

"War, Geoffrey dear. Hitler invaded Poland, remember? War. Think research and development. Think of huge grants for weapons research."

"Yes . . . ummm . . . oh, yes."

"Millions of dollars' worth of grant money. More than enough to build not just a proper lab building, but . . . think of this. An institute for theoretical studies, dedicated to pure research—a temple of science—headed by Geoffrey H. Wussman, Ph.D., at a salary of no less than twenty thousand dollars per annum."

Wussman's hands ceased their roving and he looked up. "T-twenty thousand dollars a year?"

"To start, with raises every year. Why, within five years you could be making close to fifty."

"Fifty thousand? You're joking. That's a fortune."

"For the salary of the chairman of the most important scientific research outfit in the country? A pittance. Merely an honorarium."

Geoffrey lost interest in Vivian's anatomy. He stared out the window at the peaceful quadrangle, where mild autumn zephyrs fanned the flames of the burning Lab Annex.

"Chairman of the Institute for Theoretical Studies," he mused, liking the sound of it. Presently he returned to the moment and turned his head to her. "And what's in it for you, Vivian?"

"I'd be director of research," Vivian said brightly. "And of course, the wife of the chairman." She delivered a chaste peck to his stubbly cheek.

"Yes, of course. Of course . . ."

Wussman suddenly looked crestfallen. He left the window and went back to the padded swivel chair. He sat down heavily and said, "But we're getting ahead of ourselves. We haven't even convinced the Flitheimers about the tiny little sustaining grant, much less the rest of it. I know that Sarah is very skeptical about funding science. She likes the arts. Doesn't like science, she told me at a dinner party once. Too much math, too hard to understand. 'So what good is it if nobody can understand it?' she said." Wussman rolled his eyes. "What good is it! I can't believe she said that."

"Leave the silly old bag to me," Vivian said soothingly as she massaged Wussman's insignificant shoulders. "Just you leave everything to me."

Wussman heaved a sigh. "I usually do," he said glumly as he looked around the room. "You have a

nice office here, Vivian. In fact—'' He grunted. ''It's
better than mine.''

''You insisted I take the corner office on the quadrangle. Don't you remember?''

''Oh.'' Wussman nodded. ''That's right. I did indeed. Nevertheless it seems odd that the chairman of
the department wouldn't have something better than
that cubbyhole of mine.''

''Oh, you've been good to me, Geoffrey, very good.
I'm so grateful to you for looking after my career, my
needs.''

Wussman smiled again. ''Only too happy, dearest.
Only too happy. I . . . uh, by the way, whose picture
is that?''

''Which one?''

''The one right above the desk, here.''

''Oh, that's Joseph Stalin.''

''Stalin?'' Wussman stared at the black-and-white
print. ''Vivian, I know you have progressive political
beliefs, but you should be a little more discreet about
such things. After all, this is a conservative part of the
country. People might talk.''

Vivian sneered. ''To hell with people and their little
bourgeois minds. Joseph Stalin is a great man. He's
led his country from serfdom to mass industrialization
in less than two decades. And he's a great supporter
of science. Why, only last week I was reading about
the great new discoveries made by their leading biol-
ogist, a man by the name of Lysenko—''

''Still, darling, you must be a bit more careful about
such things.'' Wussman eyed the heroic portrait of the
mustachioed Communist leader. ''Imposing man, I'll
grant you. Though I wouldn't want him staring down
at me that way.''

''I rather like it,'' Vivian told him. ''It gives me a
sense of security, of someone watching over me.''

''Stern old blighter. A father figure, perhaps?''

"No," Vivian answered, gazing at the portrait. "More like . . . a big brother."

"I don't know that I'd like my big brother always watching me either," Wussman said. "Nevertheless, if it comforts you . . ."

Miss Pelverton, Wussman's secretary, stuck her bunned head in the door to announce, "The Flitheimers have arrived, Professor. They're in the conference room now."

"Thank you, Elaine." Wussman waited till the door closed to add, "God, I hate running an outfit with a tin cup. All scientific endeavor should be financed by the government."

"That's definitely on the agenda, Geoffrey sweetest." Vivian kissed his glossy cranium, then playfully nuzzled the nape of his neck.

Eyelids at half-mast, Wussman gave a little coo of pleasure. "Vivian, you're such a tease. You really are."

She blew in his ear and said, "You love it, you filthy slave slut."

"God, don't start, Vivian. I'll want you to get into your leathers, and we don't have time."

"Who's Vivian's little love slave? Hmmm?"

"Please, dear, not now—"

She grabbed a hank of his scraggly graying hair and pulled. "Who'll do his mistress's every bidding and love it?"

"Ouch! Oh, God, me, me."

"Hmmm? Who'll get down on his chubby little knees, if his mistress tells him to, and eat dog food out of his big dirty doggy dish?"

"Me. I will."

She whacked his head with the flat of her hand. "You're damn right you will, you worthless piece of shit!"

"Vivian, the riding crop!"

She grinned. "You kinky pet. No, as you said, we

have the Flitheimers to deal with. To dominate. Besides, what would Miss Pelverton think?''

Wussman slumped. "I suppose you're right. Tonight?''

"A special session," she whispered hotly into his ear. "Fifteen extra minutes of house training, and then you hightail it home like a good little puppy.''

"I'll be there, dearest Vivian. Mistress Vivian.''

Vivian straightened her dress, adopted a primly sober mien, then strode toward the door.

"Come along, Geoffrey." When she reached the door she stopped and looked back. "What's wrong, Geoffrey?''

Wussman was daydreaming out the window again. He turned. "Hm? Nothing. Nothing's wrong. In fact, I've been inspired.''

"Inspired.''

"Yes.'' Wussman slapped the shiny top of Vivian's oiled walnut desk. "Yes! Tell Miss Pelverton to fetch me some art materials from the press. White illustration board, pencils, my pastels—''

Vivian was puzzled. "Whatever are you up to?''

"I always wanted to be an artist, you know. Have I ever told you?''

"Geoffrey, dear, you've shown me your oil paintings any number of times. Frankly—no offense—you don't have a whole lot of talent.''

"My parents didn't believe I had talent either. Refused to send me to art school, they did. One day, perhaps, I'll be able to prove them wrong. Meantime, I have enough of a flair for the visual to do the kind of thing we need—'' Wussman opened a desk drawer and rifled through it. "You have any blank paper?''

"Lower left," Vivian told him.

"Tell Pelverton to get me that stuff, and then go stall the Flitheimers. I'll work as fast as I can.''

"But, Geoffrey, they're waiting.''

"Go!'' he commanded.

Astonished, Vivian left to do his bidding. She'd rarely seen him like this.

A benign fall breeze on his back, Dr. Geoffrey Wussman began hurriedly to sketch his daydreams.

# Chapter Three

The campus fire brigade got the blaze out in short order.

Lab coat smudged and torn, Dr. Demopoulos surveyed the damage.

The gigantic tesla coil was still standing but had turned into a tower of twisted metal. Above it yawned a gaping hole, blackened and charred around the edges, that the blast had punched in the corrugated metal roof of the Annex.

Much equipment had been damaged or lost to the flames, but fortunately the time machine's exterior had survived unscathed save for some scorching along the underside. The strange machine's deliverance was a stranger turn of events, for it had seemed the focal point of the conflagration. Dr. Demopoulos gave some thought to this puzzle. Perhaps the machine had been partially shielded by the truncated wall of sandbags that the professor had bade Troy stack up against a real emergency. However, Troy had barely begun the job; thus, the mystery remained. The machine's exterior was one story, the interior another. Although fire damage inside the vessel was minimal, virtually all the electronic gear had burnt out. The ship was a useless hulk.

The fire chief chuckled as he walked past, trailing a length of still-dripping hose. "Good job this time, Doc."

"Thanks, Callahan. Next time I'll provide the weenies."

Callahan exited, laughing.

Troy slapped him on the shoulder. "Don't you worry, Professor. We'll get her working again."

Demetrios scratched his chin. "Sure, but what the hell is it? A time machine or an antigravity device?"

"Heck, Doc, that's a spaceship," Talbot stated.

"It's a time machine," Diane retorted.

"It's a spaceship!"

"It's a time machine!"

"Spaceship!"

"Time machine!"

"Spaceship!"

"You know, I hate like hell to bring up the obvious," Demetrios interjected, "but have you twits considered the possibility that it might be both?"

"Huh?" Talbot said, scratching his crew-cut head. "Doc, you've gone plumb loco."

"Come-a ti-yi-yippee yippyay, pardner. Maybe I have."

"No, he's right!" Diane said, comprehension dawning in her cerulean peepers. "It's both. It's a space-time ship!"

"Give the little lady a Kewpie doll. Yes, children, it's two—"

"Two?" Troy said dubiously.

"Two contraptions in one."

"Of course!" Diane exclaimed. "According to Einstein's special theory of relativity, time is merely one dimension of space—the fourth dimension! If the machine can travel in time, it can travel in space, too."

"And vice versa," Dr. Demopoulos added, "though you only notice it at relativistic velocities. Anyway . . ." He trailed off into deep thought.

"Wow, this is great!" Talbot enthused. "Once we get it working, we could go anywhere in this thing!"

"Or anywhen," Diane said. "Anyplace or anytime in the whole spacetime continuum."

"But the problem is controlling the craft and knowing where the heck you're going," Demetrios replied distractedly, still lost in deep cogitation.

"Hey, Doc, you got any ideas about that?" Talbot asked. "About navigation and that kinda stuff?"

"Don't bother me, I'm lost in deep cogitation."

"Oh, sorry."

Diane glanced at her watch and was dismayed. "The meeting!"

Demetrios was jogged out of his reverie. "Eh?"

"The department meeting with the Flitheimers. They've probably started already."

"Oh." Demetrios seemed uninterested. "Yeah. I'll get right over there." He began to walk away slowly.

Diane urged, "Hurry, Professor!"

"Yeah, sure."

Talbot asked Diane, "What the heck is spacetime?"

"Well," Diane began, "There was this fellow named Einstein . . ."

Demetrios wandered off, still in thrall to creative ratiocination.


Sam Flitheimer, large of bone and shiny of head, puffed on a big Cuban cigar. His dark suit was conservative and his smile seemed perpetual.

Mrs. Flitheimer was compact and cylindrical. No matter where you measured her circumference below the neck—shoulders, bust, midriff, waist, hips—it looked to be the same. Her hair was unnaturally red and cropped modishly short. She wore a flashy diamond necklace. Her dress looked fresh from the fall line of one of New York's fashionable and expensive Fifth Avenue clothing stores. In fact, most of her wardrobe had come from New York's Seventh Avenue, wholesale. Her shoes matched her dress. Besides a gold wedding band, she wore no less than four rings:

two diamond, an emerald, and a ruby. Her bracelets were eighteen-karat gold, as were her earrings.

"Science is so . . . inhuman," Mrs. Flitheimer said. "I don't like it. It's mathematical, cold. I like warm things. Human things."

"She likes those sissy dancers at the ballet," Mr. Flitheimer said.

"Sam, don't show your lack of culture."

"What culture? A bunch of skinny women up on their toes, with sissy boys picking them up and handing them around. Culture shmulture."

"My husband doesn't appreciate the finer things," Mrs. Flitheimer apologized to the assembled staff of the physics department. "He doesn't know from culture, art, refinement. He can't appreciate. All he knows from is making money."

"Which you like to spend on fairy dancers."

"Hush." Mrs. Flitheimer glanced at her eighteen-karat gold Swiss jeweled-movement wristwatch. "What's keeping Dr. Wussman?"

"He should be along any minute," Vivian prevaricated, herself at a loss to explain the delay. "He had some last-minute work to do on his presentation."

"Oh, I didn't know we were supposed to see a presentation," Sarah said. "Slides, maybe?"

"Uh, no, not that I know of. I think—"

The door to the conference room opened and in walked Geoffrey Wussman, a single large rectangle of illustration board under his left arm. He came to the table, laid the board down, and took his seat.

"Sorry, folks, sorry. Got a little behind schedule." Wussman's small face, at once cherubic and elfin, erupted into a gushy smile. "Mr. and Mrs. Flitheimer. So *nice* to see you both."

"Same here," Sam said good-naturedly.

Mrs. Flitheimer smiled briefly.

"Uh, did I miss anything?" Wussman asked of the table at large.

"My wife was just saying how she likes culture and ballet and that stuff. Science, you can stuff up your kiester."

"Sam!" The missus was indignant. "I said no such thing!"

Sam appealed to the assembled academics. "Isn't that what she said? Huh? Am I lyin' or what?"

"I certainly didn't put it in those terms! All I said was that I like the finer things of life. That's what I think is important. Science gives us many great things, like medicine and surgery and doctors—my eldest son is a doctor, you know. A urologist."

"He has a great practice, believe me," Sam corroborated. "You pee in a cup. He gives you a pill and hands you a bill. Better racket than the one I'm in." He guffawed.

"Sam, please! Like I was saying, science gives us many good things, but I think our civilization prizes it a little too highly. There are other things, higher, better things than material comforts."

"This from a woman who won't stay at a hotel in Miami unless the room is chilled like the inside of a refrigerator!"

"The heat aggravates my psoriasis."

"Then don't knock science and technology."

"So who's knocking," the missus shouted. "I'm simply saying that culture and ballet—"

"Ah—please, Mrs. Flitheimer," Wussman broke in, "if we could get this discussion on track. Forgive me." He cleared his throat and continued: "There is much to be said for culture—and ballet is certainly a wonderful example of sensitive and refined emotional expression—but I don't think that ballet is going to fuel our national engines of progress. And we certainly don't want to throw youngsters in tights and tutus against the Hun—if, God forbid, we have to participate in a war in Europe."

Dr. Karlheinz Scheissmuller, nuclear physics specialist and gray eminence in wire-rimmed spectacles, glowered a bit but said nothing. As far as anyone knew, he had no political opinions. In fact, he believed that Germany should rule the world because of its obvious scientific superiority. However, he knew it was best to keep mum.

Especially when there was grant money on the hoof and you had half a prayer of snagging it.

Scheissmuller turned to regard his Russian colleague, Dr. Kirill Vasilyevich Cherkinov, toward whom he had been feeling grudgingly more tolerant since the Führer had signed a Non-Aggression Pact with the Soviet Union.

Cherkinov, specialist in the physics of chemical processes, was a handsome man with jet-black hair and a dancer's lithe but disciplined body. He eyed his German counterpart askance. Cherkinov's dark eyes had moistened with the mention of ballet, remembering his failed audition with the Bolshoi; but he, too, remained silent. Nowadays his dreams were more practical. He wished to continue the work of his uncle Sergei Sakhnovsky, killed in the Russian civil war (fighting for the Whites). Uncle Sergei had studied the chemistry of vodka distillation, with an eye on creating alternative fuels. Because of faculty cutbacks, Dr. Cherkinov also taught freshman organic chemistry, and his classes were popular among the university's fraternity men.

"Hear, hear!" squeaked Dr. Amos Pudwicker, enthusing over Dr. Wussman's comments, his white mustache bristling. The elderly Pudwicker, who taught classical Newtonian physics and was a secret collector of women's silk underthings (some pre-owned, in a manner of speaking), had long been convinced that relativity and quantum theory were a plot to screw him out of a job. Both had come out of Germany—as had that horrid synthetic substance, nylon!—and he was all for a war against Germany just to rid the world of insidious Teutonic pseudoscience.

"Dr. Wussman is right," exclaimed Dr. Vivian Vernon, proffering a tray of sweets to the rich folks. "The Nazis are a threat to the world. Sample my homemade chocolate chip cookies, Mr. Flitheimer?" She set the tray on the table and surreptitiously ran a hand down Mr. Flitheimer's broad back in a way that was quite open to interpretation. Sam smiled up at her.

"Don't mind if I do!" said Mrs. Flitheimer, reaching in front of her husband to help herself. "You have a point about Nazis, dear. They're monsters!" She took two cookies, cramming one into her mouth, keeping it busy on nonverbal chores, which Dr. Vernon was glad to see. Vivian was also gratified to have scored a point with her.

Spying an opening, Dr. Wussman began his spiel.

"We're so happy you've decided to make a contribution to the welfare of the department, and therefore to the university and to science, not to mention—"

"It's all my husband's idea," Sarah Flitheimer said through a mouthful of cookie.

"You got that right," Sam said, complacently puffing away on his cigar.

"Uh, yes, certainly . . . uh—" Wind spilled from Geoffrey's rhetorical sails. "The money will certainly be put to good use. We haven't quite decided how to spend it yet—however, use it wisely we certainly will."

"Frankly, I couldn't care less what you do with it," the missus said. "Who made these cookies? My, they're good."

"Thank you!" Vivian said, beaming.

"You? Oh. What's a woman doing in the physics department, anyway? Physics isn't a woman's profession. It isn't feminine."

Vivian pasted a smile over clenched teeth.

Wussman continued, "I'd like to broaden this discussion a little, and talk about some long-range goals.''

Sam's right eyebrow arched. "Long-range goals?''

"Yes. I'd like to talk about the future of this department and the future of Flitheimer University—about the choices we make now, and how these will affect revenues in years to come, especially as regards government funding of scientific research.''

"I guess that's pretty important,'' Sam allowed. He looked bored.

"Right you are, Mr. Flitheimer. Let me dwell for a moment here''—a wistful smile spread across Wussman's face—"on my dreams.''

"Dreams, eh?'' Sam said with a hint of interest.

"Yes. I want to show you something. I believe, Mrs. Flitheimer, that this will also appeal to your admirable sense of esthetics.''

"Mmph,'' said Mrs. Flitheimer skeptically through a mouthful of her second mammoth chocolate chip cookie.

Dr. Wussman tilted up the illustration board. On it he had sketched his vision in a burst of rushed inspiration not ten minutes ago.

"A temple of science! The Institute for the Study of Physical Theory. A hallowed institution that will be not only a testimony to pure science but will also serve as an inspiration to the people of the world, a shining example, a beacon of enlightenment, proving that America is good for other things besides . . . well, besides making cars and air conditioners and radios and other petty material distractions! It will attract the best scientific talent from all over the globe.''

Wussman's hasty architectural rendering, in charcoal and pastel, portrayed a clutch of buildings done in a hodgepodge of pseudoclassical styles, surrounded by sweeping lawns and formal gardens.

"Oh, my,'' was the reaction from Sarah Flitheimer.

Then she frowned. Actually, the buildings were massive and rather ugly.

"Now remember, this is just a preliminary sketch," Wussman hastened to add. "An architect could do wonders with just the ideas I've doodled here. But I trust you get the general drift?"

"Yup," Sam said, nodding. "More expensive buildings. We've been noodged into building five of 'em on this campus so far."

"Yes, I know. The School of Performing Arts, the new Student Union, the Center for Humanitarian and Altruistic Studies—"

"Yeah, the Board of Trustees did a pretty good job of setting me up in the construction business—with my money, of course. Trouble is, buildings don't get to me."

"Don't get to you?" Wussman said.

"Don't get to me, don't reach me—here, in my *pupik*," Sam said, jabbing a thumb into his protruding belly. "I can't get excited about bricks and mortar."

"Oh, well." Wussman began to look a little uncomfortable. "But you haven't heard my ideas about what we'll study at this new facility. Mrs. Flitheimer, you'd be very interested to hear my theories about the merging of art and science, of esthetics and physics."

"That does sound unusual," Mrs. Flitheimer conceded.

"For instance, take the study of human kinematics."

"Uh-huh," Flitheimer said dubiously, working that big cigar around in his mouth, perplexed.

Sarah Flitheimer's face formed a petulant moue. "What in the world is that thing you said?"

"Kinematics," said Dr. Cherkinov, "is the study of pure motion."

"Exactly!" Wussman said. "Thank you, Kirill. It's a discipline that easily includes the physics of dance movement. Ballet, Mrs. Flitheimer. Can you see how the rigorous demands of science can be softened to include the investigation of something more human than atoms or galaxies?''

''I see,'' said Mrs. Flitheimer, her interest piqued the tiniest bit.

''Human kinematics!'' said Vivian Vernon. ''To say *nothing* of the electrodynamics of isotropic crystal formation!''

''Uh, yes,'' Wussman said, narrowing his eyes at Vivian.

''I wish you had something I could get really excited about,'' Sam lamented.

Just then the door crashed open. A burly, wild-haired figure hurtled through, waving his arms wildly. ''Stop the meeting! Stop the meeting!''

''What on earth's wrong?'' an alarmed Dr. Wussman asked, rising from his chair.

Dr. Demopoulos grinned impishly. ''The pizza came and I don't have enough to tip the delivery boy. Everybody pony up!'' He snagged Dr. Scheissmuller's alpine fedora from the hat rack and tossed it onto the table.

Wussman sank to his seat. ''Demetrios, please. We're having a serious discussion here. By the way, you look a mess.''

''Not to worry, this is my old lab coat. Ah, Mr. and Mrs. Flitheimer. What bamboozle has Niels Bohring, here, been trying to put over on you?''

''Hi, Demetrios!'' Sam Flitheimer said brightly. ''Hey, when you gonna come over for a swim party again?''

''Anytime, Sam. Hi, Sarah! How's tricks?''

Sarah was not amused.

''Dr. Demopoulos.'' Vivian Vernon greeted the intruder with tray in hand. ''Cookies? Milk?'' Under her breath she added, ''Hemlock?''

''Hi, Viv! Castrated anyone lately?'' Dr. Demopoulos brushed past his rival, making sure to give her a nice backhanded squeeze on the rump.

"Not so you'd notice," Vivian said casually.

Mrs. Flitheimer could only stare up at this dark apparition, half-eaten cookie in one hand, a darkly disapproving frown on her pale brow.

Mr. Flitheimer, on the other hand, seemed rather glad for the intrusion. "Actually," he said, "we've just agreed to fund a physics institute."

"No, we haven't," his wife countered. "We've agreed to study ballet. And human numismatics."

"To coin a phrase," Demopoulos said. "Anyway, you're not far wrong, Sarah honey. Thought I heard the jingle of pocket change." He winked at Dr. Wussman.

"Now see here, Demetrios," Wussman huffed. "Our project is academically and scientifically progressive and sound." Proudly, he held up the illustration board with its Greco-Roman approximations.

Dr. Demopoulos grabbed it away and held it up to the slant of afternoon light from the window, subjecting it to his withering critical eye. "What's this? Hm. Okay, I'll bite. You're starting a chain of casinos. Or brothels catering to pederasts. Which is it?"

"Dr. Demopoulos, really." Wussman was decidedly miffed.

Tossing the illustration board onto the table, Demetrios took an empty seat and slumped into it. "I'm pooped."

"You look a little ragged, Demmy," Sam observed. "What happened? Anything to do with all the fire alarms?"

"I had an argument with the Second Law of Thermodynamics. The law won. It was nothing, just a little altercation."

Flitheimer took the cigar from his mouth and leaned over the table, curiosity on his face. "What are you working on?"

"A time machine."

Sam Flitheimer's jaw dropped. "Huh?"

"Yup. Or a spaceship. Maybe an antigravity device."

"Well, I'll be. No kiddin'?"

"No kidding, Sam. Trouble is, it doesn't work all that well, yet."

"Does it work at all?"

"Well, we really haven't tested it properly."

"Spaceship! Or a time machine. Now, there's something I could sink my teeth into."

"And get into your *pupik*," Vivian grumbled under her breath.

"It'll be great if I can get it to work," Demetrios went on. "I'd win the Nobel. Edison, Tesla, Marconi, et al., forget it. Those guys were pikers. This is bigger than anything they ever did."

"Who's Ed Al?" Mrs. Flitheimer asked.

Dr. D. ignored her. "Mr. Flitheimer, is that your Lincoln Zephyr in the parking lot? The maroon one with the gleaming chrome hubcaps and the 'Alf Landon for President' bumper sticker?"

"Yeah, that's my car."

"Then, sir, you are a reader of scientific romances in the manner of H. G. Wells and Jules Verne. Maybe Buck Rogers, too."

Sam chortled. "And you're a bit of Sherlock Holmes, too. How'd you deduce that?"

"Actually there's a copy of the latest issue of *Incredible Tales of Super-Science* in the back seat. But when I espied it, I thought to myself—ah! Now there's a man who will appreciate a bit of super-science."

"I've been an *Incredible Tales* reader for years, you're right. In fact, I read all the scientific pulps."

"He stays up all night sometimes," Mrs. Flitheimer complained. "Reading and reading."

"What else do I get to do in bed besides sleep?"

"Sam, you're being such a bad one."

"Let me guess, Dr. Demopoulos," Dr. Vernon said with biting sarcasm. "You're starting your own cheap pulp magazine. *Mad Scientist Monthly?*"

"Splendid idea, Dr. Viv," Demopoulos said with a big grin, "but no . . . no . . . I have something in mind far more exciting. Something that will blow the lid off of science as we know it! Something that will not only move our minds and imaginations to outer space, but"—the doctor pointed his finger upward as though the region alluded to was hovering just above the ivy-covered walls of academe—"beyond. We are about to participate in a great adventure. We are about to . . . experience something."

Vivian rolled her eyes in disgust. "Experience what?"

Demopoulos rose and went to the open window. A tangy fall breeze stirred the graying mop that crowned his head. "The awe, the mystery, that reaches from the inner mind to—" He shrugged and gestured vaguely out the window. "Out there somewhere, you know."

"To travel in space, in time!" Sam Flitheimer was transported. "To go where no man has gone before!"

"Boldly!" Dr. D. shouted, turning and pointing a finger at him. "To *boldly* go where no man has gone before. And no tomato either."

" 'To go boldly,' " Wussman corrected. "You're splitting the infinitive."

"It's *infinity* that I want to sunder—by Krono's brazen ballocks!"

"How vulgar," Vivian muttered.

"What a journey that would be," Sam said, shaking his head in awestruck envy.

"But it's a journey not only of distance. We'll strike off in a different direction altogether. A new dimension."

Now Sam was really impressed. "Travel into other dimensions, too? Gosh, you got the whole *mishegoss* working. What dimension? The fourth?"

Dr. D. began to pace, circling the table, hands clasped at his back. "Something tells me there's another dimension, a fifth dimension, beyond that which is known to man."

"No kiddin'? What kind of dimension is it?"

"It's a dimension not only of sight and sound but of mind."

"Mind?" Wussman said. He smiled toothily at Mrs. Flitheimer. "A novel concept. He has quite an imagination."

"I know what kind of imagination he's got," Mrs. F. said. "Pure filth, that's what. A regular Don Ron."

Wussman looked embarrassed. "Tell us more about this new Demetrios, dimension . . . uh, dimension, Dem—"

"What do I know about it, weasel face? I haven't been there. All I know is that it's as vast as space and timeless as infinity. It's some sort of middle ground between light and shadow, between . . ."

"Science and superstition?" Cherkinov suggested.

"Yes! Reaching from the pit of man's fears to the something something . . . I'll have to work on that for the proposal—anyway, it'll be the greatest adventure anyone's ever undertaken. I just hope I don't wind up at the undertaker's. Ye gods, maybe I am mad."

Dr. Demopoulos halted and shook his head, suddenly fretful.

"I think it's great!" Sam Flitheimer enthused. "When do we start?"

Geoffrey Wussman was at great pains to realign himself and regain credibility. "Why, he's already started. Haven't you, Dr. Demopoulos?"

"Huh? Oh, yeah. Well, we've had a few dry runs, and then that little contretemps when I reversed phase.

Or did I reverse polarity? No, phase. Though I forget if I actually hit the switch or not. Happened so fast—''

Geoffrey noticed Vivian's smoldering eyes and felt their hot gaze. But it was obvious that Dr. D. had Flitheimer hooked, and Geoffrey was eager to help him reel the big capitalist fish in. ''Why, with the research grant, you could make repairs and try again. Uh—couldn't you, Demetrios?''

Demetrios suddenly despaired. ''Ah, it's useless. As it is now, the machine's a pile of scrap. Maybe it'll never work.''

''Don't be so hard on yourself. Don't give up.''

''Perhaps we should take Dr. Demopoulos at his word,'' Vivian said carefully, cloaking her rising alarm and anger. ''Maybe the time machine-spaceship is a device whose time has not yet come.''

''Thanks for that vote of confidence, Vivian. Hell, it could work. It just hasn't so far.''

Sam said, ''Exactly how is this contraption of yours supposed to work, Doc? Does she have rockets?''

''No, sir,'' Demetrios said. ''That would be a rocket ship. There are in fact propulsion systems in my vessel modeled on the brilliant work of Dr. Robert Goddard—but these are only used to orient the ship along its axes and maneuver short distances. No, what the ship does essentially is to take the very fabric of space and time—the whole multidimensional geometry of existence, as delineated by such lights as Hilbert, Riemann, and Einstein—''

''Eewww!'' Dr. Pudwicker said at mention of the dreaded E-word.

''—and warp, bend, and fold it in such a way as to keep the ship constantly sliding down the near side of a moving depression, a sort of mobile dimple in the continuum. The slick thing is that this dimple can move faster than the speed of light, since it's nonmaterial. Are you getting the picture?'' Demetrios stopped pacing and thought. "Either that or the ship turns quantum-uncertain and propagates itself through the interstellar medium like a wave."

"But the Michelson-Morley experiment demonstrated that there was no medium, no 'ether,' " Wussman insisted. "Einstein said—"

Dr. Pudwicker let out a moan.

"Forget Einstein!" Dr. Demopoulos exclaimed. "This is beyond Einstein, beyond anything we know."

"But how does zis machine vork?" Scheissmuller demanded.

"I don't know," Demopoulos admitted. "But I'm pretty sure . . . well, I'm not *real* sure. It's highly probable that it . . ." He thought a moment, then said, "Well, it's not *highly* probable—"

"*Gott in Himmel!* Iss zere anysing you do know?"

"Not much. But I think the time machine angle may be moot, as we have it configured now. I'd say the odds are on the spaceship side, with maybe some dimension stuff going on as a sideline."

"Do you really think the thing will travel into space, Demetrios?" Wussman wanted to know.

"Think of the market possibilities," Flitheimer mused.

Demetrios pointed to Sam. "Need I say more? I mean, isn't a market economy what America's all about?"

"You've conveniently omitted saying anything about feasibility of this machine of yours," Dr. Pudwicker sniffed. "Which seems to me is quite close to nil."

"Yes, Demopoulos," Dr. Cherkinov broke in. "Is true or not true, Lab Annex was blowink up"—he pulled out a pocket watch—"exactly one hour ago?"

"The professor, in fact, is sometimes called 'Dr. Dangerous' by his students," Dr. Vernon tattled. "They duck under their desks when he starts a lab demonstration."

" 'Dr. Dangerous.' " Demetrios considered it. "I kind of like that. But from now on my name will be . . ."

Everyone waited as Demetrios brainstormed.

"Well?" said Vivian.

Dr. D. snapped his fingers. " 'Dr. . . . Space Guy! No. Dr. . . . um, let me see."

"Dr. Dimwit," Vivian suggested.

"Kindly drop dead, Viv, darling. I'll think of something later. Meanwhile, let's not quibble about a little damage."

" 'A *little* damage,' " Wussman chided. "Come now, Demetrios."

"What's a small explosion between friends? Hm? Hey, you can't make a scientific omelet without breaking the occasional cosmic egg, or burning a few Bunsens."

"The Lab Annex is in shambles," Vivian reminded him.

"Nonsense, there's just this huge gaping hole in it. True, most of the roof's gone. But we can fix it, we can fix it. Besides . . . I hesitate to report this, since the findings are rather preliminary—"

"What findings?" Wussman asked.

"We got positive results right before things got dicey."

"Positive results? You mean the thing started to work before the explosion?"

"Well, it lifted off the ground for a second or two."

"Oh." Wussman looked disappointed. "A second or two."

Scheissmuller asked pointedly. "Do you haff recordings of zese results?"

Dr. Demopoulos's shoulders slumped. "Nah. The recording instruments burned out and all the paper tape was lost in the fire. I saw the ship rise, though. I think. On second thought, it could have been due to blast effects."

"Und zat is vhat you call positive results? Bah!"

"All the same," Sam Flitheimer said, "I think it's great. It's a project with some guts to it. I *like* it."

"I hate it," Sarah said. "From me, he won't get money."

"Well, from me he'll get it, then. Out of my own pocket. To heck with the Foundation. How much do you figure you'll need, Doc?"

Demetrios sat down again, lifted a pen from Cherkinov's breast pocket, and started scribbling on the back of Dr. Wussman's architectural maunderings.

"Really, Sam, like this I've never seen you before."

"*Nu?* Like this I should be more often!"

Dr. Vernon rose from her seat, visions of temples evaporating along with promotions and salary increases, to say nothing of her career in the overview. She flapped her hand, as though shooing away all the foregoing nonsense like a puff of noxious gas. "Whoa, gentlemen. Aren't we . . . aren't we jumping to conclusions here? I mean, Mr. Flitheimer—you're simply going to hand this lunatic a wad of money because he claims to have some gadget that can work miracles?"

Sam shrugged. "Why not? I got nothing better to do with my money."

"You can feed the hungry and shelter the homeless!"

"I've fed the hungry like nobody's business. I got three soup kitchens and one flophouse named after me. I give to charity. Oy, do I give. I'd like to do something else for a change. After all, it *is* my money."

"Money that you—" Vivian prudently bit off her anticapitalist jibe. "Yes, yes, I see. But you mustn't waste it on obvious crackpottery—on this . . . this Rube Goldberg contraption he's talking about. When you ask him how it works, all he gives you is gobbledygook!"

"And what about the automatics of ballet?" Mrs. Flitheimer complained.

There came a murmur of sympathetic agreement from the other physicists.

"Well," grumbled Flitheimer. "I suppose I should at least get a gander at this machine before I make any commitments."

Dr. Wussman said, "Perhaps another test run might be in order, after repairs are effected. I'm sure Dr. Demopoulos would be amenable. Right, Demetrios? Um, Demetrios?"

Dr. D. looked up from his figuring. "What? Hey, anybody know what nine times eight is?"

"Seventy-two," Wussman told him.

"Right. Okay, Sam, looks like four hundred bucks ought to do it."

"Four hundred dollars?" Sam was incredulous.

"Yeah. Wait, throw in another fifty for a new magneto. I don't think my lab assistant can fix the old one."

"Nonsense!" Vivian felt her grip on the entire situation slipping, slipping. . . "This is ridiculous! Absurd!"

"Too much? Okay, I can get by with just the four hundred. I'll beat up on Talbot and get him to fix the magneto. Actually, I'll settle for three-fifty."

"Too low, Demetrios," Sam insisted. "Look, from what you said, it'll take an even thousand just to get that lab back into shape. What if we make it—oh, say, four thousand instead of four hundred?"

A collective gasp went up from the assembled dons of natural philosophy.

"Four *thousand*?" Wussman whispered.

"Make it five," Sam said, nodding. "Yeah. That's more respectable for a spaceship-building project."

"Done and done!" Dr. Demetrios Demopoulos leapt to this feet and extended a hand to Sam Flitheimer. "Thanks, Sam."

"My pleasure. When you figure to get this gizmo of yours working?"

"Hard to say, Sam, hard to say. Maybe in a year or two. Maybe three."

"Or four or five," Vivian said helpfully. "Or more."

"Nah, three ought to do it."

Sam appeared mildly disappointed. "Oh. Well, I guess a thing this important takes time."

"But if we don't stop for coffee—I'd like to be ready for another static test within a week."

"A week? Say, that'd be fine. If you don't mind, I'd like to watch."

"That you shall, Sam."

Vivian said, "And of course the grant award will be contingent on an on-site inspection of the experiment."

"I suppose that's only fair," Wussman agreed.

Dr. D. wailed, "But I'll need the dough to fix the thing!"

"Why don't we trot over to the damaged lab and have a look now?" Vivian said. "All we have is your word that this improbable contraption even exists."

For the first time, the bluff Dr. D. seemed to have his bluff called. He opened and closed his mouth a few times like a fish out of water before temporizing, "Well, I don't think it's *quite* ready for public viewing."

"Just as I thought," Vivian said with smug satisfaction. "Lots of talk, but when asked to produce—nothing. How like a man."

"Demetrios, I'll have my secretary deliver the four hundred tomorrow morning," Flitheimer said. "*That* much I can get out of petty cash."

"Thanks, Sam!"

Flitheimer rose. "Well, we have to be moving along. Dr. Wussman, thanks for your fine presentation."

Wussman rose, came around the table, and pumped Sam's hand. "Only too happy."

"I'm not happy," Sarah said as she stalked out of the room.

Talking and laughing heartily, Sam and Dr. Demopoulos followed her out.

When the door shut Wussman cleared his throat and began, ''Well, I think we've all learned something today—''

''Oh, shut up!'' Vivian snarled.

She picked up the cookie tray and threw it at him.

# Chapter Four

From the time he could first remember, Delmore Demetrios Dunhill Demopoulos (Greek immigrant father, disowned Eastern Seaboard heiress mother who gave up a fortune and social standing for love) had wanted to roam the universe. As a child he had looked up from his pram in Bird-in-Hand, Pennsylvania, and gibbered in wonder at the sky even as he soiled his diapers. As a toddler his head was always in the clouds while his hand seemed always on the nanny's breast. (His father was a self-made man who had amassed a fortune in strip mining, bootlegging, scrap metal, and homeopathic medicine, and therefore could afford a full staff of servants for his beautiful Lancaster County estate.)

However, Demetrios's youth was not all daydreams and fantasy. Little Demmy (as his father called him, and no one ever called him Delmore) was forever playing with blocks, mechanical toys, and the Victorian equivalent of an Erector set, all gifts from his father, who had been trained as an engineer. However, little Demmy was forever skinning his knuckles trying to put things together; and one day, in a fit of rage, he took a balpeen hammer from the garage and smashed the shit out of all those little electric motors, blocks-and-tackle, miniature winches, and thingamabobs.

Demmy's father saw that the child had no future as a mechanic, much less as an engineer. Stavros Demopoulos, however, knew he had a bright son, and made sure, when it came time for college, that Demetrios got the best education money could buy.

Unfortunately, this ended up being literally true. It took a big bribe to get Demmy into the Frick Institute of Technology, after MIT, Cal Tech, and several other prestigious schools turned him down flat. Demetrios had daydreamed and frittered away his high school career, and his grade transcript reflected it. His aptitude test scores, on the other hand, were almost off the scale. The dean of admissions of Frick Tech took this mitigating factor into account when he decided to admit Demetrios on probation. He then cashed the huge check that Stavros had slipped him.

Demetrios turned over a new leaf. He worked hard during his undergraduate years and finally made it into Cal Tech for graduate work in applied physics. Although he had learned to keep his distractions to a minimum, every so often he would lapse into diurnal reveries about exploring the stars. He took all the undergraduate courses in astronomy and astrophysics that FIT had to offer and audited some grad courses at Cal Tech.

He worked so hard, in fact, that he didn't think about sex very much—rather he thought about it no more than six or seven times a day—which was saying a great deal for Delmore (maternal grandfather's given name) Demetrios (paternal grandfather's given name) Dunhill (mom's maiden name) Demopoulos, especially with attractive co-eds milling about all through his undergraduate years.

For all his love of women, however—or perhaps because of it—Demetrios never married.

Female grad assistants in physics turned out to be on the unprepossessing side, and his fantasy life abated for years—until the advent of the spectacularly prepossessing Diane Derry.

"Doctor," Diane said, four days into the effort of getting the spacetime ship and its auxiliary equipment back into shape, "you know, you really shouldn't work so hard. We may perfect this thing and get the grant money and wind up traveling all through time and space—but it won't do us any good if you have a heart attack."

"Heart attack?" said Dr. D., thumping his chest. "This ticker works just fine thank you. Would you care to Indian wrestle?"

Diane Derry shook her lovely blond locks. "You'd beat me."

"Of course. Do you think I'd challenge anybody who could? For instance, that strapping young simian yonder, who is, even as we speak, completely demolishing our only AC-DC rectifier. Talbot, why are you doing that?"

Soldering gun in one hand, round-nose pliers in the other, Troy Talbot was hard at work cannibalizing what was left of the spacetime ship's innards. He yanked, and out came another salvageable capacitor from a carbonized circuit board. He held the smallish cylinder up to the light and examined it as a dentist would an extracted bicuspid. "Yup, she's not burned too bad. Maybe we can use it in some other breadboard."

"Talbot," Demetrios said, "may I ask what we are going to do when the ship needs alternating current and we don't have a rectifier circuit to impart a sensual sine wave to the ebb and flow electromagnetic energy?"

"Well, Doc, you can ask, but I don't have an answer for you. All I know is, this here rectifier is shot, and we don't have enough parts to make a new one."

Demetrios threw aside his screwdriver and sat down heavily on a crate. "Unless I'm badly mistaken, that's your answer."

"Yup, I reckon it is, Doc."

"In other words, we'd be sunk."

Troy nodded and smiled, the glint of his teeth like

the sheen on polished porcelain. "That's about the size of it."

Dr. Demopoulos yawned. "On second thought, Diane, maybe you're right. What I need is a good night's sleep. Or at least some bed rest—preferably not unilateral."

"I haven't had any rest since Monday night," Diane said.

"And here it is Thursday, and the demonstration's tomorrow at ten A.M., and we *are* sunk."

"Never say die, Dr. D." Diane dropped her wire-stripper and began to massage her mentor's shoulders.

"Mmm, good. No, it's useless. Let's face it, gang, we're up the creek without an outboard. We're through. We are history. We are one with Nineveh and Tyre—oooh, God, that feels good.

Diane began to knead the professor's neck muscles. "We'll get the things back together at least to the point where we can show them something. They'll see the circuitry registering on the instruments."

"What instruments? They're all burnt-out junk."

"Well, we can at least show them that we once had instruments."

"I'm afraid the doc's right, Diane," Talbot said grimly. "To show, we got nothing but that pile of scrap metal." He pointed at the spherical spacetime ship, now smudged, scorched, and fenestrated by numerous access ports, the cover plates having been removed to extract fused circuitry.

"Well, that should be enough," Diane said with a defiant edge to her voice.

"It won't be," her physics professor said darkly. "Sam will go for it, but the rest will take one look and say, 'Very interesting, but of what scientific value is it?' And I won't have an answer except to say that I'm a Ph.D. and I ought to know what I'm doing—to which they'll reply, 'Sorry, we're not falling for any more B.S.'—which I'm perfectly capable of piling higher and higher, but there's a limit how much you can store in the barn''—he yawned again—''if you catch my drift.''

''They'll believe you, Dr. D.,'' Diane assured him. ''Sam will.''

''Sam won't be able to persuade his own foundation to fork over five thousand, because Sarah will be against it and Sam will be outvoted.''

''But it's his money!''

''When you have as much as Sam does, it doesn't belong to you anymore. It belongs to men in suits with briefcases and beady little eyes.''

''And we've spent most of the four hundred,'' Troy said.

''Yep. Should have done better damage assessment.''

''We didn't have time,'' Diane pointed out.

''True, true.''

''But we'll at least have the ship itself to show them. They'll get some idea of the possibilities.''

''The possibilities for what?'' Dr. D. asked gloomily. ''We *still* don't know what the thing will do when and if it works. I think, though I'm not sure, that it lifted off the ground. Which means it might have gone gravity-negative at that instant. Okay, say it does fly. How do we control it? I mean, the thing could go sailing off anywhere. We could land in . . .'' The professor gestured vaguely.

''Peru,'' Troy said.

''What?''

''I've always wanted to go to Peru.''

''Peru, eh? Why?''

''To see the Incan ruins. The Incas were a fascinating people, living way up there in the Andes. Some archaeologists say there're still great cities far up on the peaks. There may still be ancient Incas living there.''

"Talbot, you've been reading *National Geographic* to look at the bare breasts again."

"Aw, Doc, that's not fair. It's educational!"

"Breasts? Sure are. I've learned a lot from them. Have you ever considered a pair of breasts from a purely scientific viewpoint? It's a problem of weight distribution, potential energy, and harmonics. Did you know that when a woman runs, her breasts bounce in harmonic patterns similar to the way pendulums swing? Of course, the problem is much more complex, and the wave mechanics are very subtle—"

"Doc, you're making Diane blush."

"Why? She has them!"

Talbot laughed. "She's beet-red."

Demopoulos turned to look. Troy got the shade wrong; her face was a distinct magenta. "Sorry, Diane."

"Oh, that's all right, Dr. D. I'm a grown woman."

"Full grown, I'd say. Anyway, if we ended up in Peru, it would be tough Titicaca for all of us. We'd have no way of getting back."

"Why couldn't we take a plane?" Troy Talbot wondered.

"Because we'd be dead, because once the ship takes off, if it ever does, we won't be able to control it. Isn't that wonderful? If we succeed, we die."

"We'll tie a static line to the ship," Diane said.

"Then our data will be useless, because we—" Dr. Demopoulos was interrupted once again by a yawn. Recovering, he said, "I can't go on. To hell with it. I'm giving up."

"We can't give up now, Dr. D.!" Diane pleaded.

"Yes, we can. Before we succeed and kill ourselves. I'm calling the demonstration off."

"No!"

"Yes. Get me Wussman on the line, Diane."

"I won't."

"Do so or I will spank your nicely oblate bottom."

"You're going to make me blush again. All right, Doctor." Dejectedly, Diane crossed the lab and entered the control room, which communicated with a small office.

Under clouds of gloom, the professor watched Troy work for a while.

Presently, Troy stood, laid his tools on the workbench, and took off his work gloves. "I have to be moseying, Doc. Practice."

"Go on, desert me like a rat leaving a sinking ship."

"Squeak, squeak."

"Save that rapier wit for State U."

Talbot smiled thinly. "You know we don't have a chance against State U. We shouldn't even be playing them. We used to play them because we had an unusually good team for a small college—back when we used to be a college, and then we—"

Diane came running back into the lab.

"Did you get Wussman on the line?" Demopoulos asked.

"No. Doctor, there's a delivery truck here and they say they have a whole bunch of crates for you."

"Huh? I didn't order anything. Must be some mistake."

Diane handed him a bill of lading. "No mistake."

"What in the world—?" Incredulous, Doc D. looked the printed sheet over. " 'Electronic parts and other equipment'? Diane, you know we didn't send for this. And who the hell is this sender—'Future Unlimited'? Must be a gag."

"If it's a gag, it's an expensive one. This shipment's definitely not C.O.D."

Dr. D. shrugged. "So, all right already. Tell them to haul the junk in."

The deliverymen hauled in the junk, which consisted of five medium-size heavy-duty crates. Troy fetched a crowbar from the bench and, at the professor's urging, pried the tops off them.

What lay packed carefully within, nestled in excelsior and cotton wadding, shocked even the jaded Demetrios.

"What is this stuff?"

"Parts!" Talbot said.

"Parts for what?"

"You got me, Doc, but look at this gadget. This tag says it's a rectifier board, but it does fifteen other kinds of electronic circuit jobs!"

"That? It's nothing but a sliver of Bakelite, or plastic. Where are the tubes?"

"Beats the hell out of me, Doc. Oops! Sorry, Diane, didn't mean to swear."

"Don't worry, Troy. What's this, Dr. D.? The label says 'Y-3984-UD Nanoprocessor Cluster.' What's a nanoprocessor?"

Demetrios gave it some thought. "A miniature electronic brain? A cluster of them, no less. That's my guess."

"Processor. You mean it processes data? But it's a jelly bean with two leads coming out of it."

"Solid-state electronics on a hitherto undreamed of level of miniaturization is my next guess." Demetrios scratched his head. "But what's it all for?"

"Hey, Doc, look at this big one over here. I dunno if this is electronic or what, but it says 'Antimatter Power Plant.' Sounds potent."

"Antimatter . . . Ye gods! Contraterrene matter!" Demetrios marveled. "Matter identical to the earthly sort but of reversed electrical potential! Up to now it's only been a wild theory. And here's a technology based on it! Hey, I'm getting a little dizzy." He sat down heavily.

"Doctor, are you all right?"

"Jes' an attack of the vapors, honey chile."

"This is all rather disorienting," Diane said.

"There's only one thing all this stuff is intended for," Dr. Demopoulos said flatly.

"What?" his assistants chorused.

The professor jumped up. Following his nose, he searched each crate, finally pulling out a cardboard tube. He popped open a metal lid on one end and extracted a cylinder of rolled papers. These he unfurled and examined cursorily before pronouncing: "Assembly instructions! What's all this for, you ask?" He pointed to the copper sphere standing against the far wall. "That."

Confounded, Diane knitted her brow. "But who sent all this stuff? How did they know . . . ? And how could they—?"

Dr. D. silenced her with an upraised hand. "Don't ask!"

"Something fishy going on here, Doc," Talbot said, nodding sagely.

Demetrios slapped his forehead. "Who woulda guessed it? Brilliant deduction, Sherlock."

Diane said, "Dr. Demopoulos, do you mean to say that these parts and components were sent to us so that we could fix the spacetime ship?"

"Diane, get with the program. Yes, they're meant to go into our little jalopy, there. Someone, somewhere—don't ask me who or where—has a deep interest in this project and wants it to succeed."

Troy snapped his fingers. "The government!"

"Our government? Maybe, but I doubt they could come up with an antimatter power plant. Why, no one's even done a sustained fission reaction yet, let alone something as fancy as that."

"The Germans?"

"Let's hope not," Dr. D. said. "Otherwise you can kiss Europe good-bye."

"The Japs, then?"

Demetrios laughed. "Oh, come on. The Japanese are industrious little devils, but hardly capable of outpacing the West in technology." He sat on a small wooden box and reconsidered. "Funny thing is, they make such damned good cameras."

"Then who, Doc? Mussolini?"

"Don't be absurd. Besides, Fermi's working for us." Dr. D. scratched his chin, as was his habit. "Well, whoever it is, they have my undying thanks. I think." He pondered a moment. "Then again, I think I'd have rather done it myself."

Diane said, "But these discoveries are monumental, Doctor. This technology is years advanced over anything on Earth. We owe it to science—no, to the world!—to continue our efforts."

Dr. Demopoulos was silent for a moment. Then he slapped his knee. "Diane, you're right." He rose from the soapbox and stood on it. "Friends, I'd like to say a few words. In times like these, when we all have to pull together, it is good to take a moment to imagine ourselves in each other's shoes—which is why it's a time to try men's soles."

"Oh, groan," Diane said.

"Which reminds me of a story. When I was a lad—"

"Hey, Doc," Talbot yelled as he put his work gloves back on, "you going to make speeches or pitch in?"

"I thought you had football practice. Don't you have to go out and win one for Ronald Reagan?"

"More important things in this universe, Doc."

"Get busy screwing," Diane ordered, handing him a screwdriver.

"Anything you say."

They all set to work.


"Vivian? Oh, Vivian?"

A few hardy crickets, braving the crisp fall night, sang their dismay at the huge gothic horror of a moon that was peeking over the hills to the east of town.

Geoffrey Wussman cupped his hands to his mouth

and, in a hoarse meld of whisper and shout, tried again.

"V-i-i-i-i-viannnn! Psssssst!"

Vivian's apartment looked dark. Geoffrey took a step back and peered upward. No, some faint light; from a small table lamp, probably.

Vivian hadn't been answering her telephone. He had kept calling all day until, exasperated, he went to her place to snoop. When nothing came of the snooping, he made so bold as to knock quietly at her door. No one answered. Yet somehow he knew she was in there.

"Vivian!" he called in full voice, beyond exasperation now. He was desperate. He had to know if she still loved him.

"Vivian, please!"

"Who is that?"

The voice wasn't Dr. Vernon's. Geoffrey ran for the rhododendrons near the wall.

Light spilled out of a first-floor window. Geoffrey crouched and hid himself.

". . . I did! I heard someone out there . . ."

Snatches of conversation. Then, the window shut and the curtain was drawn. Darkness returned.

Geoffrey breathed again. After waiting a moment, he rose and stepped out from the bushes.

Suddenly he was hit by a shower of some gritty substance. Sand? He brushed the stuff out of his hair. A peculiar but familiar aroma came to him. Bringing a hand to his shoulder, he felt a soft claylike lump of something.

"Yuck!"

He looked up toward Vivian's window. It slammed shut.

She had dumped the contents of the cat box on him! He spat and choked, frantically dusting himself off.

After a quick search through the bushes, he found an outdoor spigot and cleaned himself as best he could.

Then he went back and took his former stance below the window.

"Vivian! Open up or I'll make a scene!"

After a moment the window rose a crack.

"Get your gnomish little butt up here," came Dr. Vernon's breathy contralto.

Vivian bade him enter a darkened apartment, the only light leaking through a half-closed bathroom door; but Geoffrey could pick out her dazzling figure, accented as it was by another outfit of the sort she favored. This one was a tight one-piece in dark green.

"Vivian, darling! I had to see you, I had to know if you'll forgive me, sweetest. I'm sorry for what I did, for not backing you up, for not sticking by you—but I had good reason, dearest, good reason! Demopoulos had old Sam hooked, he really did, and there was nothing—"

"Keep your voice down!"

"But, Vivian, lover, I—"

"Shhhh! Come in here."

"Vivian, what's wrong?"

Wussman took one step into the small living room and halted. The red glowing jewel of a lit cigarette moved languidly in the darkness near the opposite corner.

"Oh. I . . . I didn't know you had company. Really, I'm very sorry."

Vivian said, "Wussman, sit down and shut up."

The good doctor chose the far end of the couch and sat.

"Vivian, some light would not be great risk."

The voice was male and came from the vicinity of the glowing cigarette end.

"Perhaps, just this small one," Vivian said, going to an end table. She flicked on a piano lamp.

"Is much better."

The speaker was now revealed as a thin, mustachioed man in a dark well-tailored suit. He was thirty-five to forty years of age, perhaps a well-maintained forty-five. A dark trench coat and hat lay draped across the back of the easy chair in which he sat cross-legged, smilingly confident, and at ease.

"Dr. Geoffrey Wussman, may I present Arkady Stupolev of the Soviet Embassy in Washington."

Arkady Stupolev's smile broadened. "Is great pleasure to meet you, Dr. Wussman. I have heard much about you from Vivian." He did not rise.

Geoffrey had risen, reflexively, at the introduction, but stopped awkwardly at a crouch. "Oh? Uh, well. The pleasure is all mine, Mr. Stupolev." He sank back down.

"Arkady is an old friend," Vivian said. "He was in town, gave me a call."

"I've been calling all day," Geoffrey said.

Vivian chose the other end of the couch and sat. She took a cigarette from an inlaid box and lit it. "I was out."

"Vivian," Geoffrey said ominously, "if you don't mind my saying so, you're lying."

"Oh, be quiet. I shouldn't even be talking to you."

"We should be talking, Viv dear. I had no choice! Really, it was—"

"It doesn't matter now," Vivian broke in, waving the matter away with a flick of her burning cigarette. She shot smoke out of her thin nostrils. "Forget it. We have bigger fish to fry."

"Oh? Like what?"

"Nazi spies."

"Nazi spies, oh, well. Actually, you—" Wussman coughed and hacked for a moment. After clearing his throat he said, "Pardon me, did you say Nazi spies?"

"Is quite correct," Stupolev said. "They are lurking about, and they are very interested in secret project of your Greek colleague."

"Dr. Demopoulos? Really! Nazi spies, imagine that."

"Fascists are everywhere, my friend. Fascists have great support around the world. Even in this country."

"More than support," Vivian said. "Bourgeois democracies are little better than fascist fronts."

"Well, perhaps they are crypto-fascist," Stupolev qualified.

"Semantics."

Stupolev grinned and shrugged. "Is no time for academic discussion. What do we do?"

"Arkady, we break into that place and see what's up, that's what we do."

"Is obviously best tactic, but unfortunately I am far from my base of operations. I can give only limited support."

"We won't be needing you or Pyotr. Geoffrey and I can handle it."

Wussman said, "Me?"

Vivian turned to him. "You owe me."

"What do you want me to do?"

"We have to get into the Lab Annex and see what that shipment was."

"Shipment?"

Arkady said, "Yes. Demopoulos took big shipment of equipment from unknown source. My people have tried tracing to origin, unsuccessfully. Is quite mysterious, really."

Wussman asked, "Just what do you do at the Soviet Embassy, Mr. Stupolev?"

"Cultural and academic liaison," Stupolev said simply and didn't elaborate.

"Oh. Vivian, how do you intend to get into the Annex? Demetrios hasn't left the place for days—has he?"

"No," Vivian said.

"And both doors are bolted."

"They have to go home at some point. Then we'll get in there."

"But the campus police have standing orders from Demetrios to keep an eye on the place."

"How good are you with a broom?"

"Broom?"

Vivian got up and left the living room, returning shortly with a bundle of old clothes.

She threw some rags at him. "Try those on for size."

"What's the game?"

"We're the janitorial crew tonight. When Demopoulos and his stooges leave, we're in there."

"But the key . . ."

"Geoffrey, the Lab Annex is part of the Physical Sciences Building, to which, as head of the physics department, you have a master passkey."

Wussman snapped his fingers. "That's right. Yes, I do." He fished his house keys out of his pocket and looked at them. "Here it is. Never use it."

"You'll use it tonight."

"But what if they don't leave? Demetrios and his assistants, I mean."

"Tomorrow is the demonstration. They have to finish sometime tonight, and after that they'll all go home to get some rest, to be fresh for the test run."

"But they might not. Besides, we'll *be* at the demonstration. Why can't we wait till tomorrow?"

"I've got to get at Demetrios's notebooks. He keeps them in the lab, I'm sure of it."

"Why do you have to do that? You mean, you're going to steal them? Vivian, really, this is—"

"Not steal them, silly. Just photograph them. With Arkady's miniature camera."

Stupolev held up a tiny metal box. "Was developed in Soviet Union, but now is made in Japan."

"Damnedest thing," Wussman said. "Vivian, this is starting to sound very suspicious."

"You'd rather the Nazis got the secret?"

"The secret? But . . . Wait a minute, what Nazis are you talking about?"

"Scheissmuller," Stupolev said.

"Dr. *Scheissmuller*?" Wussman gasped. "He's a Nazi?"

"Worse than Himmler," Vivian said.

"But . . . but we should notify the government!"

"Fat chance they'll do anything. After Munich, Hitler's got the whole bunch of them bullied. Besides, the government is shot through with Nazi spies. They're everywhere. Right, Arkady?"

"They have penetrated highest levels of U.S. government," Stupolev assured her.

Wussman looked worried. "Well, I suppose we should do something to prevent Hitler from getting Demetrios's secret—if Demetrios has a secret. But I don't understand one thing."

Vivian crushed out her cigarette. "Which is?"

"Pardon me, Mr. Stupolev, but what's the Soviet government's interest in this? Didn't your Mr. Stalin just sign a treaty with Hitler?"

"Is brilliant ploy," Stupolev said with an expansive shrug. "Comrade Stalin knows what he is doing. Let West destroy itself. Is last death throes of fascist capitalism, then we pick up pieces. Soon, whole world will be workers' state."

"Right," Vivian said. "Listen, Geoffrey. Does science belong to the world, or to one selfish country?"

"Why, to the world," Geoffrey said. "To humanity!"

"Exactly. So what's your problem?"

"Uh . . . ." Geoffrey couldn't think of what his problem was.

"Good," Vivian said. "As soon as Pyotr calls in that the coast is clear, we'll move. Better get into those duds. Can you fake a Mexican accent?"

"Uh, I guess. Vivian, why you? I would have thought Dr. Cherkinov would be the Soviet . . . er, whatever you are."

"A friend of progressivism!"

"Cherkinov is émigré," Arkady said. "Old aristocratic family. Owned serfs. There is one other person in university here, Galina Savinkova, in music school."

"Oh, the pianist," Wussman said. "I've heard her play. She's brilliant."

"Yes, but is also not politically correct. Insists to play music of decadent romantic individualism." Stupolev sneered. "Rachmaninoff."

"Oh."

"So," Vivian said, crossing her long legs and lighting another cigarette, "we wait."

They waited.

# Chapter Five

In the dead of night the hum of the refurbished space-time ship was barely perceptible. No more did magnetos whine and rattle, no longer did gigantic sparks arc across heated air. All was quiet inside the ship, where, in the tight space of the central circular control room, the three hopeful spacetime travelers sat at their assigned stations.

"Would you have a look at *that*!"

"What, Doctor?"

"The graviton wave detectors."

"You mean these squiggly things?"

"Yes, Diane. They're going crazy. The electrostatic flux calibrators are up, too—and the interstitial quantum field calibrations are in undreamed of territory! I think we're close, folks! I do believe we've got something here . . ."

"Yeah, Doc," Troy Talbot said, "but what?"

Diane Derry heaved an excited breath. "A spacetime machine!"

Suddenly, the ship began to throb like some vast powerful engine. The sound grew in intensity.

"ΕΥΡΗΚΑ! I have found it!" cried Dr. Demopoulos, bouncing up and down on his seat, gray curls brushing the low overhead. "Years of work coming to fruition! The universe beckons! The stars are ours! The doors to the past and future lie open before us—"

The throbbing died as the futuristic vessel emitted a sickly cough.

The graviton wave indicators sank to zero, as did all the other digital displays.

The humming, previously an almost subliminal background presence, died pitiably. A clank; a sputter: the researchers watched one indicator spike as they felt a shudder, the death twitch of their mammoth machine as all its fibrillations flattened. Then, strangely enough, there came a report, as of a backfire, a raunchy mechanical fart—after which the spacetime ship became as pregnantly still as the air in a music hall after the last crescendo of a symphony and before applause begins. Darkness fell briefly before emergency lighting automatically switched on.

". . . unless I'm badly mistaken," Demetrios said dismally.

"It's dead, Doctor," Diane pronounced.

"Damn it, Diane, I'm a physicist, not a physician. Oh, well. Just goes to show that we can't follow assembly instructions. Insert tab A into slot B. What do you think, Talbot?"

"I think we blew another power-control nanoprocessor, is all."

"How many spares do we have left?"

"One."

"Wonderful, and there's no electronic parts house in the world that can supply replacements."

"Except where the originals came from."

"Right. Well, shit. Speaking of which, I ought to try out the head in this thing. Don't think we ever tested it, did we?"

"Uh, I did, Doc," Troy said. "Kinda cramped in there, so watch your head . . . Haw, that's pretty funny."

"Oh, you should take that routine on the road. I can book you into a club in Newark next weekend."

Demetrios rose from his chair and promptly cracked his noggin against an outcropping bulkhead. "Goddammit!"

Diane winced. "Are you okay, Doctor?"

Demetrios rubbed his cranium. "I am undamaged, captain. I think."

Grumbling, Demetrios descended through a circular hatchway in the deck, climbing down the narrow ladder that connected the control cabin with a small compartment that served as storage space and entry area.

"Ouch!"

"Watch 'er, Doc! The ceiling's even lower down there!"

The professor's hollow voice grumbled below: "Now he frigging tells me."

Troy breathed a sigh. "Well, it sure was nice watching all these pretty colored lights for a while."

"Digital displays," Diane corrected.

"Yeah. Say, Diane, are you still going to the Fall Cotillion with me?"

"The Fall—? Troy, how can you think of such trivial things when we're on the brink of a staggering scientific discovery?"

"Sorry. Well . . . tell you the truth, Diane, I think someone's pulling old doc's leg."

"What do you mean, Troy?"

"All these gadgets. Very impressive, but I can't believe this ship's going to lift off for the stars."

"Why not?"

"I dunno, but it just can't be. Things like that don't happen. It's some kind of practical joke."

"Troy, I think you need some sleep. We all do."

"Maybe you're right. All the same, Diane, I don't think this thing will ever fly."

Diane sat back and ran her hands through her hair. Then she yawned. "Excuse me. Sheesh, am I tired." She exhaled. "I'm beginning to think we'll never get it to work right. Oh, dear, oh, dear."

Diane crossed her arms on the control panel and laid her head down.

Troy yawned.

By the time Dr. D. climbed back up into the control room, both had dozed off.

"Rise and shine, everybody!"

"What?" Diane sat up and rubbed her bleary eyes. "Doctor, you scared me."

"All right, we've reached the end of our rope. No more work tonight. We need rest, no kidding this time. Let's all go home. Be back here . . ." Demetrios consulted his watch. "Ye gods."

"What it is, Doc?"

"It's nearly five A.M."

"The demonstration's at ten," Diane said. "We'll never be ready if we don't keep at it."

"Forget it. All we'll do is make more mistakes. Go home, get three hours shut-eye, be back here at eight. No, make that eight-thirty, sharp. We'll have ninety minutes to get this ship back in working order before the bigwigs get here. If we fail, we can at least get the instruments functioning and show them Christmas lights."

"That sounds great to me, Doc. I think I'll conk out on the sofa in the office. Save me walking home, and I'll get more sleep time that way."

"You do that, Talbot."

"Dr. D., there's a cot in the back of the lab. I think I'll stay, too."

"Fine, Diane. You two skedaddle. There's something I want to look at. I'll run the diagnostics on batteries."

"Doctor, you need rest, too!"

"I'm not sleepy, too keyed up. You kids get some shut-eye. That's an order."

"Aye-aye, skipper," Troy said as he descended the ladder.

"Dr. Demopoulos, you really should rest, too."

"Run along, Diane. I'm going to fiddle here for just a few more minutes, then it's off to dreamland. I'll shag it over to my faculty office and catch forty winks on the couch.''

"Okay, Dr. D. Good night.''

After Diane left, Demetrios permitted himself another yawn. Then he hunched over the controls and got to work.

The phone rang and Stupolev answered it.

"Hello? *Da. Da. Nyet. Da. Horosho.*"

He hung up and looked at Vivian.''

"Pyotr say lab is dark, very quiet. He think they leave by back door. He did not see them.'

"We'll have to risk it. Wake up, Wussman!''

"Uh! What? Oh.''

"Zero hour. Get your shoes on.'' Vivian sniffed. "Geoffrey, you need a new deodorant. You have B.O.''

Wussman mumbled something.

"Is taking big risk,'' Stupolev said.

"So what happens if we're caught? Geoffrey is the department chairman, responsible for all research. It's outrageous that he should be kept in the dark like this. Right, Geoffrey?''

"Why, yes. I resent it highly.''

"You see?''

Stupolev grinned at her. "You are better than any agent in NKVD. Fearless. Intrepid. Is word? Yes.'' He kissed Vivian on both cheeks.

Vivian returned the favor in the mouth area. "Nonsense, just helping out.''

Not enamored of the kissing one iota, Geoffrey asked, "What's the NKVD?''

Stupolev hesitated the barest second before saying, "Is cultural exchange organization.''

Geoffrey nodded. "Oh.''

Vivian handed him keys. "Geoffrey, you know where my garage is. Get the car and bring it around front. There's a good boy.''

"Anything you say, Vivian, dearest."

Geoffrey left the apartment, softly closing the door.

"Is always that stupid?"

"Always."

They embraced.

"Vivashka, you are tigress. You should have been with me in Spain, hunting Trotskyites."

"I should have loved to have bagged a few Trotskyites. Take me now, Arkady."

"We have no time."

"A tiny bit. Let me introduce you to an American custom. It's called a 'quickie.' "


Pyotr was short and stocky. Standing on the corner near the Science Building, he looked like a dark oversize fire hydrant.

Stupolev swerved to the curb and Pyotr got in the front seat. Instantly the odor of alcohol permeated the interior.

The two men in front exchanged a few harsh words in Russian. Then Arkady turned and said mildly, "Dr. Wussman, Pyotr Shlyapnikov, my assistant."

"Pleased to meet you."

Pyotr grunted, then spoke Russian again to Arkady. Arkady shrugged.

"Go around to the loading dock, Arkady," Vivian instructed.

Arkady obeyed.

The grim silence bothered Wussman and he decided to make small talk. "What city in the Soviet Union are you from, Pyotr?"

Pyotr turned his wide face to the rear and looked annoyed. "Born in St. Petersburg," he said gruffly.

"Oh. Is that where you live now?"

"No. Live in Leningrad."

"Did you go to school there?"

"No. In Petrograd."

"Oh. Do you like Leningrad? Do you think you'll stay there?"

Pyotr shook his head. "No. I will die in St. Petersburg."

Arkady stifled a chuckle.

When the car stopped again it was in a short driveway leading to the loading dock. A ramshackle enclosed walkway of weathered plywood and tar paper connected the rear of the Physical Sciences Building to the unfinished Lab Annex.

"Wish us luck," said Vivian, opening the rear door on her side.

"I should go," Arkady said. "I have diplomatic immunity."

"Let's avoid an international incident. We'll stick to our plan. Park my car in the faculty lot. Get yours and go back to my apartment. Wait there. Check?"

"Check," Arkady said.

Vivian and Geoffrey got out of the sedan.

"You took your time coming down to the car," Wussman complained.

"Be quiet, Geoffrey. And don't forget the mops."

Geoffrey's key got them into the rear of the Physical Sciences Building through a fire door next to the loading dock. However, progress was then halted by a padlock on the double doors to the Lab Annex.

"They're probably using the back entrance," Geoffrey said.

"Which will be locked from the inside. This is no problem."

Vivian reached up and took a hairpin out of her luxuriant auburn coif. She then set about picking the lock, looking as though she knew exactly what she was doing.

"Where did you learn that?" Wussman wanted to know.

Vivian didn't answer. Within a half minute, Wussman heard a click. The padlock came open. Amazed, he helped her carefully unthread the chain around the door handles.

Geoffrey's passkey worked again on the remaining lock. They went through the door, traversed the bare corridor of the connecting walkway, and paused at the next set of double doors. These were unlocked.

Vivian gave a self-satisfied smile. "Easy as pie."

Wussman stopped her before she went through. "Tell me one thing. If you wanted to steal Demetrios's secrets, why did you do everything you could to block the project?"

"I didn't think he *had* a project until he did his song and dance for Flitheimer. That persuaded me he might have stumbled onto something. When the mysterious shipment came—Arkady's men have been watching—that convinced me. There's more to this than meets the eye."

"What do you think's going on?"

"I think Demopoulos is working for the Nazis."

"No!"

"Yes."

"Vivian, did it ever occur to you that some people who aren't politically progressive might not necessarily be Nazis?"

"Shh! Spy now, politics later. Come on."

They entered a narrow corridor leading to the right. It made an L to the left and proceeded into the darkness of the three-story-high interior of the Annex, which originally had been designed to be a field house and gymnasium until the Depression put a stop to construction. A new indoor sports complex was going up across the campus to replace this more modest effort.

They stopped at the sound of snoring. Then, cautiously, they slipped past a lighted open office, where one of Demetrios's assistants lay fast asleep on a threadbare settee.

"They're still here!" Wussman whispered.

"Obviously. Ditch the janitor stuff. The disguise won't do any good now."

Wussman carefully put down the mops and brooms. He kept his silence but had trouble keeping his composure as he followed Vivian into the darkened lab. Amorphous shadows seemed to move in the corners. Above, wind sighed through the hole in the roof.

Vivian stopped him.

"What?"

"I hear breathing." Vivian went up on tiptoe. "Over there, back in that niche. Never mind, let's go."

"Where?" Geoffrey said to himself.

Then he saw the spacetime ship, a massive sphere with an open hatch on the side that leaked a faint light.

"Wow," Geoffrey said softly.

"Shh! Over here."

The place was a shambles. Odd components lay strewn all over, layers of litter and junk covered the floor. Wussman tripped over wire and nearly fell. He had to pick his way toward a table heaped with more junk, a huge twisted coil, and heaps of papers.

"At last," Vivian whispered. "Demetrios's data."

"But this is a mess. How are we going to find anything?"

"It's here, I know it."

Vivian began rifling through the snowdrift of graphs, tape, and scrap paper.

Geoffrey didn't have much to do. With one shoe he prodded a pile of debris. The top slid off and spread out over the sea of detritus on the floor, pulp lava from a paper volcano.

He ventured into the gloom, wandering toward the spacetime ship. It was impressive, he had to admit. Perhaps he should have backed Demetrios all along.

Why hadn't he? Because Vivian, for some reason, hated Demetrios, and Geoffrey loved Vivian more than his own soul. Therefore, he'd gone along with Vivian for years.

He cast a glance back toward the table as Vivian flicked on a small flashlight. She was leaning over the table, throwing her heart-stopping backside into relief. No shabby charwoman's frock could hide a body like that.

Wussman heaved a great sigh. He still loved Vivian, with all his heart and what was left of his soul.

Voices.

Vivian snapped off the light and came toward Geoffrey.

"Move! Find the back door!"

But they couldn't find the back door. It was pitch-dark to either side of the ship and all Geoffrey found was an immense stack of crates, which he bumped into and sent crashing.

"Idiot!"

"Where do we go?"

"Inside the ship!"

"But, Vivian—"

Vivian climbed the ladder to the open hatch and disappeared into it. Huffing, Geoffrey clambered up in pursuit.

It was dim inside the anomalous vessel, auxiliary lights providing a feeble glow. A hand slapped across Geoffrey's mouth and he felt Vivian's breath hot against his ear.

"He's up there, asleep."

Wussman saw a ladder leading to an upper level. Cautiously he climbed and peered over the edge of the hatchway. He saw a seated figure slumped over an instrument console on the other side of the compartment. In a moment he realized it was Demopoulos.

He felt someone tugging on his baggy pants and looked down. Vivian was beckoning.

Before he could move he saw Demetrios raise his head and in a sleepy voice say, "Hah?"—then sink back into slumber.

Geoffrey climbed down. Vivian pointed into what

looked like a narrow broom closet. He peered in. There was a seat with a hole in it and what looked like a small sink. The tiny space looked like a rest room on a miniature train.

Vivian pushed him through the narrow door and squeezed herself in. He fell backward and found himself sitting on the commode. Vivian sat on his lap, and he was instantly aware of the soft pressure of her legs and buttocks bearing down on him. The scent of her perfume filled his nostrils. Almost immediately, a subtle pressure began to assert itself against that lovely weight.

She grabbed his collar. "Don't you get any ideas, mister!"

"Miss? Hey, wake up."

Startled out of sleep, Diane was alarmed by the sight of two policemen standing over the tattered mattress on which she lay.

She jumped to her feet.

"Don't get scared, miss," the older of the two said. "We just want you to know that someone removed the padlock and chains to the door between the buildings."

"Someone broke in?"

"Well, we checked around. The back doors are still locked from the inside and there's no one here, unless they're hiding under all this garbage. Have you seen anyone? Heard anything?"

"Why, no. I was so tired, though. Dead asleep. We were working late on a project."

"Is that your boyfriend out in the office there? We couldn't get him up for love or money."

"I'll wake him."

"You'd better, just in case. The intruders could still be in the area. Anybody else here?"

"I don't know. Dr. Demopoulos probably went home. I'll call."

"Isn't that our quarterback in there?"

"Yes, that's Troy Talbot."

Both officers nodded.

"He stinks," said the younger one.

"Good morning," came a voice from the far end of the building.

It was Demopoulos, arisen.

After a further search of the Annex, the police left. Dawn broke, and there was no question of trying to get any more sleep. So the team set back to work.

"I think the diagnostic instruments have helped me get a handle on the problem," Demetrios said, once more ensconced in his pilot's chair.

"What did they say, Doctor?"

"They said, 'You got a broke machine, buster.' "

"Well, that's a lot of help." Diane fanned herself. "It's close in here."

"Open a window. Hey, wait a minute. We *do* have a window in here, don't we?"

"Sure, Doc," Talbot said. "The quartz viewport. Hit this button right here and the steel shutter rolls back."

"Why, I plumb forgot." Demopoulos pressed the button. A plate, set into the bulkhead in front of him, slid aside to reveal a circular window. The viewport was not large but afforded a view of the interior of the messy Lab Annex.

"Breathtaking. It's so light and airy in here now. All we need are a few plants, curtains . . ."

"Boy, you sure are a kidder, Doc."

"All right, let's set up all the controls to duplicate conditions as they were right before the blowout. Maybe that will tell us something. Switch to battery power."

"Right you are, Dr. D.," Diane said.

Switches snapped, buttons clicked. A few lights

blinked on the instrument panel, mostly in glaring red.
The huge spacetime ship was silent.

"Nothing," Demetrios said somberly.

"Maybe a plug's loose."

Dr. Demopoulos laughed. "Diane, you would think
of something that silly."

Diane looked down. "What's this, then?"

"What's what?"

"This thing down here next to my foot."

Troy got out of his seat and hunkered down to a get
a look.

"What is it, Talbot?"

"It's a plug. It's loose."

Diane stuck her tongue out at the boss.

"I don't believe it," Demetrios said.

"It's true, Doc. What should I do?"

"What should you do? 'What should I do?' he says.
Plug it back in, Dr. IQ! For God's sake, Talbot, you
could screw up a two-car funeral."

"Okay, Doc, here she goes."

The reaction was immediate. The ship's arcane ma-
chinery came to life, humming, and—this time—
throbbing, as it had commenced to do before the
malfunction.

The rapid heart-pulse sound quickly increased to a
bone-jarring roar, enough to vibrate eyes in the socket,
fillings in the teeth. Dr. D.'s thick spectacles jounced
around his face, fell into his lap and out, dropping to
the deck.

When every seam in the vessel screamed to pull
loose—things got worse. Weird things began to happen. Colors went off, pulsing and bleeding. Everything looked out of kilter, warped, twisted in some
odd way. Prismatic auras sprang up along surfaces and
edges; a weird light played about the tiny cabin.

And then, with a sudden wrenching, all was still.

The interior of the ship, which had previously
seemed to be bending ludicrously out of shape, now

returned to its previous state. Colors went back into their proper hues as well. Everything seemed back to normal.

Except for one thing. Outside, the Lab Annex had disappeared, replaced by a field of stars.

"Oh, my," Diane said. "What happened?"

Everything seemed rather askew.

"Gee, Doc!" said Troy Talbot, scratching his crew-cut head. "Everything seems kind of . . . well, screwy!"

"Yes," said Diane. "My thought precisely."

"Good reason for that, people." said Dr. Demopoulos. "It's because things are indeed screwy." He consulted the control panel, where all the lights were now green. "Ye gods."

"What is it, Dr. D.?"

"Wait till I find my glasses."

Dr. Demopoulos squirmed his way to the floor and rooted around. He tried to get up, cracked his head on the edge of the console, and uttered a blood-chilling oath.

"Doctor, be careful!"

"It's all right, 's all right. Only a hairline skull fracture, mild concussion." Finally the professor regained his seat and put on his thick spectacles. He scanned the instrument panel. "If I'm reading these dials and widgets correctly, we've gone ahead and done it."

"Done what?" Talbot asked.

"We've made the journey into a wondrous land whose boundaries are that of imagination. We've bought a one-way ticket on a steamboat named *Infinity*—case in point, lesson to be learned, submitted for your approval—"

"Doc, you're babbling."

"What's that out there, chopped liver? Those are *stars*, Talbot. We're in *space*."

"Oh, come on, Doc. How could we be in space? We were in the lab just a second ago."

"Nevertheless, my elaborately muscled friend, we are no longer in a large building on the campus of Flitheimer University. Nor, in fact, are we even in the United States. Nor are we on the planet Earth."

Diane put her hands to her face. "Oh, my. You mean . . . ?"

"Yes, my dear," said Demetrios, awe and excitement pushing through his usually cynical demeanor. "We're . . . elsewhere. Moreover, we may not be in the year 1939 anymore."

"Gee—" Troy said, "does this mean I'm going to miss the football season?"

"But where are we, Dr. Demopoulos?"

"Diane, you're manning the navigator's position. You tell me."

"Oh! Right." Diane examined her instruments. Then she shrugged. "I haven't the foggiest idea, Dr. D."

"Neither do I. We simply haven't had the time to figure out how to read any of this stuff. It's all so foreign, so . . . alien."

"Yes, that's the word."

"Hmmm," said Dr. Demopoulos. "We could be in another universe entirely."

"*Another* universe, Doc? That don't make sense."

"Think on it a bit, Troy, m'boy. Meanwhile, I suppose I'll have to do some calculations. Good thing this ship has a computer, the likes of which I never imagined. Too bad I haven't the slightest idea of how to use it."

"How do we get back?" Troy asked.

"That, my young friend, is the sixty-four-dollar question."

"Well," Troy said. "This little jaunt ought to be exciting, any way you look at it."

"Interesting, in the sense of the Chinese curse."

"Uh, what Chinese curse is that, Doc?"

" 'May you live in interesting times.' Get the meaning?"

"Uhhhhh!"

"No? Well, Troy, if you consider the usual sense, you'll see—"

"I got it, Doc. Give me some credit."

"Yes? Well, why did you grunt?"

"I didn't grunt."

"You didn't grunt? Someone grunted. Diane, did you grunt?"

"Dr. D., I did not grunt."

"Well, someone did."

"Uhhhhhhhh!"

"They did it again," Troy noted. "It's Martians, Doc!"

With a wry smile, Demetrios turned about in his pilot's chair. "No. Not the Martians of H. G. Wells, nor those of Orson Welles, either."

"Spacetime beings?" said Diane.

"No. Something a tad more mundane, I think," said Dr. Demetrios.

"It's coming from belowdecks!" Troy said. "I'm going down and check!"

Even as he spoke a disheveled and quite green physics professor by the name of Geoffrey Wussman came climbing up the ladder from the lower deck.

"Hello," he said sheepishly. "What happened?"

"The ship took off."

"What? Uh . . . where are we?"

Dr. Demopoulos's eyes traveled over the readout banks again. "Somewhere in outer space, hundreds, possibly thousands of light-years from Earth."

Wussman gave a nervous chuckle. "You're joking."

"Nnnnope."

"But that's impossible."

"Yuuuuuuup. But guess what."

"What?"

"We done dood it."

Wussman pouted. "Demetrios, please just let me out of this thing."

"Can't do that, Geoffrey, old bean. If we open the hatch all the air will rush out, and we'll suffocate."

"Nonsense."

"Geoffrey, just look out the viewport."

"Oh, very well." Geoffrey squeezed his way toward the pilot's station. Standing on tiptoes, he looked out.

"Oh, my God! Demetrios, we're in outer space!"

"Hundreds, possibly thousands of light-years from Earth. Wait a minute, didn't I just say that a second ago?"

In a moment a queasy-looking Dr. Vivian Vernon climbed up through the hatchway.

"What in the world is going on?"

"Hey, Viv. Join the party."

"What happened?"

"Vivian, come look!"

"Geoffrey, what is it?"

"You have to see to believe, Vivian."

Vivian peered over Demetrios's head and out the viewport.

"Oh, my God . . ."

Demetrios said, "You don't believe in God, Viv. Remember? And you didn't believe in my spacetime ship either. Well, here we be out in the middle of space. And, lordy, lordy, there be the firmament of heaven."

Vivian swallowed hard. "Where are we?"

"Uh, that is a small problem. We didn't have time to find out how the navigation gear works."

"You mean we're lost?"

Demetrios smiled. "Uh, let's not use the L word just yet. Let's just say it might take us a bit of time to get back to Earth. But then, we're in a spacetime machine—and what's time to a spacetime machine, eh?"

"Or space, for that matter," Diane chimed in.

"Oh, my God," said Dr. Vernon. "Stuck with you

people in a ship in the middle of . . . of nowhere. I think I'm going to faint.''

A fierce lightning flash flooded through the viewport. Suddenly the craft began to shake, knocking Vernon and Wussman down. Demetrios looked out the viewport but nothing was visible save the unwinking multicolored splendor of the stars. The ship did have a television viewer, which had yet to be tested. He snapped a few switches. A small screen on the console began to glow. Apparently the explosive jump through spacetime had not affected the miniature cameras set into the hull, because an image was coming through on them right now.

A moving dot registered on the television screen. He increased magnification, and the outside camera adjusted their telescopic lenses to the proper focal length. Immediately, the image of something incredible resolved to crystal clarity. Demetrios was astonished at the sharpness of the photographic detail, in full color, no less.

It was some sort of gigantic ship, a dreadnought hanging in space like a Christmas tree ornament from hell, bristling with more spines than a sea urchin. Two particularly large pointy spines shot bolts of blue-green fire.

"Look at this," he said to Diane.

Diane looked, and her jaw dropped. "What in the world is it?''

"An alien space vessel, and it's engaged in combat with something farther away. Yes, another blip on the scanner. This one is headed our way, though. If it gets too close—''

A tremendous flash lit up the area of space around the spacetime ship.

Inside the ship, the lights flickered and went out.

# Chapter Six

"Lights out!" said Dr. Demopoulos. "What a great name for a radio program. How about if we start it off with this screeching sound of a door opening? SCREEEEEEEEEEEEEEECH!"

Somebody squealed in Vivian Vernon's voice. Then, like a supernal lightning bolt, another gigantic flash lit up the interior of the ship, fading quickly. Darkness returned with a vengeance, everyone now temporarily flash-blind.

"Damned scary, any way you cut it," said Troy Talbot.

"Somebody goosed me!"

There was the sound of a slap and a resultant yowl.

"Vivian, you hit me!" Wussman whined.

"Keep your hands off me and you won't get hit."

"I didn't touch you!"

"And I suppose you didn't have your paws all over me when we were hiding in the bathroom?"

"It was *tight* in there!"

A voice of reason cut through the darkness. "People, listen," said Demetrios. "I really think we should be doing something more constructive than waging the battle of the sexes at this particular moment. We're stuck millions of miles from home in the middle not only of space, but in the midst of what very well may be the most cataclysmic battle in the history of the universe. We'll need every ounce of calm, cool, calculated rationality that we can muster."

"Dr. D. is right," Talbot said. "What should we do, Doc?"

"Pray. If we get caught in the crossfire, we're dead. *I wanna go home!*" Demetrios burst into tears.

"Then this is the end," Professor Wussman said. He wrapped his beloved in a tender embrace. "Precious one, we may well have only seconds left in this life, our final chance for the intimate embrace you've promised me for so long. Come, my Isolde, kiss your Tristan and let us have our *Liebestod*!"

"Dr. Wussman, please," said Diane Derry. "I'm not your Isolde."

"Oh, sorry. Vivian, where are you? Vivian?"

"Geoffrey, darling."

"Keep your hands to yourself, Demetrios," Wussman said disgustedly.

"Boy, you know you're a loser when the homely ones start turning you down."

"Vivian?"

"I'm warning you, Geoffrey . . ."

"Vivian, darling, we—*umph!*"

"Can't say I didn't warn you."

"Oh, that sounded wicked," Demopoulos said. "What did you do to him, Viv?"

"Kneed him in the crotch."

Something hit the deck like a sack of potatoes.

Demetrios clucked. "Geof, did you ever want to sing countertenor?"

Wussman's answer was a moan.

Vivian looked out the viewport. The battling dreadnought was now visible to the naked eye, growing ever larger and appearing all the more formidable in three dimensions. It was an immense artifact. Vivian was aghast.

"Oh, my God, look at that thing! Demetrios, you cobbled this damned crate together. What the hell do we do?"

"Hold your horses, Dr. Vernon. And your knees. First we have to do something about the lights."

Demetrios made his way along the curving bulkhead, feeling his way carefully along the nuts and bolts and wads of chewing gum (damn Talbot, anyway!), inching toward an access panel that he hoped was located where he thought it was.

"I don't know why the auxiliary lighting failed, but it could have something to do with those huge explosions. They might be releasing powerful pulses of electromagnetic energy, which would play havoc with the ship's electrical system. Ah, here we are, the circuit breakers."

Demetrios hit the button that opened the panel and began feeling inside for switches. For his trouble, he got a nasty shock.

"Φυκ!"

"Watch your filthy mouth," Vivian said coldly.

"I said it in Greek."

The lights came on to reveal a miserable Geoffrey Wussman doubled up on the deck, moaning piteously.

Talbot, standing at another panel, flicked more switches. "Circuit breakers're over here, Doc."

"Thanks, Talbot, you manually dexterous dope."

"Just trying to help."

"You could have told me where the damned things were. Never mind. Pardon me, pardon me, this is my stop."

Demopoulos sidestepped his way toward the pilot's station, inadvertently, although happily, brushing against Vivian's ample bosom.

"Oops, sorry, Viv."

"No, you're not, you wolf. You were probably the one that goosed me."

"Ah, you've fingered me at last. All right, battle stations!"

"This tub has armaments?" Vivian asked, disbelieving.

"We installed something that the instructions called weapons," Troy said. "Trouble is, not only don't we know how to shoot 'em, we don't even know what the heck they do."

"All right, let's try to get this ship away from the danger zone," Dr. Demopoulos said, frantically scanning the control board. "Um . . . um . . . yeah. Anybody have a suggestion?"

"Let's set up for another thrust," Diane said. "Just like the first."

"But we thrusted—er, thrust along an unknown vector. We have to find out how to steer this damn thing, or we'll get completely lost."

"Doctor," Diane said gravely, "we're already completely lost. Let's get away from whatever those people are doing out there."

"If they're people. You have a point, Diane."

Even as he spoke, multiple flashes dazzled all within the spacetime vessel. Seconds later, a shock wave slammed against the ship. Vivian and Troy were thrown to the deck on top of Wussman.

Demetrios stabbed a button and the steel shutter closed over the viewport.

"Those must be atomic explosions," Demopoulos said, rubbing his eyes. "Nothing else could produce that much radiation. If we were any closer we'd fry."

"The radiation meters are registering dangerously high exposure as it is," Diane said.

"All the more reason for us to vamoose. Set up for another jump. Quick!"

Outside, as viewed by the telescopic lenses of the exterior cameras, the mighty space battle seemed to intensify. Now there were two mammoth starships, looking like nothing so much as huge, pregnant, leather-clad porcupines. They had approached each other and halted, and were now exchanging rainbows of projected power, slamming back and forth with mighty force beams. That the comparatively tiny spacetime ship had not yet been melted into slag was testimony to its luck; however, from all signs, time was not on the side of the spatiotemponauts. The duking dreadnoughts displayed a profligacy of energy expenditure that made this particular neighborhood of outer space a high-risk area.

"Talbot, get off the floor. Man your station!"

"Dr. Vernon's on top of me."

"I've never cared for the missionary position either," Demetrios said, turning about to look. "You lucky stiff."

"Only part of him is stiff," Vivian said, struggling to her feet.

"Sorry, ma'am, that's my pocketknife."

"Oh? I thought you were just glad to have me sitting on you."

Talbot, greatly abashed, got up to reveal what lay under him: the slightly squashed form of Dr. Geoffrey Wussman.

Demetrios got back to work, his hands moving furiously, aping Diane's. There were any number of buttons to push, instruments to recalibrate, switches to throw, and thingees to do whatsit to.

At last he said, "Are we ready, copilot?"

Diane said, "Yes, sir!"

"Ready, Engineer?"

"Yo!"

"Engage the main gizmos."

Talbot asked, "You mean the electrogravitic thrusters?"

"Yeah, those."

"Engaged!"

The ship began to throb again, the pulsing sound mounting in intensity once more.

"All hands stand by for spatiotemporal displacement!" Demetrios announced. Then he suddenly grinned. "Hey, that sounds snazzy, doesn't it?"

"You sound just like Buck Rogers," Vivian jeered, "or any other character in the funny pages. *Now, get us the hell out of there!*"

"Madam, you'll show proper respect for the master of this vessel or be thrown in the brig!"

"Drop dead, you moron."

"Yes, nice weather we've been having," Dr. D. said, nodding pleasantly. "Yes, indeedy."

At that moment plans once more went agley. The spacetime ship again lost its nerve on the brink of delivering an unimaginable push into the unknown. The throbbing and the humming died. The engines failed, completely losing power, but this time the lights and all electrical systems remained functional.

"Come on, Talbot," Demetrios said, rising from his chair. "We need those able mitts of yours. Get to work on the bolts to the floor access plates, there's a good lad."

"Aye aye, skipper! Soon as I fetch a wrench from belowdecks."

Talbot stepped over the still-prostrate Dr. Wussman and scampered down the ladder.

"The engine's right under our feet?" Vivian asked.

"Sure is, between compartments. Geoffrey, would you mind skooching over a bit?"

Wussman groaned and complied.

Vivian asked, "How does this contraption of yours work?"

Demetrios shrugged. "I dunno."

"Huh? Well, what kind of engine is it? What are its components?"

"Couple of big coils, four gyroscopes, some rotating disks. Bunch of other little whirligigs."

" 'Whirligigs'? That's what propels this vessel?"

"Look, I had the theory all worked out, but test results never jibed with the theory. Nevertheless, the thing works to some degree. I just don't know *how* it works."

"But you must have *some* idea!"

"Well, yeah, I do. The electrogravitic thrusters are supposed to produce electrogravitic waves, which are phased transforms of electromagnetic waves. And those waves—standing waves to be exact—should set up a gravito-inertial field. Antigravity! But with the antigravity package you get all sorts of possible effects, from time travel to super-luminal travel, and even instantaneous travel in space. How does that sound?"

Vivian rubbed her forehead. "Sounds . . . goofy. The universe just doesn't work like that. There's no such thing as 'electrogravitic' waves. There's no electrogravitic radiation spectrum that I know of or anyone else knows of. And God only knows what a 'gravito-inertial' field could be. Demetrios, you're plain nuts."

"Oh, you think me mad, do you? Mwah-hah-hah-hah!"

Vivian clapped her hands over her eyes. "I must be dreaming. This is all a bad dream. All just a nightmare. I'm going to wake up soon and everything will be okay."

"Wrong, Viv. This is real, all too real. Wake up and smell the bacon."

Vivian uncovered her eyes, looked aghast at Demetrios, then gave a mock scream. "Aieeee! You're still there!"

"Sorry, Viv, but you and Geof shouldn't go snooping around other people's property."

"This pile of scrap . . . this *whatever* it is . . . belongs to the physics department of Flitheimer University, Dr. Demopoulos, and don't you forget it."

"I'm not about to with you around, my dear Dr. Vernon."

"Can it!" Vivian shouted. "Now see what you can do to get us out of this mess, and I mean pronto!"

"Yeesh," Demetrios said, wincing. "Yes, ma'am! Right away, ma'am."

"Uhhhh." Dr. Wussman got unsteadily to his feet and glowered at Vivian. "You . . . you horrid bitch!"

"Oh, dry up, you sissy. Can't you take a little kick in the balls?"

In stony silence, Wussman sulked off. Unable to find a place far enough away from his tormentor, he retreated down the hatchway.

Talbot had returned from the depths and got to work on the bolts. Now he had them all undone, and he and Demopoulos slid back the aluminum deck plate that allowed access to the engine bay.

Dr. Demopoulos peered down into the dark, machinery-clogged declivity, tools at the ready, a grin on his face.

The grin sagged.

The tools sagged as well.

"What's wrong, Doctor?" asked Diane, expecting the worst.

"Well, it appears as though that big shock we took bent one of the main rotors."

Vivian, not able to contain her curiosity, peered over the men's shoulders along with Diane.

Vivian edged closer. "Can't you, you know, bend it back?"

"Not without taking it off, setting it up in a machine shop, and hammering at it a little," Talbot said.

"But it would never be right," Dr. D. said, giving his curly head a shake. "Those blades are aligned to tolerances of a thousandth of an inch. The engine would never work right."

The television screen flashed with a tremendous starburst of light, and when the shock wave hit the crew was thrown around once again. When the rocking subsided, they all struggled to their feet and made for the television screen.

"Look!" cried Diane. "It's blowing up!"

Sure enough, one of the starships was cracking up in a soundless cataclysm of light. Dr. Demopoulos knew that if sound carried through vacuum, that explosion would have yielded enough sonic energy to destroy the ship. As it was, the spacetime vessel had been caught in the advancing front of the plasma fireball itself. Somehow, the ship had survived, and Dr. D. was now convinced that the "force-screen shield generators" that he and Troy had installed in the bowels of the ship—components no bigger than a good-size orange—had performed as advertised.

He realized quickly, though, that the shields could not guarantee complete safety. They could protect against radiation and high-energy plasma, but could not ward off everything. For the explosion had knocked the starship into jagged shards . . .

And some of the shards were headed this way.

# Chapter Seven

Demetrios scanned his instruments.

"The radio-detecting and ranging gear shows the leading edge of the cloud of debris to be about a hundred kilometers away. It's advancing at a rate of two hundred meters per second, so—"

"How do you know all that?" Vivian was curious to learn.

"Radio detecting and ranging. I had the idea for it long ago, but the mysterious shipment provided the mechanism in developed form. Essentially it tracks objects by bouncing high-frequency radio signals off them."

"Sounds farfetched."

"It works, Viv. Let's see . . . we should be mincemeat in about eight minutes. Of course, the cloud will thin out according to the inverse square law, so by the time it hits, we could have a chance. A slim chance. But that looks like a hell of a lot of wreckage to dodge, and it's all radioactive to boot. It'll be like dancing between raindrops."

"What can we do?"

Just then a strange voice sounded somewhere in the cramped compartment.

*"Whatever you do, you'd better do it quick!"*

It was an almost comical voice, tinny, coarse, but oddly familiar.

Dr. Demopoulos looked about, making sure none

of the others were playing tricks. However, no lips had moved, and no throats had quavered.

He stalked to the circular hatch in the floor and shouted down the hole.

"Wussman, is that you? Stop that nonsense!"

No answer came.

"That certainly wasn't Geoffrey," said Vivian, looking thoroughly spooked. "Sounded as though it came from inside the room, right here. Right next to me."

"Talbot, go down and see what Wussman's up to."

"Aye, cap'n!"

"And lose the nautical lingo, please, Billy Bud. Next you'll be asking me if I want to luff the main top gallant, and I don't even know what that means."

"Sorry, Doc." Talbot went below.

"Diane, go down and open the arms locker, get the shotgun and a few pistols."

"Well, at least you're prepared for some contingencies," Vivian grudgingly allowed as she watched Diane clamber down the hatch.

"I was an Eagle Scout. Of course, there are fewer eagles today and they're a heck of a lot harder to scout."

Vivian grimaced. "Spare me. I can just imagine you as an Eagle Scout."

"I used to help young women across the street."

"I thought the idea was to help old women."

"Listen, you define compassion your way, I'll define it my way."

Dr. D. wheeled around and cast a glance at the screen. Sure enough, scattered chunks of debris, visible as tiny gleamings in the starlight, were tumbling lazily toward the ship. He mentally calculated. Time was running out.

The disembodied voice spoke again.

*"Listen, people, not to worry. I realize you're*

*scared, but you got nothing to fear—until that junk arrives. Then you should worry!''*

"Dr. Wussman's locked himself in the head," Talbot said as he climbed back up.

"I'm sure he has things well in hand," Doc D. surmised. "Meanwhile, we either have a ventriloquist aboard or we're being visited by the Invisible Man."

*"Forget it, I'm neither,"* the ghostly voice informed our space-traveling professor. *"I'm flesh and blood, as you'll soon see. Of course, the flesh is weak and the blood is thicker than water . . ."*

As Diane climbed the ladder, weapons clutched to her bosom, a strange thing began to happen in the middle of the cabin. A tinkling musical sound grew to the visual accompaniment of multicolored sparkles, a microcosmic July Fourth fireworks show springing into being in the middle of the air. Slowly, the outline of a human form took shape, providing borders for the miniature display of pyrotechnics. Features and clothing colored over the flashing lights. Gradually the sparkling dispersed and the figure filled itself in. The end product was, to all appearances, a balding man with a bulbous nose, dressed in a threadbare tuxedo—black bow tie, boiled shirt, cummerbund—and holding a violin and bow.

"Good evening, ladies and germs, it's nice to be here. Hey, it's nice to be anywhere. You know, on the way across the galaxy I ran into an android who wanted a sex change. I said to him, what, you want to be female? No, he says, I'd just like some sex for a change."

*Bam!*

"But seriously, folks, it's great to be here, and to start off I'd like to play you a number, a little thing called 'She's Only a Crapshooter's Daughter But She Can Roll You for All You Have.' One and a two and a . . ."

The apparition began to play the violin, very badly.

Our dauntless spatiotemponauts, for the moment nonplussed and unable to utter a challenge, exchanged bewildered looks.

The man—or creature—scratched out only a few bars of execrable music before stopping abruptly.

"Hey, did you hear the one about the astronaut who couldn't sit down? He had asteroids. You can laugh any minute now."

*Bam!*

"Boy, this is a tough room. Is this a spaceship or the galactic morgue?"

"Who are you?" Vivian finally blurted, appalled by not only the music but the stale jokes. "And, my God, *what* are you?"

"Who am I? Who do you want me to be, honey? I'll be frank with you. And then you can be Frank with me."

*Bam!*

"What's that noise?" Diane said.

"That's a rimshot, darling," said the alien stand-up comic. "Lets the audience know I just did a joke. Otherwise, they'd laugh at my violin playing. But seriously, folks, do you know how many aliens it takes to screw in a light bulb? Depends on how many you can *fit* in a light bulb! All kidding aside, ladies and geriatrics, I want to say that it's nice to be working here at Alfredo's, formerly Nunzio's . . . formerly Vito's, formerly—"

"Arrrrgghh!" said Vivian.

"See here, you owe us an explanation," Dr. Demopoulos said indignantly, training a double-barreled shotgun on the strange visitor. "What are you doing here and what do you want with us?"

"What kind of popgun is that? You should sue Cracker Jack, you didn't get your money's worth. Play nice, junior. And now I'd like to do a little rendition of an old folk song, which I learned from a couple of old folks—"

"Talk, or I'll blast," Demopoulos threatened.

"Oh-oh, an ugly crowd. I heard of rough lounges but this is ridiculous. All right. You got any questions? Shoot . . . I mean, ask, ask!"

Demopoulos said, "Who . . . no, first tell us *what* you are."

"I'm what you call a virtual artifact. I'm projected, like an image, only I'm material."

"I don't understand that."

"Read my oral cavity. I'm a projection, like a movie, only I'm—"

"All right! Forget it, let's go to the next item. Who are you and where do you come from?"

"I was created by a great race of beings called the 'Krill.' "

"The Krill?"

"Yes, a great race, but I don't do race material, I'm a liberal."

*Bam!*

"Huh?"

"I keep pitchin' 'em and you keep swingin', but it's the last of the ninth, kid. Never mind, the moniker's 'Krill Man.' Krillman for short. Sid Krillman." The apparition smiled crookedly. "Call me Sid."

"Look, Mr. Krillman, nice of you to drop in, but we're a long way from home and in a bit of a jam."

"You're telling me! In a jam, he says. All you need is some toast and you could feed breakfast to an army. Let me ask you one. What's a load of primitives like you doing out in the middle of galactic space in a ship with technology that's a thousand years beyond you?"

Demopoulos grinned. "I thought the cheapjack comic bit was just a front. The Catskills are a long way from here. So, you have us pegged, do you?"

"Like a tool rack, pal. Actually, this getup was designed to be as innocuous as possible. We scanned your minds for language and culture and we were kinda choosy about our iconography.''

"Really? So what's your game, Krillman?"

"I was sent by the Triple-A."

"The what?"

"The Anti-Anomaly Association. We're a nonprofit group of highly advanced space intelligences who watch the proceedings in this galaxy and generally make sure that things muddle along properly and nobody gets hurt. Think of it as an interstellar B'nai B'rith. We also analyze freak occurrences. An anomalous space vessel from a low-technology level world landing in the middle of a high-tech space battle fits that category nicely.''

"So you've come to help us!" came the voice of Dr. Wussman, who was peering over the rim of the hatchway.

"Wuss!" Demetrios said. "What a time for you to rear your ugly head.''

Krillman looked and was dismayed. "Oh, boy, are most Earth creatures that handsome?''

"He's special," Demetrios told him.

"Actually, he has a sympathetic face," Krillman said. "It has my sympathy, that's for sure.''

"But he asked a good question. Do you intend to help us?''

"Well, first I'm gonna analyze the situation, and then take any action necessary. You gotta understand that this kind of thing doesn't happen terribly often, so we're a little bit rusty. Most of the time we just aid galactic travelers.''

Krillman began playing his violin.

"What gives with the fiddle, Doc?" Talbot asked his boss.

"I dunno.''

"I'm accessing my data storage areas," Krillman said. "This isn't a violin, really. It's a file cabinet with strings. Just a minute.''

Krillman played ten seconds worth of "The Minute Waltz." When he stopped he shook his balding head. "No. In fact, there are very few precedents. I'm afraid that I'm going to have to think twice about this gig. I'll have to talk to my agent."

Dr. Demopoulos, who had been surprised many times this day (Was "day" an appropriate measure of time to use in these circumstances—or could the old clock system of Earth simply be chucked in these timeless climes?), now stood regarding this undeniably real individual who had invited himself aboard the doomed spaceship—and was surprised yet again.

Meanwhile, time was running out. Massive chunks of debris loomed on the radar scope like a fusillade of thrown rocks, about to rain down.

If only he could think of something! But time for thinking was past.

"We're out of time, folks," Demetrios said. Now that he was staring the Grim Reaper right in the face, he couldn't honestly say that he was much afraid. He was more pissed off than afraid. To be on the verge of discovering a whole new universe, and then— phhhhhhtttt!

Wussman said, "Oh, well, I guess I'll go have my own one-sided *Liebestod* in my own little way." Mournfully he sulked down to the rest room and slammed the door.

Even the usually indomitable Vivian Vernon seemed on the verge of panic. She opened her mouth to say something nasty, but nothing seemed able to emerge.

Diane Derry steeled herself for sure and certain death, staring at the blips of the approaching blast debris as though she could deflect them by dint of sheer willpower. However, the various pieces of space junk, willful critters that they were, did not obey her.

Dr. Demopoulos squared his shoulders and cleared his throat. "Well, crew, it looks like we have indeed put hand money down on a piece of acreage."

"What's that, Doc?"

Demetrios's shoulders slumped. "Talbot, get a clue. We're goners, we're gonna die. The guy with the big scythe is at the door. We are soon to be former individuals. Am I getting through?"

"Sure, Doc! Uh . . . yeah."

"Good. I want to thank you all for making mine a most interesting life, and—although, speaking personally, I don't believe in such things—perhaps we'll explore the afterlife together. Just leave a note in my mailbox."

"Whoa, there, folks," said Krillman. "Don't forget about me!" He began playing his violin once again. "This is a little tune I learned at my grandmother's knee. Her name was Lilac. She could lie like crazy."

The violin began doing strange things; namely, radiating colorful emanations, coruscations of pure light that raced around the cabin, bounced off the curving walls and ceiling, and made pretty interference patterns, singing and buzzing and humming.

"How is that going to help?" Diane asked angrily.

"Well, it's pretty. Would you rather watch something ugly as you die? Tell the guy to come out of the bathroom."

As if on cue, Wussman came bounding up the ladder.

"I'm ashamed of myself," he said sheepishly.

"That makes all of us," Krillman said, still playing.

"I haven't been myself lately."

"We noticed the improvement."

*Bam!*

Wussman frowned. "God, this is so strange. Anyway, I'd like to apologize for my behavior. I'd like to apologize to you especially, Demetrios."

"Shucks, think nothing of it, Geof. Now kindly get stuffed. I've got a man's job of dying to do."

Demetrios hit the button that sent the viewport shutter retreating back into its slot. With a tombal calm that comes only to those with the sure knowledge of imminent death—or to any taxpayer on the eve of April 15—Dr. Demopoulos looked out into the vastness of space. The debris was very close, appearing as an approaching snowstorm of glitter. Somewhere at the back of his mind he believed that the alien intruder was a group delusion and should be ignored. He tried to concentrate on composing himself for death, his great mind sweeping back over the events of his life and preparing to give an account of himself should Pascal end up winning his famous wager.

The trouble was that he didn't like his life very much. In fact, he thought it sucked eggs. And Pascal was a silly ass.

Then again, maybe the alien was good for one more shot. What was it that Sherlock Holmes often said? One first eliminates the impossible; then one is left with the totally stupid (or words to that effect).

"All right," he said, turning. "Krillman. Or whatever your name is—if you really exist. Is there some sort of deal to be struck with you? You want your way with one of our women? Is that it?"

"What?" Krillman's ersatz face turned convincingly red. "Hey, you got me all wrong, pal! I don't go for alien babes."

Vivian Vernon said, "Well, it may not be a law of physics but it must be a law of the universe—you can't get something for nothing!"

"Listen, honey, I'm not a wolf."

"I'll bet you're a real Don Juan."

"That's right, women Don Juan anything to do with me!"

*Bam!*

"Sheesh!" Diane held her nose.

"Hey, really, my purposes are purely altruistic," said the strange stand-up being indignantly. "Listen, you seem like nice people. I don't want anything should happen to such nice people. I've decided to lend a helping hand, get you out of this mess, and then . . . who knows? We'll worry about the rest later.''

Dr. D. cocked a thumb toward the viewport, now nearly filled with the approaching debris. ''Well, I suggest you get on the stick and perform whatever super-science you've got planned—unless, of course, you're good at reanimating splattered protoplasm.''

''Hmm?'' The Catskill creature's beady eyes glowed briefly with a strange, far look. Then: ''Ho-boy! Have I let things get away from me!''

He placed the bow to the neck of his instrument and commenced sawing furiously. The instrument made odd noises, sounding not much like a violin anymore, but the output was music, of a sort.

The song sounded disconcertingly like ''I'm a Yankee Doodle Dandy'' by Alexsandr Scriabin as arranged by Spike Jones, but Dr. D. made no comment as he watched shimmering rainbows dance and cavort in the air around the visitor. Varicolored shapes gathered and parted. Pulsating spectra throbbed through the room, overwhelming everything and absorbing all into one gay celebration of color.

''I'm telling you, most beings are crazy,'' the Catskill eidolon quipped as he fiddled. ''Take my wife . . . please! Actually, I haven't been on speaking terms with her since we got married. On *listening* terms, yes!''

*Bam!*

''I'm going to throw up,'' Demetrios said.

A tilt, a slip, a sudden wrenching, as though the very fabric of space and time had become a rug, a rug yanked from beneath the feet of the senses.

Demetrios somersaulted into a pool of strange sensations. Normally, the doctor did not like strange sensations unless they were of or relating to sex, but out here in a strange new universe it seemed that novel sensations were the norm, not the exception. So he relaxed and let go, following the precepts of the Oriental sages, letting himself drift with the vibrational ebb and flow of the scheme of things, surge with the cosmic wash of an eternal tide, an inexorable force beyond time and space, beyond all understanding: the Cosmic All. Soon he was adrift in the ocean of Oneness, the sea of Eternity, whose sole chanty was the ever-repeating mantra of universal peace and love.

He absolutely hated it.

Nevertheless, having no choice, onward he sailed through the crisscrossing currents, the vortices of color and ripples of interference, noting this sensation and that neural response . . . until he stubbed his Tao.

Suddenly, with a gurgling noise, all the oceanic Oneness seemed to go down the drain, and the bridge of the spacetime ship coalesced into being once more; Demetrios found himself with his feet firmly planted back on metal.

It was much as he'd left it, an eternity ago, his companions still in the same poses, and the alien visitor still standing where he had before, stubby digits busy on the fingerboard of his battered violin.

However, there was a notable and significant difference now, a change that was crucial. Demetrios looked out the port and breathed an immense sigh of relief. The space that a moment ago had been clogged with masses of jagged metal and radioactive plasma was now devoid of everything but the many-jeweled glitter of star shine. In fact, there was no sign of the victorious starship, which absence also went a long way toward calming the professor's nerves.

"Well, there we go!" said Krillman. "You see! I told you there was nothing much to worry about. Now then, I suppose we should get on to the next item of business . . . but first I'd like to do another number—"

"Wait!" Vivian interrupted.. "The next item of business is getting us back to Earth."

"Earth? Yeah, of course. I register that as the name

of your home planet. Sure, Earth . . ." Krillman looked doubtful.

"Surely you can do that," said Vivian. "I mean, after all, you seem to have moved this behemoth a goodly distance with that whatever-it-is of yours."

"Could I dimensionally teleport this ship to Earth? I guess so. The question is, where is Earth?"

"Well, I'm pretty well equipped with astronomical knowledge," said the doctor. "Naturally, it's entirely geocentric, but as long as we're in our home galaxy, the Milky Way—"

Krillman blinked. "You name your galaxies after candy bars?"

"Candy bars," said Troy Talbot. "Gosh, I could use a candy bar. Come to think of it, I could eat a horse!"

Demopoulos gave his assistant a sharp look. "Talbot, at a time like this, how can you think of—?" He stopped, realizing how absolutely famished he was. "Food. Hmm, food. Talbot, I think you've hit on something. Maybe we should invite our new friend Krillman of the AAA to stay for supper."

Krillman scowled. "I hate dinner shows, but never mind. Uh, what's cooking?" The alien sniffed the cabin's already stale air.

"Nothing yet. Diane, you were in charge of laying in provisions."

"I sent Troy out to shop. Troy, what did you get?"

"Beans," Troy said.

"Beans?" Demetrios said archly. "That's all?"

"Didn't have time to do a proper job of shopping. Just went to the grocery store, and there was this case of canned beans lying in the aisle, there. Mr. Goodman was about to shelve them, so I bought the case to make it easy. Why is everybody looking at me? Don't you like beans?"

"You couldn't have varied the menu a little?" Diane asked, not pleased.

"Sorry. Like I said, there wasn't time."

"Do we have a can opener?" Demetrios inquired.

Troy fished out his pocketknife and pried it open. "Got one right here on my Boy Scout Camper Special."

"Score one for the Boy Scouts," Demetrios said. "Well, beans it is. Krillman, you're welcome to stay for supper."

"Beans, huh?" said Krillman. "I know what those are. What kinda beans?"

"What kind? Is there any other kind?" said Troy. "Why, pork 'n' beans!"

"Pork?" Krillman chuckled, "Oy, have you got the wrong alien."

# Chapter Eight

"Well, all right, since I'm not *really* Jewish . . ."

Seated on the metal deck of the control cabin, the alien creature called Krillman spooned up a steaming mound of pork and beans and examined it dispassionately, his long nose twitching as it sampled the odor. Then he shrugged, smacked his lips, and directed the spoon and its contents to his quite human, though overlarge, mouth.

He chewed, his face first registering surprise, then going into contortions of pure pleasure. Swallowing, he sighed and seemed absolutely overwhelmed by the experience. "Say, this is good. I heard of this stuff but I never had any. What vintage is it?"

"Uh . . . gee," said Troy. "A couple months ago?"

"Only wine has a vintage," Vivian informed the creature.

"Oh, right. Little glitch in my data files. Sorry. Gosh, this stuff is great. A little strange. Exotic. Yeah, exotic. But wonderful! My compliments to the chef, whoever he or she may be."

"H. J. Heinz."

"Well, he sure knows how to cook. Of course, almost any food would taste good to me. I never get to eat. I mean, it's rough being an artifact." Krillman took another mouthful and said through it, "Jeez, I'm happy."

"Heinz's pork and beans makes you happy?" Vivian scoffed.

"Like I said, it's rough."

"Don't the Krill feed you?"

"Feed me? I've never eaten before in my life?"

"How old are you?"

Krillman looked at his wristwatch. "By your time, about fifteen minutes." He smiled wanly. "I don't look my age."

"That's absurd. How can you be only fifteen minutes old?"

"This getup was created on the spot for your benefit, like I told you. Before, I was just a bunch of electrons whirling around inside a big computer."

Diane shivered. "Sounds so . . . cold."

"It ain't no picnic, lady."

"If you're just a computer artifact," Demetrios asked, "how can you eat?"

"Oh, I'm material, all right. But I'm still dangling at the end of a teleporter beam in case you guys turn nasty and I gotta duck out the kitchen. I remember one club I worked . . . I think it was in Cleveland—"

"I thought you were only ten minutes old," Diane Derry said, a confused twist to her palely beautiful brow.

"Sorry. I got implanted memories to make me more believable. They get in the way sometimes. Make me feel human, too human. It's rough being human."

Krillman worked his spoon into the dish, lifted out another moundlet of beans, and ate with as much relish as before.

Dr. Demopoulos solemnly regarded his own hill of beans. The brown legumes in their watery tomato medium, speckled with glutinous cubes of pig fat, were hardly tip-top in a gourmet's choice of comestibles. Although his appetite was considerable, he hated pork and beans. However, his intellect reminded him that proper nutrition was necessary to insure optimum functioning of the all-important gray cells floating lan-

guidly beneath his skull. Heaving a vast sigh, he word-
lessly ordered his intellect to shut the hell up.

He began to eat his meal. With the exception of
Troy, the other terrestrials ate dourly. The strapping
quarterback seemed to be enjoying himself, but the
thought of being millions of miles from home had
clearly damped everyone's spirits.

All human eyes were on the spacecraft's savior and
guest—with Talbot included, his gusto notwithstanding—but the humanlike creature who called himself
Krillman seemed oblivious. He savored each morsel
of food; then, having gobbled up everything, he examined the bowl to make sure he'd gotten it all. Thus
satisfied, he smiled contentedly.

"Hey, thanks for dinner. I really enjoyed it. Thank
you very much. Now, I guess we can talk about the
business of getting you back to your home planet."

The crew of the ship immediately brightened.

"You ain't got a chance," Krillman said, shaking
his head.

Demetrios spat beans. "Huh? Why not?"

"Because I've scanned your minds and your data
files and you don't have a clue as to where Earth is in
relation to where we are."

Everyone looked woebegone.

Krillman went on, "But . . ."

Hope sprang.

"We'll work on it. We—the Krill, that is—we gotta
be able to find this Earth place of yours. I mean, it's
gotta be on the map—*some* map. Someone must have
noticed your race by now. You're a reasonably intelligent species—maybe a little slow on the uptake, but
you're not total dummies."

"You're so kind," Wussman said dryly.

"Don't mention it. Actually, you guys aren't bad at
all. I actually wish my IQ were lower so I could enjoy
your company more."

"Big of you," Demetrios murmured, moodily picking at his beans.

"I have a gift for people. Anyway, give us a little time, we'll get back to you."

"Excellent," Demetrios said. "But we're safe here for a while, right?"

"Yeah, sure. That is, if your atmosphere mixture is correct and your life-support mechanisms continue working."

"They'll be fine," Dr. D. assured him, looking abstractedly at his beans. A thought suddenly struck him. "You know, I'll bet you could heat food by zapping it with radar waves. You might even be able to cook an entire meal using radar."

Vivian guffawed. "What a ridiculous idea."

"That cooker I installed in the mess does a pretty good job," Talbot stated.

Demetrios emitted a grunt. " 'Mess.' A drawer with some plates and spoons under a counter with a hot plate. Well, when we redesign the ship—" Something occurred to him. "Hey. We never named this vessel."

"How about the S.S. *Disaster*?" Vivian said sardonically.

"Not bad, not bad," Doc D. said, nodding approval. "Though I'd rather *Prometheus* or something a little more classy."

"How about the *Skylark*?"

Everyone thought it over.

"Nahhh," was the consensus.

"*Mudlark* is more like it," Dr. Demopoulos said. "Any other suggestions?"

A few more names were proposed; all were rejected.

"Okay, then, *Mudlark* it is until we come up with something better. Meanwhile, we'll put our heads together on that cosmological map."

Wussman said, "First, though, I was rather hoping

that our guest would tell us exactly who owned those space-going battleships."

"Of course. Least I can do." Krillman swiveled his head, examining the ship around him. "Yeah, I'm sure that creatures that can put together a vessel like this from a primitive technology can comprehend what—" Krillman noticed the look of discomfort exchanged among the crew.

"What's the matter? Did I put my foot in it?"

"Uh, well, it's like this," Dr. Demopoulos confessed. "I came up with the general idea for the electrogravitic thruster, and Talbot, here, cobbled it together from parts we designed and had fabricated at a machine shop. Cost a small mint, those parts. Anyway, the first problem we had was power. We had to deliver . . ." Demetrios took a drink of water from a paper cup. "Let's skip the technical details. Suffice to say the damned thing didn't work. There were simply too many engineering problems in the way. In principle, the theory was sound, but a working prototype was years away, on the other side of about two dozen technological breakthroughs. That was the state of things before somebody, somewhere, sent us all the internal guidance and power components we needed to construct a real working prototype, with all those engineering problems solved and all those barriers broken through."

"No kidding?" Krillman said, intrigued. "And you don't know who sent the stuff?"

"Haven't a clue," Demetrios said, shaking his head.

"Very interesting—very, very interesting. Obviously there's been some intervention here."

"By whom? Do you know?"

"Got some suspects in mind."

"Was it the Krill, by any chance?"

Krillman shook his head. "Not a chance. The Krill don't give away good technology."

"I thought they were humani—well, whatever the word is. Good-deed-doers?"

"You mean do they help people out now and then? Sure. Do they give away the store? Like I said, not a chance. No. I have to fill in some background for you before I can tell you what my suspicions are."

"Well, please do."

"In time, in time," Krillman said, taking a sip from his paper cup. Then he looked into it. "Pretty strange, this habit you humans have, ingesting large amounts of water. Kinda weird. Kinky."

"At least now we know," Vivian said, "what a fraud you are, Dr. Demopoulos."

"Huh? I said the theory was basically sound! I'm telling you, right before the explosion I saw this buggy levitate!"

"A likely story. When you pitched this whole business to the Flitheimers you had nothing, absolutely nothing. You've admitted it!"

"But we were on the right track. We had the basic idea."

"You have two tons of junk, cluttering up valuable laboratory space. Why don't you admit where the shipment came from!"

"Okay, I admit it," Demetrios said. "Now, you tell me where it came from."

Vivian spat out. "The Nazis!"

"The . . . ? Viv, baby, you've taken leave of your senses."

"Well, who else? The Germans lead the world in science. What other country can claim so many famous scientists?"

"Most of whom have left Germany by now," Diane put in.

"True, Vivian," Wussman pointed out.

"After the Nazis milked them of their secrets. I'll bet this whole ship is based on the work of men who now rot in concentration camps! Nazis steal everything, why not science?"

"I stole from no one," Demetrios protested. "And I don't have anything to do with Nazis. The basic principles propelling this vessel are mine."

"You certainly didn't filch any good tips on construction," said Wussman. "This thing is absolutely creaky. And there's no toilet paper in the bathroom."

"Oh, stuff it, Geoffrey. That goes for you, too, Viv."

"Eat shit and die, Demopoulos."

"Ladylike, isn't she?"

Wussman looked hurt. "Go stuff yourself, you big Greek jerk."

"Oh, now we're getting ethnic?"

With her spoon, Vivian flicked a bean at Demetrios. "Shut up, you fraud."

"By the way, Viv, did I tell you the dress is a knockout? Is that a Paris original or did you mug a cleaning lady at Saks?"

"How would you like to eat this tin plate, garlic breath?"

"Watch it, Viv, your male hormones are showing."

"At least I have some, which is more than I can say for some men!"

"Oh, come on, Geof has hormones somewhere in that pudgy body. And you're probably the whore he moans for."

"You bastard! Geoffrey, are you going to let him talk to me that way?"

"Uh . . . that was completely out of line, Demetrios."

"Olé! What a hero. Viv, you have great taste in men."

"I certainly do!"

"In fact, your tastes in men are uniform—army, navy, and marines."

"You rotten creep." Vivian threw the plate at Demetrios, who ducked and rolled. Still on her knees, she lunged for him.

"Whoa there, Professor Vernon," Talbot said, restraining her.

"Get your big dumb hands off me, hayseed!"

Diane jumped to her feet. "People, *people!* Let's show our guest that we're civilized human beings!"

"Right!" said Wussman. "Looks like lots of civilization out here in space. Ships blasting each other apart!"

"That's simply war," said Krillman. "All civilizations got war. You mean, your planet doesn't?"

Wussman could say nothing to that.

Krillman made a haughty face. "Mr. Goody-Two-Shoes."

"I'll let you go if you settle down," Talbot offered.

"Let me go or you won't have any hormones in your body either!"

"Let her go, Talbot," Demetrios said.

Talbot did. Dignity regained, Vivian seemed to lose her appetite for combat. She straightened her rag of a dress and sat primly back down on the deck.

"Of course we have war," said Dr. D. "Got a doozy going in Europe at this very moment. But we're not talking about us, we're talking about those ships we saw. Whose were they?"

The creature called Krillman cleared his throat. Then he took out a handkerchief and honked into it.

"Okay, I gotta fill you in on some background. But first, did you hear the one about the traveling biomass salesman who ran out of liquid fuel out in the galactic boondocks?"

"Please," Vivian pleaded, "don't go on."

"Sorry, that's my blue material. My agent books me into the class joints and I never get to use any of it. Okay, forget the jokes. Here's how it is . . . In the beginning, there was Darkness, Nothingness, Chaos, and Heinz Fifty-seven Varieties . . ."

"What?" the humans chorused.

"Huh? Oh, I was trying to put it in terms you'd understand. I'm talking about way back at the beginning of the universe, when things were pretty elemental. Says here on this can that these 'Fifty-seven Varieties' go back a long way.''

"Assume we know at least the rudiments of physical science and cosmology," Dr. Wussman instructed the alien comic.

"Gotcha. Like I was saying," the strange comedian went on, "all this chaos was stirring around back then, pretty much formless and hard to put a finger on. But let's skip ahead a few eons from the Beginning to the Big Kaboom, the cosmological dry run for the Big Blooey. As cosmological events go, the Big Kaboom was rather a dud. All this chaotic goo in the universe had gotten all clunked up together, you know, like hair in a bathroom sink, thick as Heinz ketchup, which I hear is pretty thick . . . sorry, never mind . . . which all made it very crowded. The laws of the universe hadn't been invented yet, things like the law of gravitation, the speed-of-light limit, and right-hand turn on red with caution. So there was *everything* that there was, all cheek to jowl and really not getting along too well, especially since language hadn't been invented yet and it was all energy and matter, soup, ketchup, and chunky chili sauce.

"Something had to give. A blowup was inevitable.

"This was the Big Kaboom, in which Energy attempted to get the hell away from Matter, especially since it was sick to death of baked beans for supper every night. Energy plotted. Energy planned. And then, one nanosecond, it made its break—and discovered, to its chagrin, that it had been so moribund for so long that in fact it had gotten its nose caught in an equation and so much of it had turned to matter that it really couldn't do anything but go 'Ka-boom!'

"Which was the first sound, the very first word created. But since there was no one around to hear it, it didn't count. No, the development of language had to wait for living, breathing beings to really get started. But before that, however, protons, neutrons, photons, quarks, leptons, and other particles had to coalesce into matter, and then they had to do the galaxy thing, you know, get themselves all crunched together—''

''Hey, wait a minute,'' Dr. Demopoulos complained. ''You're leaving out a whole lot of good stuff! Why, the problem of galaxy formation has plagued cosmologists for years!''

''Hey, who's telling this story? I gotta skip some details or we'll be here all night. Continue? Sure, no problem. Like I said . . . all that stuff got together into stars and stars grouped into galaxies and nebulas and like that, and the stars developed planets, and then the stage was pretty much set for life. I had a brother-in-law, wanted to go on the stage, be an actor in legitimate theater. Poor schmuck never had two dimes to rub together . . . but I digress . . .''

''For God's sake,'' Vivian said, rising, ''you're all mad if you listen to another word of this nonsense!''

''Why doncha sit down, Dr. Vernon?'' Talbot gently urged as he tugged her back down.

''Thank you,'' Krillman continued. ''So, for the first time, life began in the universe, only it wasn't so common as it is now. Now, intelligent races are a dime a dozen; but then, you could hardly find intelligence in the universe. In fact, there were only two really brainy races, one inhabiting a planet named 'Aspera'; and the other renting a planet (because they didn't think real estate was such a hot investment in a hard-money economy, as most economies were at that time) called 'Dharva.' Now, both these races were totally unlike life is today. They made 'em really strange back in those days. Both were pretty powerful, almost godlike. You couldn't quite tell whether they were made of matter or energy or what. They were kinda halfway.

Anyway, between the two of 'em, they pretty much
ran everything in the universe. Okay, it's pretty hard
to talk about good guys and bad guys when you're
dealing with gods or near gods, but the Dharvans were,
how shall I put it, nasty critters. I mean, they were
hard-nosed. They liked to play hardball. They'd spike
you sliding into second base anytime. Know what I'm
drivin' at? Albert Schweitzers they weren't. All they
could talk about was how great everything was when
Chaos was the only law and you could get a decent
egg cream with your matzoh ball soup at the deli down
at the corner. On the other hand, the Asperans only
wanted for the universe to be at peace. They liked joy
and happiness, universal harmony, and that stuff.

"That was exactly the kinda stuff that made the
Dharvans puke.

"Well, eventually these two races found out about
each other. The Asperans were willing to live and let
live, but the Dharvans weren't. They started a war.
(Scrapping is universal, you see. Goes way back.) The
Asperans didn't fight back at first, being peaceable
types. But then they started to get wiped out, and they
said, hey, enough with the whole pacifism schmear.
There was this big debate in the government. The
peace guys, the doves, said, we gotta hold to principles. The hawks said, principles, shminciples. Principles don't matter to a corpse—what, are you kidding
me? So there was a vote and the hawks won, and the
Asperans started fighting back. And then war broke
out with a vengeance. I mean, these two races kicked
the living crap out of each other from one end of the
universe to the other. Don't ask me how they fought,
'cause it wasn't like wars today. It was done mostly
mentally. But before long, things really got mental,
absolutely crazy. The whole *mishegoss* went nuts there
for a while. Another advanced race, that wasn't as far
advanced as the other two, from the galaxy of Thoraz,
tried to intervene. They succeeded in negotiating a

brief cease-fire. But as far as dealing with the craziness, the Thorazenes accomplished *bubkes*.

"Well, to make a long story short, as a result of this war, which kinda got outta hand, the universe blew up again. And that was called the Big Blooey. Chaos returned, sort of, and it was all kinda muddy. But pretty soon the universe began to sort itself out again, and regroup and re-form. And what d'you know, the Asperans and Dharvans were still around—scattered, admittedly—but as time and gravity began to coagulate things again back to a semblance of the original cosmic egg cream, the Asperans and the Dharvans began to form again. Only this time they were mostly energy. You could call them ghosts if you want.

"Ghosts they may have been, but they continued to fight it out. Only this time, instead of doing it directly, they fought the war by proxy, using as puppets all the new races coming along in the new, improved universe. Down through the ages, these puppet races mixed it up with one another, here an uppercut, there a left jab. There have been thousands of pairs of them, tussling, and feuding. The little scuffle back there that you witnessed was fought by two of their current proxy races, the Pizons and the Proons."

"Absolutely astonishing," said Dr. D. "But let me get this straight. There are two basic but opposing forces in the universe—the Asperans and the Dharvans?"

"Embodying the principles of good and evil?" Diane added.

"You got it," Krillman told them. "More or less."

Diane went on, "And these forces, constantly at odds, are presently doing battle in the forms of two space-faring races—the Pizons and the Proons, who we just witnessed battling."

"Nice recapitulation job, there," Krillman said admiringly. "Now we can get along with the plot."

"It's all very interesting," said Vivian Vernon. "But

don't you think we could wrap this up and get this ship back to Earth, like you promised?''

"No, no wait," said Diane. "This could all be very important in the scheme of things. The Nazis, for instance, Doctor. Do you think that they could be in thrall to the Dharvans?''

"Hey, it's possible," said Krillman, "but since your planet isn't mapped on my charts, I couldn't say for sure.''

"In any case," Diane said, "this is a situation that we of Earth should be aware of—and prepared for.''

"True," Dr. Demopoulos said.

"The Dharvans gobble up planets like after-dinner mints. Funny thing is, though, these puppet races don't know it. Don't have a clue they're being used.'' The alien peered around the cabin. "By the way, you wouldn't have any after-dinner mints, would you? I'd like to try more human food.''

"All we got is beans," Troy Talbot said, craving seconds.

"Oh, well. Too bad. Where was I? Oh, yeah—the Dharvans. That's why I'm telling you about them, to warn you. It's best to be prepared. So when I do give you a lift back to Earth or whatever you call your planet, you should acquaint people with the situation out here. Be prepared for contact within a few eons.''

Vivian grunted. "Right. That'll do our academic reputations loads of good, spouting off about godlike aliens in outer space. They'll lock us up and throw away the key.''

Dr. Demopoulos said, "Not if we show them the recordings the ship has automatically made and the data it's gathered and stored.''

"Right, hit 'em with the facts," Krillman said. "They gotta believe you.''

"Can you tell us more about these Pizons and . . . what did you call them?''

"Proons. Yeah, sure, it's just that I hate to do it in another expository lump."

"Oh, go ahead."

"Well, all right. Are you sure you don't want to hear a few jokes first, just to break it up?"

"We're sure!" Vivian screamed.

"All right, already. Okay, what I'm gonna do is just look up the material in the Encyclopedia Galactica."

"Where are they?" Talbot asked.

"Where're what?"

"Where are the books, the encyclopedias?"

Krillman tapped his head. "They're up here, kid. In my noggin. I'll just turn it on and let it talk. I got this little speaker embedded in my head, so the next voice you hear will be that of the Encyclopedia Galactica. Listen up."

Sure enough, a strange, artificial-sounding voice emanated from the top of Krillman's head.

*The Asperans and the Dharvans,* the voice said, *the two great godlike races of the universe, had battled each other for eons. There was another race called the 'Kwaaleuds,' which we have neglected to mention heretofore, but they were neutral, preferring to keep to themselves while pursuing their two chief racial crotchets: speculating in precious metals and amassing one of the most extensive pornography collections in the known universe.*

*As eternities of time passed, these mortal enemies and eternal combatants—Asperans and Dharvans— took to fighting their intergalactic wars through proxy races, the latest of which are the Pizons and the Proons.*

*The Pizons are a fun-loving race of quasi-avian beings whose home world is a tropical paradise featuring thousands of casinos and lots of little strip joints that don't charge a cover or try to stiff customers with overpriced drinks. The Proons are the indigenous race of the planet Hahmiroid and have a decidedly expansion-*

ist universe view; they are wont to raid strip joints and shut down gambling operations and generally spoil the hell out of everyone else's fun. A race of joyless blue-noses, the Proons roam the galaxies, on the lookout for anyone committing the capital offense of having a good time.

In time the Proons encountered the far outposts of the Pizon Confederation, a loose association of friendly worlds that shared a taste for gambling, rec-reational chemicals, and a glimpse of bare wing. With gimlet eyes, the Proons scrutinized this new civiliza-tion and did not like what they saw. Pleasure! Cheap thrills! Naked anatomical parts!

Horrors!

Coldly and deliberate calculation, the Proons began to draw up plans for invasion of the Pizon Confeder-ation. They struck first at an outlying solar system, that of a star called "That Big Shiny Thing Up There"—the native population, nice enough blokes for the most part, being a little on the unimaginative side. In a brilliant sneak attack, the Proon star fleet devastated the system, scorching every planet after smashing all the slot machines and subjecting all the females in the joy houses to a good lecturing. As a nasty fillip, they sowed the soil of all the planets with salt.

And then they spit on everything!

Disoriented by shock, the Pizon response was slow. But respond they did, fighting the invaders to a stand-off at the battle of Dirt (another planet whose native race was a bit on the dull side) and actually winning an encounter that came to be known in the history files as "The Battle of What If They Gave a Battle and No One Knew Where It Was?" The Proons, new to the neighborhood and not members of the local chapter of the Triple-A, got lost. The Pizon fleet got lost as well, but one feckless reconnaissance vessel did blunder into the correct sector of space and demolished a wayward *enemy garbage drone.* Thus, the Pizons won by default.

The Proon "defeat," such as it was, came as a stunning blow to the bluenosed interlopers, who had never lost a major battle. They regrouped and sent out peace feelers. One of these was arrested on a Pizon world for sexual harassment; but after this minor contretemps, the feeler—actually a robot diplomat programmed to give feather massages while emitting soothing cooing noises designed to placate birdlike beings—was admitted to the High Council of the Pizon government, where it negotiated a peace treaty. This nonaggression pact, referred to in history files as the "Treaty of Euplaibalwimee/Alplebalwichu" (the double star system where the agreement was finally signed) lasted for thirty standard years and ushered in an era of peace and prosperity for the Pizons.

However, it was the false peace of induced slumber. All during that time, the invaders violated every clause of the arms limitation accords and built up their armed forces until they had overwhelming superiority in both combat readiness and numbers. Then, once more without warning, they struck.

Fortunately, a right-wing faction of the Pizon military (who favored clipping their right wings short and ate only organic birdseed washed down with pure rainwater) had been expecting an attack all along and had repeatedly warned of it. In blatant violation of standing High Council orders, they launched a counterattack across the Demilitarized Zunn ("Zunn" being the name of the galactic neighborhood) as soon as the first enemy star cruiser crossed the interface. This lone ship transmitted a curious distress call—something about running out of a certain kind of pungent condiment. The Pizon Joint Command was immediately suspicious and gave orders to blast the ship out of space and follow up with an attack. The right-wingers were indeed proven right. The cruiser was in no way experi-

*encing gastronomical distress, this ruse being the
opening gambit of a full-scale invasion.*

*The battle raged back and forth. And it is at this
point that our story impinges on that of Dr. Demopoulos and his pals . . .*

"Not bad for an expository lump," said Dr. Demopoulos when the voice had ceased reciting. "Had
rather a dramatic surge to it. But how did it know
about *us* at the end, there?"

"I just threw that in as a gag," Krillman said. "After all, I am a comedian. I do it for a living."

"Why don't you start thinking about your job as a
Good Samaritan?" said Vivian Vernon, her eyes flaring hotly.

"Eh?"

"Your promise?"

"Promise?" Krillman yawned and patted his mouth
sleepily. "Oy, excuse me. Like a day-old *latke* I feel.
But you've been excellent hosts, I gotta give you credit.
You got a good thing going there with those beans.
You ever think of exporting? I got an uncle in the food
business."

Vivian Vernon could hardly contain herself. "You
promised to get us back to Earth, remember?"

"Earth. Oh, yeah! Earth. Just a minute." Krillman
took up his fiddle and put it to his chin. He bowed and
stroked tentatively, then played a sequence of notes.
Before long a 3-D panoramic display of stars and nebulas appeared above his head.

"A thousand points of light!" Troy marveled.

"It's a holograph," said Krillman. "A star chart."
He patted Dr. D.'s shoulder familiarly. "Now, if you'd
care to shoot me that astronomical information you
said you had, we got a chance of pegging the exact
location of your star system."

Demetrios seemed at pains to say something. "Uh
. . . well."

"What?"

Demetrios studied the myriad swarms of stars and clusters and galaxies. "None of that looks familiar. I'm really not so sure we're in our home galaxy."

"Is this your galaxy?" Krillman asked, pointing.

"Well, it doesn't look familiar. Do you know where Andromeda is?"

"Andromeda?"

Demetrios lifted his arms. "Well, now, that's silly of me, isn't it? 'Andromeda' is our name for it. You wouldn't know it by that name."

"This it here?"

"Nope. At least I don't think so."

"You guys anywhere near the Lucite Nebula?"

"Not hardly."

"How about this fine globular cluster over here?"

"Can't say I recognize it."

Krillman frowned. "We're gettin' nowhere fast. What kind of star is it—what, red, blue, yellow?"

"Yellow."

"Okay, that narrows it down some," Krillman said as he eyed the glittering map. "Down to about six trillion trillion stars."

Diane said, "Oh, dear."

"Yeah, it's gonna be rough. We could do it, though. It'd take about a century of searching by computer."

Wussman collapsed back onto the deck. "We're lost, doomed!"

"That's the fighting spirit. Never say die. Well, this ain't doing us a bit of good."

The three-dimensional star chart disappeared.

"Listen," Krillman said, "there's only one thing I can do under the circumstances. According to Triple-A regulations, you get one free tow to the nearest garage, or the equivalent."

"Well, that's something," Dr. Demopoulos. "Maybe we can get this crate fixed. How we're going to pay for repairs is another matter. Maybe we can work the bill off.''

"Good luck. Well, that's it then, folks," Krillman said as he stood up. He took a bow. "One free tow coming up. Hey, it's been great meeting you all. Before I wind it up, though, I'd like to leave you with this one little thought.''

"Oh, God," Vivian said with quiet desperation.

"A guy walks into a doctor's office with a chicken on his head. The doctor says, 'What are you doing with that chicken on your head?' And the chicken says to the doctor, 'Hey, not with my wife you don't!' ''

Silence.

"I don't get it," Troy Talbot said.

"Neither do I," Krillman said, scowling and shaking his head. "Another glitch. Oh, well, nothing's perfect. Anyway, now I'd like to finish up with a big number, an original composition of my own by Felix Mendelssohn. And a one and a two and a . . .''

Krillman began to play.

# Chapter Nine

Out of control again!

The ship seemed to tumble end over end as Dr. Demopoulos hurtled along with it, awash in a painter's palette of color. Garish pink and blue light invaded his eyes, swirled into his brain, taking root there to blossom into a nosegay of phantasmagoric flowers.

Desperately he clung to consciousness, but consciousness had other ideas. It slipped from his grasp, and the good doctor plummeted, splashing into the dark river of oblivion that gurgled and churned below.

At length, oblivion ceased being a river. The darkness sprouted streamers, confetti, and paper hats, twirling like a barbershop pole into a carnival of sights and sounds and smells. Ferris wheels tumbled and carousels turned; there came the smell of popcorn. The taste of cotton candy lingered on the tongue and rollercoaster screams of delight carried over the festive din.

He enjoyed himself for a longish bit of eternity, riding a wooden horse painted green and red with a long yellow mane. The horse went up and down, up and down; the calliope played "O Dem Golden Slippers" as a mechanical band clanged and tooted a raucous accompaniment.

He reached for the brass ring . . .

And then everything stopped. The carousel died with a wheeze, the band ceased. Colors faded like Fourth of July banners left up till autumn . . .

Reality, such as it was, returned, and he found himself sprawled on the deck of the *Mudlark*. Although a bit dizzy, he tried to stand up.

Everyone else was busy at the same task with varying degrees of success. Demetrios was the first to get unsteadily on his feet; he counted heads. Everyone accounted for, with the exception of Krillman. He wondered if the alien had ever really been present.

He sat at the control console and took a look out the viewport. Good-bye, stars. Instead of the glitter of distant suns against the dark velvet of space there appeared a network of shadowy tunnels, like the interior of an anthill or termite mound. Curious.

"Doc," Troy said, "that doesn't look like Flitheimer University to me."

"Talbot, you've a knack for the pithy but obvious."

"Where the hell are we?" Vivian asked, peering over Talbot's broad shoulder.

"Beats the pith out of me," said Demetrios.

"Krillman, would you care to explain—?" Vivian whirled around, searching. "Hey. Where's Krillman?"

Diane came scrambling up the interconnecting ladder. "He's not anywhere in the ship."

"Did you check the bathroom?" said Wussman.

"The door reads 'Occupé—Occupied—Occupado' but there's no one in there."

"I didn't see him go anywhere," said Troy. "He must have left the way he came."

After a look out the viewport Diane frowned. "Dr. D., where in the world is this place?"

Demetrios adjusted his thick glasses. "This place isn't in our world, I'm willing to bet." Demetrios felt obliged, as leader of the ad hoc expedition, to say something authoritative, lest his assistant lose all faith in him. "It does appear, though, that we're inside some sort of . . . enclosure with, um, tunnels."

"Brilliant observation," Vivian said mordantly.

"Sorry. Okay, Viv, you take a guess."

"Looks like we're underground."

"Maybe. What I was thinking. Caves? But those walls look too smooth. That's not rock, surely. Nor is it dirt."

"Looks like—intestines," Troy said.

"Yeah," Demetrios concurred. "Odd."

"Yuck," Diane said. "A huge space monster swallowed us?"

"Krillman said he'd 'tow' us to a garage, so this must be it."

"Funny kind of garage," Talbot commented.

"Yup." Demetrios folded his arms and looked thoughtful. "Well, we can sit here and wait for the mechanic, if there's one here. Or we can go out and take a look around."

"I volunteer, Doc."

Demetrios smiled up at his assistant. "Brave Talbot, stout Talbot. Stupid Talbot."

"Guess I went and did it again. What did I do this time, Doc?"

"For one thing, we don't know what the atmosphere's like out there. For another . . . but you volunteered, Troy, m'boy. Why don't you just trot on out there and check?"

"Sure, Doc!"

For her mentor, Diane had an admonishing frown. "Dr. Demopoulos, you *know* that if there's no atmosphere or the wrong atmosphere Troy will be in horrible trouble."

"He's a healthy lad, he'll recover."

"Just one problem, Doc. When I spring the hatch, everyone gets a whiff of what I'm breathing. You'd better seal off the upper compartment."

"I have a better idea. Why don't we consult the atmosphere sensors?" Demetrios scanned the console. "Here we are. Remember these dials? We installed them but didn't have time to figure them out."

Diane bent to look. "I think they're reading oxygen, nitrogen, and carbon dioxide."

"Right you are," Demetrios concurred. "And in a tolerable mixture at tolerable pressure—though it does look a little thin on the oxy and rich on the carbon dioxide. But not enough to worry."

Talbot was already down the ladder, humming "Swanee River."

"Doctor, pardon me," Vivian said, looking annoyed and worried at the same time, "but speaking as a fellow physicist, I don't think it's wise to open a door to a totally unknown and alien environment. Are you sure those instruments are calibrated correctly?"

Dr. D. shrugged. "What choice do we have?" But he had to admit to himself that Vernon's venality notwithstanding, her methodology was sound. "Maybe you've got a point." He rose from his seat.

"You mean you're going to stop him?" said Diane.

"Hell no. Help me seal off this hatch."

Demetrios, however, had not counted on Troy Talbot's gridiron quickness. Before they could crank the hatch out of its slot between the floor plates they heard a whoosh of air from below. There was a grunt and a clang and then a sound like a dull gong.

"Ouch!"

Demetrios shouted, "What happened?"

"Banged my head against the bulkhead," came Talbot's reply from belowdecks.

Demetrios, Wussman, Diane, and Vivian sprawled on the deck and peered down through the hatchway.

A faintly rancid stench wafted up from below.

"Pee-yoo!" Diane said, holding her nose.

"Well, no vacuum," said Dr. D., pleased. "And a breathable, though stinky, atmosphere. What's it look like out there, son?"

Talbot squatted and looked out the hatch. "Don't look much different from what's out the viewport."

"See anything at all different from your angle?"

"Stars."

"Huh? Not swimming in front of your face, numbskull. Beyond the ship!"

"My skull ain't numb, Doc. It *hurts*. Lemme see . . . Well, we're in some sort of chamber—yeah, and there's lots of tunnels going in and out of it . . . and that's about it, I guess."

"That much we can see. Anything to indicate this might be a garage? Equipment, other craft?"

"Nope. There's this sign, though."

"A sign? What does it say?"

"It says, 'Do Not Open While Vehicle Is In Operation.' "

"Intriguing. In fact . . ." Dr. D. did a take. "You moron, that's stenciled on the hatch."

"Oh, yeah. Guess that bump on the head's got me all goofy. I'm going to climb out. Here goes."

Talbot disappeared from view. They waited apprehensively.

"Okay, I'm outside the ship. Floor's a little slick. Otherwise . . ."

"Troy!" called Diane. "Do you see any living beings down there?"

"Nope."

"How about Krillman?" Vivian yelled.

"How about some toilet paper?" Wussman asked. "I've really got to go!"

"Nope. I don't see anything, guys. Whoops!"

Troy fell silent.

"Talbot? Report!"

"I see something now."

"What is it?"

"Get away from there, you bugger!"

"Troy! Troy, get back in here!" Diane yelled, all feminine concern.

"Get in now, or we close the hatch!" Vivian barked, not very femininely.

"All clear," said Troy. "It's gone now."

"What was it, Troy?" Diane asked fearfully. "Some awful slithering dragon? Some skulking beast with tentacles? Some monster with bugs in its eyes?"

Demetrios corrected, "Diane, the term is 'bug-eyed monster.' "

"Isn't that what I said?"

Dr. D. directed his voice downward. "Talbot, report! What did you see?"

"It was a snake, sir."

"A snake?"

"Strangest snake I ever saw, sticking its head out of its hole."

"What hole? In the deck?"

"Yup. Went right back in when I yelled. Funny thing, the hole's not there now."

"What did it do to you?"

"It sniffed me."

"Sniffed you?"

"Yeah, and in some embarrassing places, too. Darned thing."

"What did you do?"

"Swatted at it. Missed it, though."

"That might have been the mechanic, for all we know." Dr. D. sighed, shaking his head. "Are you sure it was a snake, Talbot?"

"Well, it was a funny-looking one. It had metal scales from the looks of it. Oh, yeah, and there were these big lenses sticking out of its head."

Dr. D. and Diane exchanged significant glances.

"Could it be some sort of alien life-form, Doctor?"

"Maybe. Sounds more like a robot, though. Whatever it was, I don't believe it was the mechanic."

"Then we have to make contact with whatever intelligent life form is in charge here."

"But where *are* we," Vivian wailed. "That's what I want to know."

Demetrios said, "My guess is we're aboard an alien

space vessel. Possibly the survivor of the two we saw slugging it out.''

''You mean that idiot Krillman didn't tow us to a garage?'' an irate Vivian complained. ''I'd like to get my fingers around that chubby neck of his!''

''Well, forget the toilet paper,'' Wussman said.

''If this ship belongs to the Proons, forget ever getting back to Earth,'' Demetrios said.

''Definitely forget about the toilet paper. Vivian, I want to go home now. Wake me up.''

''Be quiet, Geoffrey. Demopoulos, speaking of H. J. Heinz, this is quite a pickle you've gotten us into.''

Demetrios nodded. ''I'd say one worthy of old man Heinz himself.''

''And just what do you propose to do about it?''

''Well, I don't know about you, but I'm feeling kind of claustrophobic. Our trusty servant Troy Talbot has valiantly shown us that the air outside is safe to—''

''Achoo!''

''—breathe, and I would like to head up a party—''

''Sniff sniff,'' said Troy.

''—to go and explore the environs before environs explore us. And then—''

''AHCHOO!!''

''Oh, hell. Everything all right down there, Talbot?''

Talbot came climbing up the ladder. ''Yesh, shir . . . Must be one of my allergies . . . Shooo! Acting up. Sniff.''

''What exactly are you allergic to, Talbot?''

''Milk, sir.''

''Milk. There's *milk* in the atmosphere?''

''It doesn't smell particularly dairylike, Doc. And I sure don't see any cows. I mean, I haven't stepped in anything.''

''Well, see that you don't. Think you can take it?''

''Yes, sir, but I sure could use some tissue paper. I'm a little drippy.''

"Then we'll simply have to go on that trek for toilet paper." He turned to the rest of the stranded party. "Are you up to it?"

"Count me in, Doctor," said Diane.

"Actually, I think I could use a nap," said Vivian. "Why don't you three shuffle off and Geoffrey and I will guard the fort."

"Doctor . . . they're stowaways," said Diane. "Worse, they're academic rivals. Do you think it wise to leave them here?"

Dr. D. shrugged. "Someone has to keep an eye on the ship, Diane. Vivian's quite right." He got to his feet, as did the others.

"Are we going out, Doc?" Talbot asked.

"We are, the three of us. Let's get together what supplies we can. Vivian, if we don't report back within two hours . . ."

Vivian arched one eyebrow. "Yes?"

"You're shit out of luck. What's the matter, Viv? You look a little green about the gills."

Vivian made a face. "Those beans didn't agree with me."

"Sorry to hear it. I, for one, am looking forward to the olfactory possibilities of being cooped up in a tiny space with a bunch of people who have nothing to eat but beans. Okay, let's get cracking." Suddenly weary, Demetrios took off his ponderous spectacles and rubbed his eyes. "There's just one thing I can't figure, though."

"What's that?" Diane said.

"Krillman. He said he was tailor-made by the Krill to human specifications, based on knowledge of our culture that they gleaned from our minds. My question is, who the hell among us is Jewish?"

"Certainly not I," Vivian said.

"My name sounds Jewish, but I'm not," Geoffrey said, then added emphatically, "Really, I'm not."

"Geoffrey, your protestations are a mite suspect.

Because I know I'm not, and there's no way in the world a blondie like Diane could be, and Talbot, here—"

"I am, Doc."

"—couldn't possibly . . . What did you say, Talbot?"

"I'm Jewish."

They all looked at Demopoulos's footballing assistant.

"It's true," he said. "My dad changed the family name. I was born with the moniker 'Tully Tarnopol.' "

"Tully Tarnopol? But don't you come from a Midwest farming family?"

"Yup, in Nebraska."

"And they're Jewish?"

"Why not? My dad started out in dry goods but went broke. He borrowed some money to buy a farm, and . . . well, that's how we got into the farming business."

"But you don't—" Demetrios ran a hand through his salt-and-pepper curls. "Forget it. Talbot, you ought to write a novel. I have the title for you. *Good-bye, Omaha*. Never mind. Right. Let's get cracking, marines."

"Right you are, Doc. I'll get another pistol out of the ordnance locker and meet you outside."

"Check. Geoffrey, hand me that shotgun."

Geoffrey did, saying, "Seriously, Demetrios, what do you suggest we do if you people don't come back?"

"Come looking for us."

Wussman swallowed hard. "Oh."

"You asked. Otherwise, I think there's a deck of cards somewhere around here. Come to think of it, though, it's a pinochle deck. Why do they make those, did you ever wonder? Who the hell plays pinochle?"

"I'm sure I don't know. Well, good luck, Demetrios."

Demetrios swiveled his gaze between Wussman and Vernon. Then, in an impulsive burst of sentiment, he gathered them into a hug. "God, you've both been bricks through this. I just want to say that if we never see one another again . . . well, we'll always have Paris."

Wussman was confused. "But I've never been to Paris."

Vivian disentangled herself as though from the tentacles of something repulsive. "Oh, just *go*, please, before I throw up those goddamned beans!"

"Viv, you have no sense of camaraderie. You also have no sense of adventure, because this is one of the grandest adventures any human beings have ever undertaken. And you two look like you have a date with the undertaker."

"Just . . . *go*."

"All right, throw me out like a worn-out shoe. Use me, abuse me! I'm just a toy to you, just a toy."

Vivian's green eyes flashed. "You're a lunatic, that's what you are. Look what you've done to us. Here we are, light-years away from our planet, stuck inside the middle of God knows what monstrous thing, and all you can do is *joke* about it."

Demetrios struck a dramatic pose. "I was born with the gift of laughter and a sense that the world was mad."

"Dr. Demopoulos, please, for God's sake—"

Eyes suddenly glazing, Vivian put a hand to her stomach. "Geoffrey, I'm going to be sick. Fetch something for me to be sick into."

"Uh, I . . ."

Demetrios handed him the shotgun. "See here, Wussman, do the right thing. Poor girl can't make it. Put her out of her misery. One shot to the head, there's a good chap."

"But . . . huh?"

Vivian bent over and belched. "Oh, do it, Geoffrey. I want to die."

"Don't be silly. Demetrios, take this thing back!"

"Keep it, Geof. I just realized you'll need something to defend yourself . . . when they attack."

"When *who* attacks? Vivian, are you all right? Vivian, you look positively green. Demetrios, who is going to attack? Demetrios!"

As he climbed down the ladder Demetrios hollered back, "Whoever owns this crazy rocket ship, that's who! Good luck, kids!"

"BLEEEEECHHHH!"

"Oh, dear," Wussman said. "And I left the mop in the Annex."

# Chapter Ten

The walls of the giant spaceship were not exactly featureless. They bulged here and there, and in places they bore odd, ill-defined contours. Some sections were blotched and mottled; in other places the surfaces were rippled or warped. But for the most part the environment was a warren of tubelike tunnels, like the inside of a pile of congealed pink spaghetti.

"Gee, Doc, not much to this place, is there?"

"It does have a rather . . . *minimal* look to it," Demetrios agreed.

"Creepy," was Diane's word for it. "I could swear these walls are moving."

"They are, and their movement resembles peristaltic action. Heaving, like an intestine. Maybe we are stuck inside the gullet of some giant creature, like space-faring Jonahs."

"Wouldn't that be something," Troy marveled.

"It'd explain the foul odor—which seems to have abated a bit." Demetrios sniffed. "Can't seem to get much of a whiff now."

"You get used to smells," Diane said.

"You're right. Vivian's perfume used to knock me over. Now it just makes me gag."

They'd been walking along for perhaps fifteen minutes, searching for landmarks but not finding any. Troy had wanted to leave a trail of beans and had brought along a can in his knapsack for just that purpose. However, Dr. D.'s wisdom had prevailed. After all, he reasoned, the floors were spotless; surely there were mechanized janitors sweeping along regularly.

Failing to leave some kind of trail was a sure and certain way to get lost, the good doctor had to admit, but he thought the tactic unnecessary.

"We're bound to find the occupants of this ship," Dr. Demopoulos had argued, "if they don't find us first. They probably already know about us. No sense in leaving a trail. We have to find help or there's no sense going back to the *Mudlark*. I can't imagine getting lost inside a ship, space-going or otherwise. Besides, it's compounding bad manners to barge into someone's place and then litter it."

Nevertheless, as the minutes ticked past and as the three explorers padded over the mushy floors—turning bend after bend to find essentially what they had just left behind—Dr. Demopoulos began to wish they had dropped those beans or trailed a thread like Theseus in the labyrinth. The occasional vague markings on the bulkhead, which he had been selecting and mentally filing, had begun to repeat.

He shrugged off his doubts and pressed on. He was feeling more or less confident, still flushed with the wonder of being among the first of Earth to travel into space—deep space at that.

"Hey, Doc," said Troy. "What do you suppose it is we're inside—really?"

Diane said, "It must be a creature, because if it were a ship, the occupants would have shown themselves by now. Right, Doctor? I mean, they've just ignored us."

"We've been observed, if that 'snake' that bothered Talbot was some kind of remote viewing instrument, as I suspect."

"You mean the lenses, Doc? Yeah, some kind of camera. 'Course, cameras don't usually talk."

Dr. Demopoulos halted. "It talked?" He glanced at Diane, then said, "Talbot, you incredible bone brain, you didn't mention anything about it *talking* to you.''

"I didn't? Sorry. Well, it talked, all right.''

"What did it say?'' asked Diane eagerly.

"It said, 'Buzz,' '' said Troy. '' 'Buzzzzzzz . . .' ''

The doctor nodded sagely. "Buzz. Did you hear that, Diane? Talbot said the snake went buzz.'' He laughed. "Buzz. Imagine that. Open to interpretation, of course, but semantically it's loaded as hell.''

"No, you don't understand,'' Talbot protested. "It didn't *go* buzz.''

"I thought you said it went buzz.''

"I said that it *said*, 'Buzz.' ''

"Oh, it *said*, 'Buzz.' It told you to buzz off?''

"No! It just said, 'Buzz'!''

"Is that a nickname of yours?''

"Huh?''

"I mean, are you saying it *called* you 'Buzz.'?''

"I dunno. Maybe it did. My name's not Buzz, though.''

"So you're saying then that the word it said was 'buzz'?''

"I said what it said.''

"What did you say it said?''

"I said that it said, 'Buzz.' That's what it said to me.''

"It said the word 'buzz' to you.''

"Yup, it said the word 'buzz' to me.''

"Or did it say, 'The word "buzz" to you'?''

"Huh? No! It said the word 'buzz' to me.''

"It said the word 'buzz' to you?''

"That's what I said. It said, 'Buzz.' ''

'' 'Buzz.' ''

"Yep. And then it said, 'Buzzzzzzz.' Like that.''

Dr. D. heaved a great sigh. "Why is communication always such a problem?''

Diane said, "This is the first time humans have ever tried to communicate with alien beings, Doctor.''

"I'm talking about human-to-human communication. It gives me headaches."

"Oh."

"Well, let's keep buzzing along—as it were."

They began walking again.

"So, what do you think, then, Dr. D.? Are we in a spaceship or inside an alien space creature?"

"Diane, you're not paying attention. Maybe a bit of both." Dr. D. sniffed the air. "Do you smell something new?"

Diane got a snootful and turned up her pretty nose. "Sour milk?"

"That's it, then," the professor declared. "We're on the mother ship."

"The mother ship?" said Diane.

"The *mother* of all mother ships, from the size of it."

Troy said, "Wonder where all the little baby ships are."

Dr. D. shrugged. "I'm just free-associating, Talbot, don't pay it any mind, as vast and powerful as that mind of yours may be. Frankly, I don't know what to make of this dump, but I have a number of theories. The problem is putting them to empirical test."

Diane said, "Seems to me the simplest way to find out something about this place would be to ask the people who live here."

"If there were anyone to ask. Damn it, there must be some way of announcing ourselves."

"Hallo, thar!" cried Troy, cupping his hands to his mouth. "Hallo-o-o-o! Is anybody here?"

"Not *that* way, Troy!" said Diane.

"Talbot, how gauche," said Dr. D. "How boorish. You're a guest here. No, an intruder! Please show a little diplomatic protocol. Use proper terminology and appropriate honorifics when dealing with aliens." He cupped his hand. "Yo! Hey, tentacle breath! Anybody home or didja just leave your goddamn lights on?"

No answer came.

"Wait a sec," Troy thought to ask, "where *is* all the light coming from anyway? I don't see any fixtures."

"Light seems to be coming from the entire ceiling," Diane said. "It glows."

"What an innovation," Dr. D. said.

"A cool chemical light," Diane marveled. "Probably generated by biological means, like the way fireflies do it."

"What are you talking about, Diane?"

"Isn't that what you meant, Doctor?"

"I meant indirect lighting. Can't you see those little flaps running along both sides of the tunnel? The lights must be inside, shooting up toward the ceiling. We can't see them from this angle."

"Oh, right. Gosh, I hadn't noticed."

"Ah, you see, but you do not observe. Let's go."

And so they trudged onward, the good doctor's curiosity and awe slightly diminished, his disenchantment growing.

Where were these flaky aliens, anyway?


"I'm really disappointed in you, Geoffrey. No. Strike that. I'm absolutely ashamed."

"I don't suppose there's any coffee aboard this boat. I'd kill for a cup of coffee. Coffee always makes me move my bowels."

"You've displayed nothing but absolute cowardice throughout this whole affair."

"You're going to beat me?"

"You don't deserve such pleasure. And you certainly don't deserve any coffee. Even if there were some aboard this barge."

Dr. Wussman passed gas explosively.

"For God's sake, get back into the toilet if you're going to be doing that."

"I always get gas when I travel. And I always get

constipated. My system simply can't abide beans. And that's all there is to eat.''

"Don't remind me. I'm still nauseated. And I think I'm getting my period.''

"Darling, I love it when you're about to get your period. You always get so . . . wild. Are you wearing your leather undies?''

"How can you think of leather undies when we're stranded in the middle of outer space?''

"Sorry. Can I have a kiss?''

"Certainly not! Figure out how to get us out of this fine mess you got us into!''

"You were the one who insisted on burglarizing the lab,'' Geoffrey said.

She slapped his face. "And if you hadn't lost control of the Flitheimers there wouldn't have been any need to do it!''

Geoffrey rubbed his reddened cheek. "I think you still love me.''

"Oh, snap out of it!''

"But I adore you, Vivian, dearest. I can't think of anything but you.'' Wussman lunged for her.

She body-checked him and slapped him twice, both hands, the old one-two. His eyes wobbled.

"There.''

"Uh, thanks. I needed that. Where are we? Who am I?''

"That's the Wussie I know and love! Now, let me bounce some things off your head.''

Wussman cringed.

"Listen up, idiot. First of all, we're going to have to dump Demetrios and his idiotic sidekicks.''

Geoffrey was watching pretty lights. "Of course, my love.''

"And then we're going to have to get this boat back to the university.''

"Naturally.''

"It's our ticket to not just control of the physics

department—it could make us famous . . . and absolutely stinking rich!''

''Could I just be rich?''

''A figure of speech.'' Maybe she'd slapped him a bit too hard? That strand of spittle sliding down from his lips was a bit troubling.

''Oh. I like figures. I like to add and multiply and play with my slide rule. And I certainly like your figure, my darling.''

She *had* hit too hard.

''That's sweet, dear. So, are you for it?''

''For your figure?'' Life showed again in Wussman's eyes. ''I certainly *am*.''

''No. For rubbing out Detritus and company.''

''Rubbing?''

''Making them walk the plank!''

''You mean . . . ?''

''Actually, all I mean is leaving them here.''

''Oh.''

''Yes. We'll get the ship fixed and leave on our own. We'll get back to Earth, make up some story about our valiant companions getting lost, and take all the credit. I hate to admit it, but this insane contraption just might be the scientific breakthrough of all time.''

''Yes, yes. Uh, but it wouldn't do to just go off and leave Demetrios and his assistants—well, I just don't know.''

Vivian thought about it. ''You're right. We should kill them.''

''Kill th—?'' Geoffrey laughed nervously. ''You shouldn't joke like that. Why, we could get the electric chair.''

''Geoffrey, think. We're light-years beyond the silly laws of Earth. Out here, in deepest space, it's the survival of the fittest.''

''I thought that was in the jungle.''

''That's the way it is out here, too, my dear.'' She wiggled up close to him, her ample anatomy rubbing provocatively against his shoulder. "Don't you think that even as we speak, the doctor and those dimwit assistants of his are plotting our demise?"

"I don't believe it."

"Wandering out there was just an excuse to regroup. They're going to come back, probably in league with hideous space monsters."

Wussman suddenly turned and ducked into the head.

"Geoffrey, no use in hiding."

"I'm trying to move my bowels."

"Close the door, for pity's sake."

Geoffrey shut the door and was alone. "Aliens coming," he mumbled. "And I bet they won't even have any toilet paper either. What a universe."

An immense feeling of futility came over him. He felt like an insignificant speck floating in the infinitely immense blackness of space. Just a bit of fluff drifting, drifting in eternal darkness.

He thought: I really could use some Milk of Magnesia.


Vivian Vernon, on the other hand, was absolutely invigorated by the challenge. Now that she had some time to think, she realized what was at stake. No longer was it just a matter of a paltry grant. Now there was a world—no, a *cosmos* of power to contend for!

All she had to do was to find the right set of gonads to grab! She thought of the glittering stars she had seen. To think that her destiny was woven into the stars!

She loved that phrase. It was so . . . so mystical.

Although she had never breathed a word of it to anyone, Vivian Vernon, B.S., M.S., Ph.D.—quite at odds with her philosophical commitment to dialectical materialism—was enthralled by the occult. She owned a padlocked hope chest jammed with tarot decks, Ouija boards, and astrological charts, all of which she consulted quite often. Very often the stars and the spirits had foretold crucial events in her life. True, she'd never seen anything about a trip light-years away from Earth—but the readings always insisted that she would have interesting travels. Granted, there'd never been anything much about fame and fortune achieved by knocking off a crazy inventor and appropriating his spacetime machine—but they'd always insisted that there was some kind of pot of gold at the end of the rainbow. Well, sort of . . . if she fudged things a bit. Actually, in truth, her natal horoscopic chart had always strongly suggested marriage, a house in suburbia, a husband and five kids. But she had always taken these homey prognostications as a metaphor for her almost nuptial bond with the field of solid-state physics.

In any event, her moment was at hand! *Carpe diem!* Seize the day—and squeeze every last ounce of possibility from it.

Now, what to do first? First, she would have to go up and get a good look at that twisted rotor blade. There must be some way of bending it back . . .

This plan of action was immediately interrupted by a loud banging against the hatch.

She got up, went to the hatch, and listened. Hearing nothing, she said, "Hello? Who's there?"

Geoffrey cracked the door to the head. "Who is it, Vivian?"

"I don't know!" Vivian bent nearer the hatch. "Who's out there?"

The sound of a familiar voice conducted through the thin titanium plate. "Who else could it be? It's me, Demetrios, back with Geoffrey's toilet paper."

"That was fast," said Viv, puzzled.

Geoffrey yelled, "Let him in, Viv!"

"But I don't think we ought to—"

"Viv, please, I'm really going to need it soon. I hope."

"Oh, very well."

Vivian turned the crank that undogged the hatch. She opened it.

She screamed.

# Chapter Eleven

Geoffrey Wussman, Ph.D., heard Vivian's screams and was afraid. Very afraid.

In a sudden deliverance, his constipation problem was solved. He groaned with relief. But now another problem immediately presented itself.

"Geoffrey, help! He-e-e-e-e-lp!"

"Be right out!" Geoffrey yelled.

"It's got me! Help me, Geoffrey!"

"If you'll wait just a sec . . ."

Really, this was the awfulest thing he could imagine. The love of his life was out there, in the clutches of who knew what hideous creature, and here he was, embarrassingly indisposed and unable to help.

Unless—

He rooted in the pockets of his patched work pants. "Hooray!"

He pulled out a wad of tissue paper. After unraveling the crumpled mass into something usable, he used it. In just a few seconds he had himself hitched up and ready to dash to the rescue.

But he hesitated, listening to Vivian's horrid shrieking. What exactly was out there? He had no weapon. What could he do?

Then, quickly, something rose in him. His gorge, for one thing; but also something resembling courage. He loved that woman. If she died, he couldn't face life. He was sure of that.

Well, at least that's how he felt in calmer times. Did he feel that way now?

"Get hold of yourself, man," he heard someone say, then realized he had said it. Steeling himself, he grasped the door handle and pushed.

"What the hell took you so long?"

Stepping out into the compartment, Wussman beheld a strange sight. Vivian was the prisoner of pink spaghetti, wrapped head to foot in thousands of tiny strands of wriggling, writhing vermicelli. The entire bunched-together bundle of it, congealed and glistening, trailed out the hatch and downward in a long trunklike mass.

"What is that stuff?" Geoffrey asked, appalled.

"How the hell would I know? Get it off me!"

"But . . ."

"Get a knife or something! Cut it!"

"Right! Uh . . . know where they keep the knives?"

"You stupid jerk, how the hell should I know where they keep the knives? Look for them! Try those storage compartments!"

Geoffrey looked to his left. "Oh."

He rummaged through a bin containing blankets and nothing else immediately useful. He reached for another drawer.

"Geoffrey, look out!"

He turned his head. "What?"

"Your foot!"

He looked down. One strand of pink linguine had wrapped itself about his ankle. He felt it constrict. He tugged, and it tugged back. As he watched in horror, several reinforcing strands metastasized outward to join the first, encircling his ankle and calf. Whatever the stuff was, it had him. As more of the vermicules snared his other leg, he felt himself inexorably pulled toward the larger mass.

"Viv, dear, I'm afraid it's got me, too."

"That I can see, dummy."

In no time Geoffrey was completely enwrapped, hog-tied and helpless. The whole pink mess then began to withdraw, spilling out the hatch. Grim-faced but resigned to their fate, Vivian and Geoffrey flowed out with the noodly ebbtide.

"Where do you think they're taking us, Viv?"

"After the spaghetti comes the main course. Us!"

"Do you think? Uh, where's the sauce? I wonder."

"Wussman, you utter fool."


"Talbot, you utter fool."

"What'd I do now?"

"You brought the beans but not the can opener."

"Sure I did! It's right in my—"

Searching his pockets. Talbot suddenly looked chagrined. "Hey."

Demetrios eyed him sardonically. "You were saying?"

"Heck, left my Boy Scout Knife back in the ship. Somewhere."

"On the deck where you set it down," Dr. Demopoulos said with a sigh, throwing Troy's rucksack aside. "I'm famished."

They had stopped wandering and sat down to rest, more disheartened than weary. The floor of the tunnel throbbed unpleasantly.

"Hard to keep your head with so much happening," Talbot grumbled.

Demetrios stretched his legs. "As the poet said, 'If you can keep your head about you when everyone else is going nuts, you're a better man than I am, Gunga Din.' "

"Dr. D.," Diane said reprovingly, "that's not how that poem goes."

"I'm a poet of science, not a scientist of poetry."

"Don't you know anything about Kipling?"

"Having never kippled, no."

Diane shut her eyes. "Groan."

"Just kidding—of course I know Kipling. Knew him when I was a Bengal Lancer. Went tiger hunting with him once—me, old Ruddy, and the Raja of Chandrapore."

"Oh, go on."

"The British Raj! 'Lest we forget, lest we forget!' Khyber Pass, pukka sahib, and all that. Bloody marvelous, what?"

"Dr. Demopoulos, you can be such a silly scientist."

"You doubt me, woman? Why, I've the trophy in my study to prove it. Handsome beast. Got him with my .505 Gibbs, center shot. Winged one of the bush beaters, poor blighter. But the cat dropped and I had my trophy. The Raja was fit to be tied. He—"

"Uh-oh."

"Huh?" Demetrios turned his head. "Talbot, did you say 'Uh-oh'?"

"Yup."

"Why did—? Uh-oh."

Demetrios saw it now. A hand, quite disembodied but growing up mysteriously from the floor, had materialized next to Talbot. It held his left upper arm in a tight grip.

"What in the world . . . ?" Demetrios rose and took a few steps toward his assistant, but was halted by something that grabbed his leg. He looked down.

Another floor-spawned hand had him by the ankle.

"Ye gods."

Diane yelped as a pair of hands sprang up to pin her thighs.

All these mysterious appendages were alike: three-fingered, narrow, and of the same color as the tunnel walls, if a bit lighter. Although they did not appear especially powerful, they were nonetheless capable of exerting a circulation-pinching grip.

The hands multiplied quickly. Some grew long, rubbery arms and extended upward, taking handholds on the upper body. Soon the tunnel was thick with phantom arms and ghostly mitts, and the three Earthlings were helpless prisoners.

"Darn it all to heck, this is nuts!" Talbot complained. "Darn place gets crazier every darn minute."

"Heck and shucks," Demetrios said. "You sure have hit the nail on the darn head, there, Troy old son."

Diane squealed. "Some of these hands are getting awfully fresh!"

"I doubt that any aliens would be interested—hey!"

"What is it, Doc?"

"This one's measuring my inseam. Listen, pal, I love the way you do clothes but don't get any ideas."

The anomalous appendages began to urge their captives forward, hands handing off to hands, as it were, in a slow but steady relaying action. The three prisoners moved willy-nilly through the tunnel in this strange way.

"This is slick," the professor said, "you've got to hand it to them."

"I *knew* you'd say that," Diane moaned.

"If I had my writers here I could ad lib something better."

Vivian Vernon shouted demands to see her lawyer, the resident United States diplomat, or both; Wussman merely whimpered. When it became clear that her demands would remain unmet, Vivian began detailing the hypothetical and improbable sexual proclivities of the pair's unseen captives. This tactic proved fruitless as well, and Wussman began to pray.

The moving pasta mass whisked them through tunnel after tunnel, seeming to move knowingly through the maze.

"I'll sue! I'll sue you for everything you've got! You won't have two pennies to rub together after I get done with you, you rotten creeps!"

"Vivian?"

"I know people in Washington! Important people!"

"Vivian, please."

"If you had any idea of the number of important and influential people in the United States government that I happen to personally know and even be friends with, you'd be shaking in your boots, you lousy, no-good sons of—"

"Vivian!"

"*What?*"

"Who are you talking to?"

"I'm talking to whoever the hell is—" Vivian was suddenly crushed by despair. "Oh, God, I think I'm going insane."

"Vivian, darling, keep your chin up. We'll get through this. We will. I promise!"

"Oh, shut up, you little twerp! When I get out of this I'm going to cut your nuts off and play racket ball with them!"

"Let's not go too far, Vivian."

At long last they reached a destination, of sorts. It was a large chamber into which several tunnels converged. Here they were unceremoniously dumped and set loose. The squirmy vermiform mass dispersed, withdrawing into the walls and disappearing without a trace. The two captives were free, but not free to go. Strange tubular appendages extruded from the walls and surrounded them, blocking escape. Some had lenses on their ends, and these bizarre instruments proceeded to scan, scrutinize, and examine.

A rose-colored light flooded the chamber. Arms with three-fingered hands reached out from the walls, poked and prodded the captives, then withdrew.

Finally, a disembodied nasal voice said, "What sort of creatures *are* you?"

"We're human beings," said Vivian, who had ceased her litany of complaints, withdrawing into a sullen monotone.

"You are very *odd* creatures," said the voice. "You don't look like one another."

"I'm male and she's female," said Wussman.

"Bipolar sexuality," the voice sneered. "How perverted. Well, at least you can communicate half intelligibly. However, you have a lot of explaining to do. Just how did that primitive ship of yours get onto Level 7, Tunnel 192, right in our empty storage areas?"

"Actually, it isn't our ship," said Wussman, suddenly at home in a sea of talk rather than the nebulous regions of space. "It belongs to Demetrios Demopoulos."

"What a strange-sounding name. But of course creatures as perverse and unnatural as you would have an outrageous language and nomenclature. Where is this misbegotten creature?"

"Er, you mean Demopoulos? He went out to explore this . . . place you have here."

"This is a space vessel."

"Oh. Well, he went out to explore it."

"Attack it, you mean. From within."

"Uh, well, I don't think he had that in mind."

"He—that is the masculine designation?—he carries weapons."

"Oh, those. Well, he . . . ." Wussman didn't know what to say. So he asked, "Um, what space vessel is this?"

"You are aboard the Imperial Super-Outrageously Humungous Star-Straddling Flagship of the Cosmos, the *Vindicator,* owned and operated by none other than we, the Universal Keepers of True Morality, the Feared and Just-This-Side-of-Immortal Proons of the Heavenly and Tasteful Planet Nofunatal!"

Proons! thought Dr. Vernon. Of course! These were the nasty creatures that Krillman had spoken so negatively about. How wonderful of him to plop their ship right in their midst. But then, at least there was communication happening here, and even though they were plainly immune to her feminine attributes (indeed, seemed to find them rather disgusting), at least they might be vulnerable to her feminine wiles!

"Proons! You're the guys who are fighting the Pizons, right?" said Wussman, who, even though he'd been in that toilet, had pretty much followed the whole proceedings. "You're the folks who've been carrying on such a noble and excellent crusade in the cosmos!"

Good old Wussman, thought Vernon. A rank coward, but put him with a superior and the right words would flow out slicker than snake droppings.

"You've heard of us, even though you are clearly from a planet not of our knowledge?"

"That's right!" piped Vernon, eager to cast her own two cents into a winning hand. "And you know what . . . There's a very good chance that we can *help* you!"

"Hmmm! It is questionable that a superior race like ours actually needs help—but your sentiment is politically correct and you bear the marks of creatures who are willing to be educated."

"Communication!" said Wussman. "It's all a matter of proper education! Now, can we talk this over—face-to-face. We're feeling a little uneasy here . . . like bugs under a microscope, you know?"

"But you *are* bugs under a microscope. You are intellectual filth that we have just wiped off our boots. You are common space bacteria who cannot even aspire to our lofty range of morality and intellect!"

"Yes, but we know something that you don't!"

Pause. "You do?"

"Hmmm hmm. Something really, really juicy," said Vernon.

"Oh? What?"

"We know where there's a planet that's quite the *naughty* planet!" said Wussman.

"Yes!" said Vernon. "A planet that could really use a good spanking!" She slapped her hand on her thigh.

"And you just might be the big and noble creatures just right to give it to them."

"Hmmm. Yes . . . We're also looking for naughty planets. Which one is this?"

"It's called 'Earth.' "

# Chapter Twelve

The mysterious alien hands bore them ever onward. The walls sprouted new appendages, these looking more like the "snake" Talbot had conversed with.

Dr. Demopoulos ruminated on all this awhile, weighing all the various factors and considerations. Then he said, "Yes, yes, it's definite."

"What is?" Diane asked.

"I'm really getting tired of this crap."

"You're not a girl," Diane said. "These jokers are still pawing me in sensitive places."

"I'd enjoy being a girl, if I were a girl."

"No you wouldn't."

Finally, they seemed to have arrived at some destination. A membrane ahead dilated and admitted them into another spacious, irregularly shaped chamber, and in the middle of it stood something surprising.

A spaceship.

This was no great surprise as such, and actually it was a relief from the monotony of all those endless corridors. And after all, a large mother ship was bound to have tiny little baby ships—Demetrios had already hypothesized as much.

However, there were definitely incongruous things about this ship—unexpectedly incongruous.

For one, the lines and angles of the ship were decidedly at odds with those of the hallway. It was obvious that the shipwrights were just as different for this boat as they were for Dr. D.'s.

For another, it somehow was fitted into a cavern of the hallway, rather like a crab in a seashell, its nose poking out only slightly.

Suddenly, the phantom appendages released their captives and withdrew.

"Wow!" said Troy. "Another ship! What do you think, Doc? Another bunch of hapless space travelers, lost in space and time?"

"Speak for yourself, Talbot," said Dr. D. "I feel quite comfortable in this situation. I am not lost, only exploring. Now then, let's have a look."

"Okeydoke!" Without compunction or pause, Troy Talbot loped up to the vessel, found something resembling a door, and knocked a 'shave and a haircut—two bits' rap upon the metal.

"He didn't say wake up the inhabitants!" Diane stepped back, looking as though she were ready to run for her life.

"Let's just hope the thing isn't filled with tentacled beasties who go for full-breasted beautiful assistants," Dr. D. said, not at all adverse to the idea of meeting someone who might tell him something—anything— about where exactly they were.

As it happened, they were in luck.

The door opened with a squeak of rusty hinges.

Eyes peeked out from the gloom.

Four eyes.

"Yeah?" said a wary voice. "Stand a little farther back . . . I'll warn ye—I've got a pretty big blaster here."

"If you and your friend would care to step out so we can see you," said Dr. D., raising his hands in the air to show they were unarmed and nodded to his companions to do the same. "We can make friends."

The four eyes stepped out from the spaceship. They were attached to one being. They wiggled above a bald dome like a hunchback who uses his hump for a head.

Two arms, two legs, draped with a kind of purple velvet with tassles.

And as promised, the triple-jointed arm held a weapon like a weirdly assembled bunch of Tinkertoys with a multicolored lamp in its middle.

"Howdy!" said the affable athlete, grinning. "I'm Troy Talbot, and you must be an alien! This trip just keeps on getting better and better."

"An alien that speaks English," said Diane. "Pretty curious."

"The same variety of English as dizzy old Krillman, I bet," said Dr. D. "Utilizing the same kind of translator, I shouldn't be surprised."

The effect of that name upon the alien was immediate.

"Krillman! That bastard!" The eyestalks wobbled excitedly, the eyes blinking and turning a variety of unusual colors. "Are you in cohoots with that villain?" It extended the weapon so that the business end touched the tip of Troy Talbot's nose.

"No, no!" said Troy. "He was supposed to send us back to Earth. Instead we landed here."

"Right," concurred Diane. "The problem is, we don't know exactly where *'here'* is!"

The alien pulled the bore of the gun away from Troy Talbot's nose. "Hmmmpf!" it said. "Another bunch of goofs in the same situation as I'm in! Well, I'm not surprised. That Krillman fellow is an absolute menace. He should be reported to the Triple-A place he claims he's from!"

"Perhaps he's some sort of recruiter for rats to run this maze," said Diane sardonically.

"Rats?" said Troy. "I don't see any rats!"

"Eat your cheese and shut up, Talbot." The doctor turned back to the alien. "Listen, nice to meet you. Uh, say. Do you have any clue where we are?"

"You really don't know?" The particolored eyes

blinked incredulously. Bits of its body wobbled gelat-
inously.

Dr. D. presumed this was the display for some sort
of emotion, but its exact nature was difficult to determine.

"We only just got here," said the doctor.

"Well, folks. Sorry to break it to you this way, but
you've just landed on the biggest ship in the universe—
a ship about the size of a small planet. It's a mother
ship—"

"Just like we thought!" Troy burbled.

"—and it belongs to the meanest mother shippers
in the whole universe."

"You don't mean . . ." said Diane, grimacing.

"Yes, I do mean, and I do mean *mean*!" An intake
of breath, a flutter of gills, a significant widening of
four eyes. "The Proons!"

"Yes, the planet is called Earth and that's where
we're from," said Dr. Vivian Vernon. "And we're
just the people who can tell you how to get there and
how to run it and who the really naughty people are
there. And taking it over will be a lot easier than duking it out with those difficult Pizon creatures. Not only
are morals low on Earth. So is technology!"

"Oh, dear yes!" babbled Wussman, catching onto
the drift of the proceedings and clearly approving totally. "And all the universities there are in sore need
of better guidance than they're getting!"

"Absolutely! So what about a deal! We help you
conquer Earth," said Vivian. "And you put us in
charge of the universities there!"

Perfect! Absolutely wonderful! No sooner had the
thought sprung to her mind than it blasted off out of
her mind, fully formed and complete. Why, this was
turning out even better than she'd possibly imagined.
There'd be no need now to show off a silly new kind
of engine and grapple their way on some ladder to

success. They'd just help these weird beings, show them the way, whatever, and then deign to accept the spoils. Oh, there may be some death rays blasted here and there (and maybe directed at a few bothersome professors—oops!), a little muss and fuss, maybe some casual genocide, but hey! As Joe Stalin had said, you gotta break a few eggs to make an omelet! (Well, he didn't exactly say that, but never mind.) Besides, in the end, Earth would be a far better planet.

And certainly it would have better universities.

"Indeed. How intriguing!" said the voice.

"So, is it a deal?" said Wussman in the tried and true American tradition, trying to close the same. He almost even extended his paw for a glad-handing shake, but fortunately managed to suppress the urge.

"Maybe the superior beings would rather get to know us first, Geoff." she stepped forward. "I am Dr. Vivian Vernon. This is Dr. Geoffrey Wussman. We are both physicists of high standing on the planet Earth. We admit we are not as advanced as your clearly superior culture. But perhaps we can learn." She thought for a moment, scratching her nose, casting her mind back to what had been said by both this voice and the other beings. "Certainly we are willing to aspire to your excellent moral caliber."

"Excellent!" said the voice.

Bull's eye! thought Vivian.

The voice went on, "You have very far to go, mind you. But it is good that you are willing to assay a moral turnabout. And by the way—conquering this planet of yours and putting it upon the path to proper conduct is an excellent concept. We are always on the lookout for worlds needy of our firm hand!"

"Then we can talk about this?" Vivian said brightly.

"Yes, let's *do* talk. We've already examined you anyway, and you seem harmless enough!"

A door irised.

"Nice irises," said Vivian, bending over to smell

the pretty flowers ringing the door that had just opened.

"You have excellent taste in flowers!" said Wussman, making sure they knew he admired the purple blooms as well.

They walked through the door into another room.

"Excellent, Geoffrey," said Vivian. "I think we've concocted a superior plan!"

"I get Harvard!" piped up Wussman, very pleased with himself.

Vernon elbowed him in the side. "Shut up. Don't count your universities before they're hatched. We've got a long way to go yet."

They walked into a room with considerably more furniture than an examination/interrogation room, but somehow just as severe. There was a door on the other side of the room marked RECREATION ROOM. A sign across it read: CLOSED INDEFINITELY.

Instruments like tinny trumpets tootled.

With great ceremonial dignity a creature much like the ones that had carted the doctors there entered, with two other Proons by his/her/its side. The creature was wearing a long flowing robe, completely hiding its body. Its face was partially hidden behind what looked for all the world to be a Groucho Marx mask—bushy eyebrows, spectacles, hooked nose, and mustache.

Wussman giggled.

Vernon kicked him in the shin. "Quiet, you fool!"

The head Proon pointed a tentacle at the prisoners. "Release them of their fetters!" he commanded.

The other creatures, masked like the one who commanded them, scurried forward and unlatched the cuffs on Vernon and Wussman. Their robes had sleeves that accommodated multiple tentacles. Vivian tried to count them but they moved too fast.

"Thank you!" said Vivian. She was tempted to smile, but she decided that a smile would not be taken well by these sorts of creatures, so she simply nodded very seriously.

"Yes, thank you," said Wussman. "I don't suppose you'd have an Alka-Seltzer, would you?"

Vivian kicked him again.

"Excellent," said the creature. "I approve of your chastisements. Clearly you keep your lackey in line, Vernon being. A true sign of the rudiments of civilization." He cleared his voice self-importantly. "I am the Grand Proon, resident counselor and general head of the Proons hereabout, and also, by the by, head Inquisitor."

"Why's he wearing that Groucho Marx mask, anyway?" whispered Wussman. "Do they get comedy movies out here?"

"Must be purely coincidence. Anyway, shhh!"

"Yes, darling. But you really must—"

She kicked him again for good measure.

"Ow. That one hurt."

The Grand Proon cleared his throat. "Is this some rite of human beings that I'm not familiar with!"

"We were just admiring the nobility of your carriage and the courage that shows on your face," said Vivian. "To say nothing of your integrity."

"Ah. I am glad that it shows through this regal mask I wear. Thank you. And how, by the way, do you like our masks . . . Items that you do not seem to have . . . You go about with naked faces . . . although, in truth, you do not seem to have much to hide."

Vernon and Wussman exchanged glances.

"Wonderful!"

"Gorgeous."

"Excellent. Then you will be honored to wear the same, so that we will no longer be subjected to the stark and shameful, ugly nakedness of your human faces."

"Er . . . well, I really don't think . . ."

Vivian kicked him in the shin again.

"We'd be *happy* to wear the masks. Indeed it would be a wonderful honor."

The Grand Proon nodded and then clapped his hands. Immediately, a Proon servant trundled out, carrying two Groucho Marx masks and handing them to Drs. Vernon and Wussman.

Vivian checked hers. They seemed to be made of plastic, and on closer inspection they were different from the Earth version. The spectacles were bigger and the eyebrows weren't really eyebrows but some sort of decoration. The nose was gigantic, and she wondered what it was supposed to hide. The whole affair was held in place by a wide elastic band around the head. She put hers on and then looked over at Wussman, who had also donned his.

She had to suppress a giggle of her own.

"You don't exactly look dignified yourself, honeybun," said Wussman.

"I once shot an elephant in my pajamas," said Vernon in an uncharacteristic lapse of humor. "What it was doing in my pajamas I'll never know."

It broke the tension, but seemed to annoy the Grand Proon.

"Stop that this minute! I cannot abide laughter!" he stormed. "It signifies *fun*! And fun inevitably implies immorality and degradation!"

He stomped up and down, his Groucho Marx mask wobbling precariously on his face.

Vivian Vernon could not help but wonder what the mask hid. What kind of nose did the thing have? Curious . . . Did all advanced interstellar species have nose problems?

She and Wussman stopped chuckling immediately. No sense in spoiling a good thing.

"A thousand apologies!" said Wussman.

"You can see that we need instruction, but we shall aspire to your high achievements," said Vernon. "You may beat my companion here, if you like, even though it will cause me great pain!''

"Uh," said Wussman. "Now, wait a minute . . .''

"Just as well. Keep the fellows busy." The Grand Proon nodded at his henchmen, who ran over and dragged Wussman kicking and screaming from the room.

"Oh, the pain! But thank you, thank you for your wonderful instruction!" said Vernon as Wussman's yowls filtered through from the next room.

"Now then," said the Grand Proon. "Let us discuss the best way to get to Earth."

"Well, first off," said Dr. Vernon, her voice slightly muffled by the Groucho Marx mask. "We're going to have to deal with a certain troublesome doctor and his fellow stowaways about our spaceship. And my goodness," she leered. "Have *they* ever been naughty!"

Dr. Demopoulos had to admit that in the entirety of his admittedly dodgy career he'd never before careened and kiltered from disastrous event to disastrous event with such speed. The explosion. The near success of his rivals to ruin the physics department. The catapulting into Who-Knows-When/Who-Knows-Where utilizing the (let's face it) Who-Knows-What-Drive. Bumbling into a space battle, nearly getting crunched—and then saved by a being with the strange name of Krillman, who in turn handily delivered them from the atomic frying pan into the atomic fire . . .

If it all wasn't so exhilarating, it would all simply be too much.

Running into this alien here, of course, could not be considered disastrous—but it nonetheless had that definite potentiality.

Dr. D. wasn't sure whether it was the way the thing's eyes tilted, and the way it would froth at its mouth on certain words . . . But it definitely felt like trouble.

"The Proons," said Troy. "I don't suppose they're the good guys, huh?"

"You don't listen! You *never* listen!" wailed Diane. The pressure was plainly getting to her. She looked like she was about to blow a gasket.

"Go ahead. Belt him if it'll make you feel better," said Dr. D.

Diane hit Troy in the arm.

He looked puzzled, but not terribly hurt.

"Hey. What'd you do *that* for?"

"For your good, for my good. But mostly *my* good. You know, we've got enough comic relief in this farce of an adventure. We don't need any more really stupid comments from you."

"Actually, I rather enjoy them," said Dr. D. "Keep it up, Troy. We're not quite sure what logic this world runs by, and you could well turn up something positively brilliant that will save our butts."

"What did you have me hit him for?" said Diane.

"Better him, my dear, than me . . . or, certainly, our current host."

"Strange, violent beings," said the alien.

"Yes. Sorry. But let's get back on track here. We're on the Proons' mother ship . . . presumably that ship that launches the other ships that battle the Pizons and generally make menacing forays into the universe."

"That's correct." The eyes wobbled as the thing agreed.

"I guess the first appropriate thing to ask," said Dr. Demopoulos, "is A, how do we get hold of Krillman, and B, what do we do with him when we *do* get hold of him?"

"I've got a few suggestions on that one," Diane said. "And two involve a caldron of boiling oil."

"I sense much anger here," said the alien. "I, too, was angry until I ascertained that I should get even. And then, when I examined fully the nature of the universe in my meditations here in the belly of this space whale, I concluded that I should not blame the being known as Krillman. For is it not true, as one of the Ancient Masters of our universe said—Squigley, I believe his name was—that the underlying principles of the universe are not merely absurd, they are goofy.''

"Oh. And who made them goofy? What does Squigley say about that?''

"His answer would have been, 'The sound of one tentacle slapping.' ''

"An alien Zen master! How fascinating,'' said Dr. D. "Although philosophy hasn't seemed to do you much good in getting you out of this place.''

"No, this is true. But it has given me further time to mentally delve into the conceptual secrets of the universe. So far I am a bit gummed up in ontology, metaphysics, and the cosmic implications of the Altairan Bubble Gum trees, but hey, it's been something to while away the time with.''

"Well, as long as the Proons haven't found you or found us, I would rather imagine that time is something we've got plenty of.''

"Speak for yourself! I'd like to get back to Earth!'' said Diane.

"Yeah! The football team *needs* me!''

"Talbot, they need you like they need a bad cold. How can you think of football at a time like this? This is mankind's greatest adventure. The awe, the mystery, remember? Don't you want to travel to the farthest end of the universe?''

"I'd rather do an end run and score a touchdown.''

"You're hopeless.''

"We have not yet exchanged names,'' the alien said.

The doctor made introductions. "And what are you called, sir?''

"My name is Spon,'' the alien said.

"Spon, eh? Well, pleased to meet you.''

"Gladness is in my circulatory pump. Please enter my humble abode. I shall serve tea.''

Silently mouthing "Tea?" and exchanging baffled looks, the Earthmen went in. The inside of the ship was peculiar, but hardly stranger than the weirdness outside. In fact, it looked positively homey.

The doctor stretched and sat down on one of the globular-shaped pillows that the alien indicated. The effect was immediate: the extended report of flatulence. Dr. D. looked absolutely stunned.

His companions broke into laughter.

"A whoopee cushion!" said Troy.

"Boy, I needed that!" said Diane. "You sure got the doc, Spon!"

The alien looked bemused. "Why the hilarity? These are merely the sounds of hospitality. As the old saying goes, the wind itself must take a break in order to relax. Please—you must sit as well. You do not wish to offend, do you, gentle guests?"

"Yes! Sit. Right here, two more cushions," offered Dr. D. "Just waiting for you."

Troy shrugged. "Okeydoke." He plopped down onto his cushion, and the sound, if anything, was louder. He laughed.

"I'm sorry. But I refuse to be responsible for such a rude noise!" said Diane, folding her arms stubbornly over her chest.

"Come on, Diane! When in Rome!"

"You know these lovely sounds of company," said Spon. "They are increasing my concentration. I am seeing all kinds of possibilities now that I am factoring others into my equation. Memories are unfolding like flowers."

"Okay, okay, but you'd better not laugh."

Diane sat down with predictable explosive results.

Troy and Dr. D. did not laugh, but it was clear that they were hard-pressed not to.

"So go ahead," said Diane, after their tea had been served. It reminded Dr. D. more of cod liver oil floating in water than actual tea, but he did not say anything to offend their alien.

Troy, who was a big cod liver oil fan, slurped happily. "Hmmmm! Dee-lish!"

"Yes! Perhaps that will go a long way in explaining myself and why I am here."

"Actually what we need to know is how we get *out* of here . . ." said Diane.

"No, you misunderstand," said Spon. "I need to figure this out myself. My memory is not what it used to be, and perhaps if I just work this through, I'll be able to get the clue needed to bail us *all* out."

"We need a rest anyway," said Dr. D. "We're down, we're comfortable." He gestured. "What could it hurt? You want to wander those weird corridors some more?"

Chastened, Diane shook her head no.

"What else have we got," said Dr. D. "Go ahead, Spon. Carry on."

"Yeah," said Troy, "and tell us some more about Bubble Gum trees. I forgot to take along my supply of Bazooka, and boy, do I miss it."

The alien sat down on a cushion that gave a particularly fruity Bronx cheer in commentary.

"It all began when I was a tertiary umbilical tadpole in my brood's mud waddle . . ."


An hour or so later Dr. D. and friends were still listening to Spon's expositions on alien philosophy, their cod liver tea long since gone cold.

All having something to do with the Eternal Cycle of Door-to-Door Karma Salesmen.

Dr. D., who'd used the opportunity to take a short cat nap, feeling refreshed and more than a little bored, interrupted the proceedings politely by asking for a warm-up on his tea and then gently prodding Spon on exactly what alien philosophy really had to do with getting them all out of the clutches of the bad guys.

"After all, it *is* a fairly basic plot situation. A problem that indicates the need for a solution," said Dr. D, accepting the additional tea.

"You clearly don't understand, Doctor. But perhaps you're right . . . I could expedite my summary somewhat," said Spon. "I guess what I'm getting at is that I was so frustrated by the loop de loops of philosophy that I just got inside my spaceship and split—searching for the Truth. What I ran smack into, though, was this huge space battle."

"Hey, Doc! Just like us!"

"And that's when old Krillman popped into your ship's cabin, saying that he was going to solve all your problems," suggested Diane sarcastically.

"This is true. Although it was some time ago. And if I can only unwind our discussion about philosophy and ethics and the basics of the Meaning of Life and the warring parties of the cosmos, then maybe I'd have a clue on how to get us *all* out of this situation."

"Seems to me that's a dialogue that could go on for a very long time indeed," pointed out Dr. D., feeling a little discouraged.

"It's already been going on long enough that I'm *hungry* again!" said Troy. "I sure could use some more of those Heinz pork and beans. I lost that can I had."

The effect on Spon was like a stroke of lightning!

All four of his eyestalks erected like exclamation points in a paragraph of pulp fiction!

"*What* did you say?"

"I said I was *hungry!*" said Troy hopefully. "You wouldn't have any human being food around here, would you?"

"No—I mean what you said about what you were hungry *for!*" said Spon hopefully.

"Well, Heinz beans, of course! Pork 'n' beans, to be precise!"

"That's it! That's what I've been looking for!" The

alien got up and danced about happily. He whirled and grabbed Troy by his lapels. "You say you've got Heinz beans?"

"Yep, but not a lot of other of the Fifty-seven Varieties." said Troy, a little nonplussed.

The alien looked as though he were about to explode with glee. "The sacred Fifty-seven Varieties. The very foundation of our Metaphysical Alchemy. How can this be? This is too wonderful!"

"That's all well and good, and I suppose it's always nice to have a philosopher's stone hanging around to throw . . ." said Dr. D. "But exactly how is this going to help us get out of here?"

"Where did you get that wonderful stuff?" demanded Spon, grabbing Troy by his arm.

"Huh? Well . . . it's all over Earth," said Troy. "In lots of stores and restaurants!"

"Hmmm," said Diane. "Krillman was excited about the beans, too—but all he wanted to do was to eat them!"

"That's because he hasn't done the in-depth quantum philosophic studies that I have concerning the Heinz Fifty-seven Varieties! They're the very foundation of *everything*. Matter, energy. Life, death. To say nothing of the makings of the consummate picnic."

"I don't understand, Spon . . . What does this have to do with getting away from the Proons?"

"I'm sorry! You couldn't possibly understand. . . . You see, most of my problem wasn't being lost when I ran into that space battle. My engine runs on Heinz tomato soup or pork and beans and water . . . And I ran out!"

"You mean . . ."

"Yes. It makes great rocket fuel."

There was a blatting sound and an immediate foul fragrance. No one had sat on one of the cushions. Everyone turned toward Troy who had the grace to blush.

"I wonder why," said Troy to change the subject.

"So what you're saying is . . ." said Diane.

"Yes," the alien declared. "Take me back to your ship, get me some of your supplies of that wonderful stuff . . . And I can save us all . . ." His eyestalks twisted together, so great was his joy.

"To say nothing of delving once more into the very nature of things."

"I can see," said Dr. Demopoulos, "that I'm going to have to reexamine certain of my fundamental assumptions about physics."

# Chapter Thirteen

As it happened, Dr. Vivian Vernon was having exactly the same kind of thought, albeit in a decidedly different set of circumstances.

"I can see that my fundamental assumptions are going to have to be reexamined," she said.

*"Fun?"* said the Grand Proon, glowering down at her through his Groucho Marx eyeglass. "Did you say 'fun'? I thought I told you we don't allow such words here!"

Dr. Vivian Vernon hastily explained what she really meant.

" 'Basic.' I mean 'basic.' "

" 'Base' is a suspicious word as well. And sick? It sounds as though you have a very twisted planet."

It sounded like what was *twisted* was whatever device these guys used as a translator, but Vivian thought it best not to make an issue of it. Best to go with the old electron flow.

"Yes, and we need help, as I have said."

"Good. I'm glad we're understood. We've practically crushed the Pizons. Only a few more space fleets to mop up." Those bloodshot eyes bored up at her. "You're really going to have to stop protruding if you're going to get along here!"

"Protruding?"

"Forward and aft."

She looked down. She'd never considered the juts of her chest and her butt anything but assets, no pun intended. Even back at the university, her climb up the academic ladder had been just as much physical as it had been mental. To have her feminine attributes held in something less than awe was a bit disorienting.

"Yes. Disgusting."

"Would you like us to remove them?"

"Ah—no, that won't be necessary," she said, controlling her panic. "Maybe if you could just—ah—let me have one of those robes there, I won't offend you so much."

"We have excellent surgical procedures. It will do you a world of good." The Grand Proon tut-tutted—a maneuver of his mouth that splattered the floor and Vivian with spittle. "Besides, it will improve your looks immensely!"

"Your offer is most gracious—but I really would prefer a robe."

"How about your companion's protuberances?"

"Oh, I've already dealt with those."

The Grand Proon shrugged and let the matter pass.

Vivian breathed a sigh of relief—as inconspicuously as possible.

"Well then . . . This evil doctor and his fellows. We have not yet been able to locate them."

"It's your ship. Why not?" Best defense . . .

"It's a *big* ship!"

"As I told you, we're here by accident. I've no idea where Earth is. Once you get us there, there will be no problem . . . I can tell you exactly what to do."

"Your vessel—do you think anything in it might jog your memory. Navigational equipment, perhaps?"

Navigational equipment, thought Vivian. *What* navigational equipment?

Still, she had to act as though she knew something . . . otherwise, what good would she be to the Proons.

"Yes. That might be of help."

"Excellent. We will procure your ship for you then. You will have plenty of time to determine how to use it—and your evil doctor—to get back to your native planet.''

"Fine. Meantime, have you beaten Dr. Wussman properly?"

"Thrashed him. Would you like a blow or two?"

"That's all right. I'll get my licks in verbally. Can you give him back to me?"

"Certainly. He made the most curious range of noises."

"Yes. He does that."

"We had no fun at all, of course."

"Of course not. What a shocking thought."

"And I trust you will not."

"I have forsaken the very concept!"

"True, our ways our decidedly superior. Nonetheless, you are an unusually quick convert!" said the Grand Proon suspiciously.

"Only because, in my heart, I have known the path you Proons tread as the correct one!"

"That's all well and good, but how do I know we can trust you? You won't even willingly undergo plastic surgery for us."

"Hmm. How about an ear piercing. Will that make you happy."

"No, but get this robe on quickly. You still bother me."

The Grand Proon clapped his hands.

Two servants brought in a robe, which Vivian hastily donned. She even assumed a bent-over position so that her breasts would not bulge.

"Much better," said the head Proon. "Now that we have finished with your companion, would you like him back?"

"Sure."

Vivian did not know what to expect, but hopefully it was going to be a more pliable Wussman—a more docile and quieter Geoffrey.

Certainly she did not expect the man who actually lumbered into the room.

Dr. Geoffrey Wussman, held up by two Proons, was actually *smiling*. Smiling in a decidedly silly fashion, true, but grinning nonetheless. Why, was he seeing little stars flutter around his head? His seeming happiness annoyed Vivian terribly.

"What's going on with you?"

Wussman found his feet and stumbled toward his love.

"It was *wonderful*!"

"What, the beating? That was wonderful? Better than mine?" She felt a pang of jealousy growing under her (hidden) breasts.

"No, of course not, my love."

"What is it then? Why have you got that dopey smile on your face?"

"It's what they gave me to drink after that whipping."

"What they gave you to—" She turned to the Grand Proon, a question mark in her eyes.

"He must mean the Eternal Elixir of Life Liquid, Stirred and Diluted," said the Grand Proon. "It is meant merely as tonic for us to cleanse our minds and hearts . . . and put a little hair on our chests. The effect upon your fellow is most curious. We find his smiles most upsetting . . ." The Grand Proon waddled over to Wussman, sniffing. "You're not having *fun* . . . are you?"

"Fun? Of course he's not having fun. His smiles are those of a creature upon whom the truth of right living has just dawned . . . Isn't that true, Geoffrey?"

She gave him a swift kick in the shin to underline the directional point of her speech.

Geoffrey, thank God, seemed to snap out of his trance, his smile bending into a decided frown. "Ouch. Yes. I guess so . . ."

"Good. Well, then it's agreed," said the Grand

Proon. "We shall go off and get your ship. We shall bring it back. Utilizing it, we will determine where your home planet of Earth is. We will then make plans for its conquest. In the meantime, you will be taken to your quarters for now and given food and drink. We will come for you when we need you." The Grand Proon sniffed disapprovingly on general principles. "Any questions?"

"Yes. Can I have some more of that LSD stuff?" said Wussman. "I need to get a little more straightened out."

"We'll see," said the Grand Proon. "Guards! Take them to the room that has been prepared for them. And take them by the very least entertaining path!"

Vernon and Wussman were unceremoniously shuffled out, down the most boring, long corridor that Vivian had ever seen and then ushered into a small room with a chair, a bed, a pitcher of water, and two glasses.

The door closed.

After waiting an appropriate period of time, Vivian attempted to open it, without luck.

Wussman slumped, exhausted, on the bed.

"Well, this is another fine mess Dr. Demopoulos has gotten us into," said Vernon, turning away, frustrated, from the door.

"Viv, you weren't the one that got the beating."

"Don't fool me. You loved it. And you got to drink that stuff . . . whatever it was. Speaking of which, just what *was* it?"

"I don't know, but it sure threw me for a loop, I'll tell you."

"What was it . . . alcohol?"

"No. I know a martini from a milk shake and that was neither. I sure saw some pink elephants!"

"Pink elephants? What are pink elephants doing on an alien spaceship?"

"Just a phrase, Viv. You know . . . like when drunks

go on the wagon and get delirium tremens. They see pink elephants.''

"I told you we should have tried to act like Nick and Nora Charles and drink all those martinis! Hammett all . . . I mean, dammit all, Geoffrey. We need to have all our mental faculties about us.''

It was Wussman's turn to smile. ''Dashiell it all, Viv. I'm not an alchy. You really haven't any sense of figurative language, do you? I'm talking about hallucinations. The stuff the aliens had me drink gave me hallucinations!''

Vivian Vernon mulled this over a moment. ''Just what *kind* of hallucinations. You really saw colored elephants?''

"I'm not sure *what* I saw. I don't really think I can express it in words.''

"Well, we've got plenty of time, Geoffrey. You think how you can put it in words and you tell me and we'll work out any possible meanings from that.'' It seemed like the intelligent thing to do in this situation. Besides, it was better than sitting around, twiddling your thumbs.

Geoffrey Wussman slid an arm around Dr. Vernon's waist. ''Gee, Viv—I was kinda hoping we could sort of . . . you know . . . fool around. Especially since now we're going to be powerful and we make our own rules . . .''

"One moment you're quivering and quailing in the bathroom, the next you want to rut like a rabbit.'' She raised her eyebrows at him. ''That stuff must have also had aphrodisiac qualities, Geoffrey.''

"Maybe it just relaxed me. Maybe I just see things as they really are now . . . You're a beautiful woman. I'm a man with burning desires. We're millions of miles from our home planet, in the direst of straits. What could be more natural than falling into each other's arms testing out the laws of biological physics!''

Uh-oh, thought Vivian.

When Dr. Geoffrey Wussman started talking about the "laws of biological physics" it meant that he was not only in a randy mood, but in a particularly aggressive randy mood.

Dr. Wussman's "laws of biological physics" utilized Newtonian and Einsteinian formulas to particularly nefarious purposes. It perverted the equations that governed the very nature of the universe, and made it all look like the entirety of the cosmos had sex on its mind.

Vivian had heard it all before, and had no patience for it.

Especially not now.

"You've got to be out of your mind, Geoffrey," she said. "For one thing you're wrong. I feel about as sexy as a doorknob right about now. And for the other thing, haven't you been listening to these guys? They're *bluenoses*! They're probably watching us right now. If we even start *acting* like we're about to do something untoward they'll come in and hose us down like a couple of dogs." She smiled, leaned over, and gave him a juicy peck on the cheek. Sweet torment! "Otherwise I'd be happy to oblige you!"

"I'll take that chance! I'll take that chance!" shouted Wussman, jumping on her.

Vivian slugged him. He stumbled back, then went down like a sack of potatoes.

"Sorry to cool your ardor, dearest, but it's all for the best!"

Geoffrey got up, rubbing his jaw. But instead of pain in his eyes, some sort of light gleamed.

"I remember!" he said.

"You remember? You remember *what*?"

"The vision!"

"What are you talking about, man?"

Geoffrey Wussman got up, his eyes far, far away, staring off onto some infinite panarama. "That drink they gave me. It gave me a vision of the Proonian

conceptual philosophy of the universe! And that pop
on the jaw—it made it all fall into place. I see it all
now! It's beautiful! Spectacular! It all falls into place!
Oh, catharsis! Oh, holy vision! Oh, hallelujah!''

Vernon, however, was not terribly impressed. ''You
want to spit it out?''

Geoffrey Wussman nodded and began to narrate a
translation of his astonishing cosmic vision.

''Yea and verily! I walketh out into the wilderness
and above me were the stars and . . .''

''Come on, Jeremiah Wussman,'' said Vivian in her
most deadly sarcastic tone. ''Cut the pseudo-biblical
stuff and tell me what you saw . . .''

Pure awe showed on Geoffrey Wussman's face. He
looked positively inspired, as though the entirety of
his brain were lit up by some sort of light-streaming,
numinous presence and shone forth majestically.

''I'll try, but it really all does deserve to be described in those kinds of terms.''

''Spare me. What did you see? The Virgin Mary?
Some Apostle. The Buddha? The Holy Grail? The Face
of God? The One and True Tenure?'' Some amount of
reverence crept into her voice on the last term.

''No, nothing so glorious as *that*,'' said Wussman.

''Well, then, is it bigger than a bread box?''

''Bigger than the universe, yet microcosmically
speaking able to fit into a single Rice Krispies!''

''Okay. The new Geoffrey. No more physics, no
more 'Let's Get Physical.' The phrase flavor of the day
is 'Let's Get Meta*physical*.' ''

''You scoff. Oh, ye of little faith.''

She stepped forward and slapped him a couple of
times . . . purely medicinally, taking no pleasure in
the act. ''Okay! Okay. Get on with it. Any way you
like—just for God's sake, *get on with it*!''

Geoffrey bravely turned the other cheek.

Which happened also to be on the other end of his body.

"What is *that* supposed to mean?" said Vivian, staring down at Wussman's bare bottom, unsleeved from its pants.

"It is a holy gesture, meant as a supreme sign of respect from practicers of the New Way of the Practicers of the Holy Order of the Bearers of a Full Deck, Minus One Card."

"Well, thank you, I suppose . . . But you were supposed to tell me about that religious experience . . . Not show me your pink and hairy bum!"

"You're supposed to kiss it now. To finish the Cherished Circuit of Concussion."

She booted him smartly, propelling his head into a wall. Geoffrey swiveled around, blearily looking back at her. "Sacrilege!"

"Oh, I'm so sorry!" said Vivian with only the slightest of smirks. "I thought you said *'kick'* it!"

Wussman pulled his pants up, belted them, and rubbed his head and behind, both apparently sore. He looked disoriented.

"I'm listening!"

"Hmm. Oh, yes. Just a little fuzzy. You wanted to hear about my religious experience."

"It would seem that it's more than a religious experience! You've been converted to something!"

"Yes. And you need worry no longer about my amorous advances."

"I never worried . . . I mean . . . what's that supposed to . . ."

"I have taken a vow of Total Nofoolingaroundhood."

"What?"

"Holy and Just Folks do not exchange precious bodily fluids in carnal and craven acts! It's a part of the Proons' bible, which somehow, quite mystically,

was engraved on my sensibilities with the drinking of
that potion.''

Vivian twitched her nose. She wasn't sure if this
news was good or bad. On the one hand, no longer
would she have to suffer the advances of this clown.
On the other, it was a distinct blow to her self-image
as an irresistible femme fatale.

"Go on," she prompted.

"Anyway, like I stated, I found myself in the wilderness. To make a long story short, it was wasn't
really all that much of a wilderness. There were hot
dog and Coke stands all around, so I didn't go hungry
or thirsty.''

"I *am* relieved.''

"I stopped at a hot dog stand and ordered a New
York frank with sauerkraut and ketchup. The waiter
was offended. He made me take the frank with Grey
Poupon instead. He turned out to be an archangel who
looked just like Proon. He pointed a blazing sword at
a mountain just down the block. 'Get ye hence and
find truth upon the peak!' So I did just that, hiked all
the way up, and noticed all kinds of funny critters
dancing around on the periphery of my vision . . .
Symbolic creatures . . . you know, like armadillos and
kangaroos and porcupines and aardvarks. Symbolic of
exactly *what* I really couldn't say. And any rate, they
*seemed* important. So I got up to the top of the mountain and waiting there was this creature—definitely a
Proon—in flowing chartreuse robes. 'I'm looking for
Truth,'' I said. 'That's me,' she said. 'T. Ruth The T
is for Tyrannosaur.' '' How odd, I thought, but then
who was I to question what was clearly a deeply important religious experience. 'Now that I've found you,
what have you got to say to me that will enrich my
spirit and change my life.' 'First off,' she said, 'you've
got to ditch that bitch you're lusting after. Then
you've got to ditch lust itself. Here,' she said. 'Take
my hand.' And I took her hand and we went aloft,

flying not only through the air but through the entirety of the universe. Through the stardust of nebulas and the gases of magnificent planets we drifted, and upon every world which she showed me life, she also showed me how heterosexual reproduction brought nothing but misery and war and pestilence upon the poor biological beasties—like human beings—whom it had been visited upon.

"And then she showed me many of the levels of the cosmic religious mysteries . . . Sherlock Holmes and Agatha Christie were my own personal favorites.

"The ultimate truth, I learned, however, was that sex was the reason why we human beings cannot concentrate upon the more mystical aspects of existence that our minds were meant for . . . Mystical states that the Proons can achieve with ease, with only the aid of a good nonillustrated technical manual very densely printed and readable only with very thick glasses!

"And so, you see, Dr. Vernon, thus am I rid of the petty shackles of my life. I did not remember, but in my religious conversion I forsook the pleasures of the flesh. I realize now that the Proons are truly on a righteous path, and I long to aid them to conquer the Earth, not to achieve status and power myself, but for the sake of my fellow human beings!"

Vivian Vernon stared at him for a moment, not quite believing what she'd heard. But she saw the sincerity in Wussman's eyes, and shrugged.

Oh, well, all the more universities for her!

"Congratulations!" she said, shaking his hand.

"You, too, should drink that wondrous fluid? And you, too, shall experience the cosmic mysteries."

"Hmmm. No thanks. I'm just fine the way I am." Though that was a thought—why hadn't they given her any of that stuff. Maybe they were using her as a testing control . . .

Or maybe—just maybe—her sex appeal had not been lost upon the seemingly asexual Proon.

"Oh, by the way, there was one more thing that I noticed in my vision."

"Do tell."

"There's even more to those Heinz baked beans than even that guy called Krillman knows! And oh, yes . . . Dr. D.? He's the Devil Incarnate!"

The man's eyes burned fiercely.

"I could have told you that, my dear." She bent over and give him a sloppy kiss full on his bloodless lips.

Geoffrey Wussman cringed.

# Chapter Fourteen

In the company of their new ally, Spon, our intrepid heroes made their way back to the *Mudlark*.

It was by no means an easy affair. Dr. D. half wished now that indeed he had left a trail of beans or string or something. There were so many twists and turns and side tunnels, and they all looked pretty much the same. Without the aid of compass or sextant (which was Dr. D.'s favorite choice of direction finder, purely because of its name) or even a Heinz baked bean detector trying to figure out which was the right way was quite difficult.

Fortunately, Diane Derry's sense of direction was the absolutely best the doctor had ever seen a woman possessed of.

Before long, the *Mudlark* loomed before them.

"Must have some kind of device in that delightful bra of yours!" said Dr. D., his eyes twinkling, patting Diane fondly on the fanny. After nimbly dodging her blow, the doctor pointed up ahead proudly to his invention. "Well, there it is, Spon—the *Mudlark*. Stranded, but absolutely full of beans."

"Thanks to me, Doc!" said Troy.

The alien capered up, his eyestalks wiggling about with great curiosity. It examined the bolted metalwork of the ship's hull, then rapped it hard with one of its four-digit hands, making a small dent. "What sort of ridiculous alloy is *this*?"

"Aluminum mixed with titanium!" boasted Dr. D., proud of his accomplishment.

"Feh! It sounds more like cookware than a space vessel!" said Spon, wriggling his lips with disapproval.

"And the port?"

"It's at the base."

"No, no, no. You said you'd get me a drink when I got here, and I prefer a large glass of port!"

"Sorry. Didn't bring any alcoholic beverages, alas. Most certainly would have if I knew we were going to meet you . . ." Dr. D. grimaced. "I could use a drink right about now."

"As could we all. So, how do you get into this thing?"

"The hole in the bottom," said Diane.

"How anal dementive," said Spon.

"You mean anal retentive? That's our two stowaways we left behind."

"No. Anal dementive."

"I don't think I'm going to ask what that means," said Diane.

"Hey, Doc . . ." said Troy, looking up the ladder. "The barn door's open. Dr. Vernon! Dr. Wussman! We're back . . ."

No sounds emerged from the *Mudlark*.

"Maybe they're snoozing."

"You go first and check, Talbot," said Dr. D. "I believe we're sufficiently well announced."

"Okay, Doc. Right away!" Troy Talbot happily clamored up the ladder.

"A brave soul!" said Spon approvingly.

"No, just very dumb," said Diane. "You know, Doc, if you keep on going like this, you're going to get that big darling of mine *killed*."

Rattling and banging sounds sounded from the cabin.

"Ooops!" said Troy.

"Why do I get the feeling that he's going to get *us* killed before I manage to get *him* killed?" said Dr. D.

Spon stepped under the portal, odd oculars ogling. "We have a saying among our race—the clumsy are often the charmed. Small pricks at the karma bubble are better than gigantic blows."

*Clang! Klonk!*

An empty can tumbled down and smacked him on the forehead.

"What a *doofus*!" said Spon, rubbing himself.

"Watch out down there! I think some stuff fell down!" called Troy.

"Amazingly distorted time sense," said Spon, wisely stepping away from the ladder. "I can see your companion is one of the big pricks at your karma bubble."

"Ah, Troy means well," said Dr. D.

"And I've certainly met bigger pricks . . ." Diane colored. "Ah . . ."

"Yes, my dear. And I'm the biggest prick of all . . . At that pretty karma bubble of yours, anyway." Dr. D. smacked a kiss into the air toward her, eyeing her attributes with his usual goat eyes.

"I distinctly detect the release of pheronomes!" said Spon, wiggling and squiggling his alien nostrils.

"I think the doctor's are called phero-gnomes," said Diane.

"Touché!"

"You're more of a douche, I think."

"We're getting a little *talkie* down there!" snorted Troy. "By the way I don't see hide nor hairy nor heiny of Drs. Vernon or Wussman."

"You checked the bathroom?"

"Yeah. Nothing."

"The bar."

"We haven't got a bar."

"First order of business, Diane. Next time we head out for the hinterlands of outer space, we stock a bar."

"Check, Dr. D. But I didn't think you were a drinking man."

"I'm taking it up, as of the first chance I get. Come on, let's get up into the ship."

Spon said as he slithered up the ladder, "Do you think your friends wandered off, exploring?"

"They're not really our friends," said Diane, following the alien and ducking a hanging tentacle or two. "And they were specifically ordered not to!"

"Well then, how can we explain this?" said Dr. D., now inside the ship. He was holding up a high-heeled shoe.

"Dr. Vernon's?" said Diane as she slid inside the hatch.

"Who else wears stiletto heels? Hmmm. Curious . . ." The doctor, noticing that one of the heels was cocked at an odd angle, examined it. It came off in his hand and something fell out of the hollow heel. Some sort of capsule or long lozenge-shaped thing.

"A spare tampon?" wondered Diane.

"No . . . it looks like some kind of code book . . ." Dr. D. unfurled it. "Hmmm. It appears to be Russian." He looked up at Diane. "It would appear that our Dr. Vivian Vernon is even busier than we thought!"

Troy looked over Dr. D.'s shoulder. "Gosh . . . She's taking Russian studies, too. Smart lady."

Diane glowered at him.

"She's moonlighting as a Russian professor?"

"She's a Soviet spy, you nincompoop!"

"Oh. So? I thought they were on our side."

"Well . . ."

"I mean, aren't they pioneering a new social system that's based on compassion and caring and brotherhood, and like that?"

Diane shrugged, then did a take. "Troy, you sound like a radical."

"I'm a card-carrying member of the Students',

Workers', and Farmers' Alliance for Peace, Prosperity, and Social Equality. Have been for years.''

''What's that?''

''A student radical socialist group.''

Diane frowned. ''I dunno, Troy. It sounds a little un-American.''

''Heck, radical socialism is as American as cherry pie!''

The professor said, ''That political stuff is millions of miles away. To hell with it. Right now we've got other things to think about.''

''You mean how it's apparent that the Proons have carried off Vernon and Wussman?'' said Diane.

''No, to hell with them, too! We want to get out of this stinking place. And fast!''

''I think in light of this discovery that's not a bad idea,'' said Diane. ''It looks as though we may have done our country a service without realizing it.''

Dr. D. sighed. ''What a waste.'' He sighed. ''What a bust and hips, too. Oh, well. *C'est la vie. C'est la guerre.* Berma-Shave. Come on. Spon. Let's show you what we're packing inside this boat!''

Gesturing for the alien to follow him, Dr. Demopoulos began to ascend the ladder.

Time to exit the slapstick dimension and head back to some good old-fashioned serials . . . the way life was supposed to be!

The alien was making that strange laughter noise again.

''Brrappp!''

The laugh that sounded like a Bronx cheer by a bunch of monkeys in a swimming pool of raspberries. Fortunately, no alien saliva sprayed on Dr. D. Otherwise, he would have really been ticked off, and not quite annoyed.

''You've got a problem with my spacetime drive?'' he said.

"Oh, no, not at all! Pardon my mirth!" said Spon. "I am being much too rude, I see. You appear about to grow stalks with your eyes as well!"

"Gee, Doc . . . That sure would be a sight," said Troy in a nonrequested contribution to the conversation.

They were hovered over the very heart, the quintessential core of the *Mudlark*.

"I'm surprised," Spon said. "Your technology is more sophisticated than I thought."

"Yeah, well," Dr. D. said, but did not expand on this.

"Clearly you are quite influenced by the internal commotion machine!" said Spon.

Dr. D. pouted. "You mean, the internal combustion machine."

"Wasn't that what you were working on *last* year, Doc—the eternal commotion machine."

"No, you dunce . . . that was the perpetual commotion . . . I mean perpetual *motion* machine!"

"Oh. Right. Yeah. Whatever it was it made a bunch of noise."

Spon's nose turned in what was clearly a universal sign of disapproval. "Well, you've jammed all your roto-gyros and your gravito-initial stabilizers are absolutely useless. I'm afraid that this engine is totally screwed up. However, not to despair, for it just so happens that with those Heinz beans you promised me, hope is available."

"You mean to fix it?"

"No, to inspire me to tinker together an entirely *new* kind of space drive," said Spon, clearly very pleased with himself. "The Quantum Fuzzy Drive!"

"Can you do that without new parts?"

"Well, it's just a matter of taking *out* some parts from your drive."

"That's strange," the professor said.

"There are some disadvantages that way," Spon allowed.

"Oh? Such as?"

"Navigation problems."

"That's nothing new with us. If you can fix this crate, do so, please. With our blessing."

"I can't do beans without the Heinz," Spon said. "Must have spiritual inspiration."

"Diane, serve 'em up!"

# Chapter Fifteen

"Beans!" said Diane Derry, carrying a tray filled with dishes.

Dr. D.'s appetite, however, was not exactly keen for anything, much less beans, and so as Troy and Spon happily took their steaming mugs of the delicious and nutritious (and, heaven knows, cosmic) treat, he just looked down mopily at his tattered spacetime drive, and then back up at their alien guest technician.

"Quantum Fuzzy Drive?"

"Quantum Fuzzy Drive," Spon said.

"I've often thought of the possibility. How exactly does it work?"

"Well, you see, it's quite simple," said Spon after a sip of his soup. "It's a machine that gives to gross objects the same quantum uncertainty that little sub-atomic thingees have . . . i.e. you never know what the heck they're doing; they're here, they're there, you don't know their momentum, you don't know beans about 'em . . . Oh. I made a funny."

The Earthmen (nongender specifically speaking) laughed politely.

"And thus," Spon continued, "they propel your vessel through fantastic distances of space."

"Sounds good to me!" said Troy.

"And you can rebuild my engine to do this?" said Dr. D. doubtfully.

"In a trice!"

Troy frowned. "Yeah, but can you do it fast?"

"Absolutely. However, there is just one little eensy weensy kind of a problem . . ."

"You did speak of some disadvantages," Diane said.

"Isn't really a disadvantage," said Spon, his eyestalks drooping slightly. "Actually, it's a major problem. Trouble is, when the ship goes quantum fuzzy, you never know where it's going to wind up."

"Oh, dear," said Diane. "How precise we scientists are in this universe."

"Yeah, but it'll be away from here, right?" said Troy, peering out the vu-plate.

"True, very true." Spon nodded. His eyestalks bobbed, decidedly more erect.

"Well, that's all right then!" said Dr. D. in a suddenly gay mood. "We can modify it to our specifications. And besides, it's really *not* much different from the way it worked before. But now we have a *name* for it."

Diane Derry made a wry face at the doctor's rationalization. "So you're hoping to end up in the middle of another space battle so that we can attract Krillman's attention again?"

"Well, hopefully not Krillman per se—but definitely the Triple-A. And then they can take me back here and jump start *my* ship!"

"You can fool with this, but not with your own?" said Dr. D.

"This is *much* simpler. Besides, you've got the baked beans. A vital inspiration for contemplating the essential chaos that underlies all natural phenomena."

"Gee—you better make it quick," said Troy. "We've got company."

Dr. D. looked out the vu-port. Sure enough, trooping down the corridor were a batch of strange-looking aliens in robes, with holsters bearing ray guns.

"Yikes. I need more time than that!" said Spon. "Doctor, you've got to stall them. Just a few minutes. That's all I need."

"Stall them. They're coming to take us away!" Dr. D. could feel the decided tread of panic upon the nether regions of his spine—an unusual sensation, not one that he experienced often.

Spon grabbed the tool case and proceeded to work away with lightning speed upon the motor under the open hood.

"Hey, Doc . . . They all look like Groucho Marx," said Troy.

"Those look like masks, Troy," said Diane. "And not very good ones at that!"

"They mostly just use it to hide their noses," Spon said. "Sordid details later." Spark plugs and distributor cables were flying from the motor. Squirts of oil. A charred copy of *Screen Stars* that Dr. D. had been using for temporary insulation.

"What can we do to *stall* them?" said Dr. D. "Where's that shotgun of mine?"

"Violence is not recommended. They have far more firepower than you."

"What can we do?" Demetrios asked. "Are they vulnerable in any way?"

"Well, no, they're fairly powerful," Spon said. "Oh, wait. I remember something about them. They don't like music."

"Music? How can that help us?"

"I mean, they *really* hate it, along with a lot of other things."

"Well, I really . . ."

"Here, Doc." Troy handed the professor a small metal object.

"A harmonica? This is yours, Talbot?"

"Yup. Carry it with me always."

"But I've never heard you play."

"Do it alone, mostly, Doc."

"You shouldn't play with yourself, alone," the physicist said. "Okay, it so happens I used to play a little when I was a lad."

Demetrios put the harmonica to his lips and blew a wheezing chord in C major. "I'm a little rusty, but it will have to do. Diane, do you sing?"

"Sing? Why, I really never . . ."

"You're about to make your debut. Come on!"

"But, Dr. D., I really can't—"

"The show must go on! Act like a trouper, Diane."

"Never thought I'd end up as a starship trouper," Diane said.

"There's always time enough for love songs," Dr. Demopoulos said. "Let's go!"

# Chapter Sixteen

Diane and Demetrios were clambering down the ladder as another party of Proonish creatures, clustered around a Proon in a different colored robe who looked authoritarian, came down the main tube.

Behind them marched none other than Drs. Vivian Vernon and Geoffrey Wussman.

"It's the professors!" Diane said, looking over her shoulder as she climbed down. "They're back!"

Vivian Vernon shouted out, "Those are the Earthian wretches! They should be seized immediately. They are deviants and sinners of the highest order."

Wussman waddled up to Demetrios. "The Proonian mind cannot conceive of the evil they spawn! Lewdness and lechery are their stock in trade . . ." He pointed at his erstwhile colleague. "Especially *that* one!"

"Stuff it, Wussman. Into a little treachery, now, are you? And what's with the getup, Viv? That dress just isn't you."

"I have given up nasty thoughts and actions of all sorts!" proclaimed Dr. Vernon. "And no longer will I wantonly display secondary sexual characteristics!"

Demetrios thought, Brain washed?

But as Vernon shot him a look of hatred and pure academic rivalry, Dr. D. could see no sign of brainwashing whatsoever in their eyes.

They'd betrayed their companions.

"Diane, I think we've been sold down the river.

And speaking of rivers, here's our little chanteuse to ask the musical question, 'Swanee River.' " He put the harmonica to his lips and began to belt out the tune, interrupting only long enough to whisper hoarsely, *"Diane, sing!"*

"They've got something up their sleeves," Vivian said suspiciously. "Grand Proon, they—"

The Grand Proon already had his ear orifices covered, his wrinkled face a mask of pain. *"No!"* He emitted a high-pitched squeal. "NO, NO, NO!"

Diane began to sing "Swanee River." Her professor-boss tapped his foot against the greasy deck, not quite in time. It struck Dr. D. that Diane's voice wasn't so bad, for an amateur.

The other Proons mimicked him, their rotund bodies contorting in agony.

"What's the matter, guys?" Dr. D. said between blowing chords on the harmonica. "Got . . . something against . . . music?"

"Oh, foul, egregious noise!" the Grand Proon cried. "Oh, horror, oh, terror!"

" 'Oh-h, say can you see, by the dawn's early light . . .' " sang Diane when she had run out of lyrics on "Swanee River."

"Tough tune," Demetrios muttered, but did his best to fake it.

After Diane got through three stanzas of the "Star-Spangled Banner," the duo did an eclectic medley of five numbers: "Shortin' Bread," "I Dream of Jeannie," "Fascinating Rhythm," "Begin the Beguine," and the Flitheimer University alma mater.

They danced, soft-shoeing, then went into a tap routine.

"Seize them!" Vivian commanded the guards. "Don't let them get away!"

But the guards were incapacitated by this impromptu concert of Earthly music.

Wussman approached Demetrios menacingly and got stiff-armed hard in the face for his trouble.

"Ow," Wussman complained.

"Doc, Diane!" It was Troy, above. "We're ready!"

"Glad you made your new affiliation known, Doctors," Demetrios huffed as he pushed the still-singing Diane up the ladder. "We won't feel so guilty in leaving you behind."

"They're getting away!" Vivian howled.

Still wheezing harmonically, Dr. D. grabbed the bottom rung and started pulling himself up after his assistant.

"Demetrios, don't!" called Wussman after him.

"Surrender! This is the Way of Truth and Righteousness!"

"Come back!" cried Vernon. "Come back, Doctor, and we'll give you Stanford University!"

What in the world are these weirdos talking about? the Greek physicist wondered.

One of the guards apparently had more willpower than the rest. A badly aimed power ray buzzed past Demetrios, sizzling into the hull.

He shinnied up the ladder, the air around him distinctly warmer.

Something grabbed his leg. He managed to shake it off, and flopped into the hatch with the help of Troy's brawny pull.

Hastily Diane pushed the hatch closed.

A satisfying *Boink!* of metal sounded. Then they battened the thing down.

Dr. D. turned back. "I don't know how long we can hold them . . . Spon . . . What's going on in there!"

"Almost finished, Doctor!" called the alien's voice from the engine room. "Just need to tear out one more superfluous component!"

"Superfluous?"

They could hear the sizzling of rays against the bulkhead. He put his hand against the hatch. It was heating up.

"Hurry up!"

As the professor climbed the ladder to the control room, a strange throbbing filled the ship. Dr. D. cocked his ear. A great deal noisier than previously, too, if that really meant anything.

"Sounds like he took the muffler off."

"I asked about that, Doctor. He said that controls—"

The entirety of the *Mudlark* shook as though it had been hit by a 8.1 Richter-scale earthquake.

Dr. D. slipped and slid back down the ladder, tumbling with Troy and Diane to the deck. The ship rocked and rolled about. Everything began to spin in front of Dr. D.'s eyes. He grew faint, dizzy . . .

There was a terrible *wrenching,* like the A train makes pulling into Times Square after a particularly jazzy night in Harlem. Dr. D. could feel his body's protons getting jammed into his neutrons. His electrons seemed to be kicked right out of their orbits, sailing around his head dizzily.

*Quantum Fuzzy Drive.*

That's what Spon had called it, and clearly for good reason. Everything around him, the whole ship and its passengers were getting, well, *fuzzy,* smeary colors slipping out of their normal outlines and bleeding into the atmosphere. Troy wore a surprised look on his big face. Diane was clinging for dear life on to a handhold. In the compartment above, Spon was rolling around on the floor, making some sort of apparently *gleeful* chortling noises, looking like some kind of demented anemone in an undersea storm.

*"What's happening?"* Dr. D. cried to him. *"Is this right, is this* supposed *to be occurring?"*

"Hard to say," Spon called out, his voice warbling. "Tell you what, though, friend. We aren't going to be on the Proons' ship much longer!"

The colors seemed to pulse, shake, and then splinter into a thousand variations of themselves. All in all, Dr. D. realized it was rather like that strange chemical he'd worked on with that Swiss chemist and they'd taken while listening to Richard Wagner records. What was his name? Hoffman, that was right! The guy had claimed he was going to name it after what Dr. D. had hallucinated: his childhood dog Lucy, capering in the sky among a field of diamonds. Dr. D. had also heard a particularly distasteful sort of music in his head during the ingestion of the chemical, and it was based on this that he'd decided the chemical was bad. Electrified guitars jangling with feedback overtop a driving jungle beat. Horrible! He'd called it troll music. Rocking troll music! Ugh.

Now was no time for musical criticism, however. It was time to hang on to one's sanity. He felt like a beetle in a field of rolling stones, clashing about who knew which way, smashing into doors and hammering and rapping about, his very soul ripping his body, splattered by guns and roses.

God, I hate puns, the good doctor thought.

Then he got locked into some exploding bass drum and his consciousness escaped like a terrified melody, in a manner of speaking.

# Chapter Seventeen

Dr. Demopoulos woke up.

At first, after his usual moments of disorientation, he thought he was on the bridge of the *Mudlark*. However, when the usual odors of burnt oil, old seat cushions, Troy's smelly gym socks, and Heinz baked beans did not assail his nostrils, he knew he was somewhere else.

His private little universe of imagination, calculation, and ideas? No, it would appear not.

He looked around from where he lay, seeing that he was sitting in some kind of straight-backed chair and the hard thing that he'd been lying against upon awakening was a big black Olympia typewriter, atop a desk. The only light in the room was a desk lamp.

There was a piece of paper in the typewriter. Dr. D. looked at it. It was twenty-pound bond paper. Two sheets, with a carbon in between. The paper was half-filled with typing. The last sentence of the typing read:

"Then he got locked into some exploding bass drum and his consciousness escaped like a terrified melody."

"Ugh!" said Dr. D. "What purple prose!"

Still, it had a faintly familiar ring to it.

And now that you mention it, Doctor, he thought, perturbed, why do your fingers ache so? He looked down at them. The pads of his fingers were typewriter-ribbon black. How peculiar . . . how very strange.

At his side was a neat stack of papers. He rifled

through them, caught the names. Diane Derry. Troy Talbot. Dr. Geoffrey Wussman. Dr. Vivian Vernon . . .

"Thanks for the mammaries," he said under his breath.

Now why had he said that? These names . . . they meant something . . . they were very significant. And these flashes of words here . . . starship . . . *Mudlark* . . . vu-plate . . . tractor beam . . . Eyestalks . . . Cosmic mind-boggling space battle . . .

Of course! It all rushed back to him now in a torrent, from the first trembling attempts of the *Mudlark*'s space drive to wobble into destiny to the raucous efforts of the Spon's Quantum Fuzzy Drive.

But what in the name of Aristotle's hot water bottle was he doing here?

He looked around at his environs. There was the smell of pipe tobacco and cigarettes in the air. He saw a standing ashtray, bulging with butts. The room was pure middle thirties Americana, from doilies on the arms of a thickly stuffed chair to a wooden rocking chair, to the copies of the *Saturday Evening Post* and *Argosy* on the coffee table. The place smelled also of old books, and Dr. D.'s eyes quickly found the source: several bookcases filled with leather and cardboard jacket volumes, yes . . . but also more.

Several shelves appeared devoted to old pulp magazines.

Hmmmm.

It was then that he realized what he'd taken for street noise seemed to focus into voices from another room. Voices, backed by the sound of Benny Goodman's orchestra. Dr. D. could tell that they were from the next room, and being of the philosophically empirical school, he went to see who it was who was talking.

Getting up, he noted that he was dressed as before; his absentminded professor's garb of wool trousers, checked shirt, and the prerequisite lab coat. However, they lacked some of the rips and tears he'd had before.

And wait . . . this was odd. The last thing he'd been wearing before wasn't this, but a Chico Marx getup!

The old door squeaked plaintively as he opened it. He found himself at the edge of a dining room. Upon a table on the far wall was a big RCA radio: the source of the Benny Goodman music. Sitting at the dining-room table were a bunch of men, playing poker.

Smoke hung heavy in the air. There was the smell of booze, and Dr. D. peripherally noticed a well-stocked wet bar in the corner. Each of the players either had glasses filled with whiskey and ice near them, or cans of Schlitz beer.

A single lamp hung over them like a single alien eye, examining the proceedings below.

"Raise you four bits."

"I fold!"

"Me, too!"

"I'll call." Clink of poker chips. "What do you have, John?"

A man with a crew cut and thick glasses smiled around a cigarette holder. "Full house. Jacks over fives."

"Damn!" Toss and flutter of cards over the table. Three kings, ace high. "Can't blame me for staying in!"

The speaker was an older man, wearing wire-rimmed glasses and a grin. "You're cutting pretty deep into my last payment from my serial, John."

"Well, Doc, we all got to make a living some way," said the man who had been called "John" as he raked in the chips.

"Doc?" *He* was Doc. Confusing, but then again, he didn't exactly own the name. No reason to get excited. The thing to do now was to figure out what he was doing here and where the hell he was.

He advanced upon the table. "Excuse me."

The man who'd been called "John" looked up, his cigarette holder wobbling cockily as he smoked.

"Well, well. So are you finished with the sixteenth chapter, then?"

"Uh . . ." Then he remembered that the piece of paper in the typewriter had been marked "SIXTEEN." Then he *had* written it! "Yes, apparently I have . . . though I must say, I'm not quite sure which reality is legitimate!"

"There you go!' said a young man with a goatee. "That's the wave of the future for you. Identity crisis. The nature of Truth." He tapped his head. "The mind."

"No, sorry, Ted," said a serious, mustached man with a navy hair cut and strong, serious eyes. "Extrapolation. Serious logical extrapolation, populated by believable characters. If this goes on, I promise you, I'm going to make a bundle on it. A *bundle*." He coughed into a handkerchief, then started counting the chips in front of him.

"Well, the future of this crap is, Bob, what the reader wants *now* is space opera." The eyes gleamed behind the horn rims. The cigarette holder waggled happily. "And that's what we're giving them, right, Demetrios." The man wheeled around and nailed Dr. D. with a smirking look. They knew his name! However did they know his name? "So how are the Proons doing? Have our heroes escaped yet?"

"More importantly, have you come up with at least one new cosmic idea for each and every thousand words?" said one bespectacled fellow, eyes bleary between yet another pair of spectacles. What was this, four-eyes anonymous?

"Oh, A.E., would you come off that crap!" said another of the players. "Now would you cut the cards and deal."

"Well?" demanded the imperious man authoritatively, signifying his seriousness by taking the cigarette holder from his thin lips and leaning his crewcut toward Dr. D. "Those Proons are my babies, and I'm very interested in how our folks escape them!"

"Spon," said Dr. D., a bit at a loss. "The alien . . . he installed a 'Quantum Fuzzy Drive.' "

"Oh, excellent!" said the man who had been called "A.E." "Smells like a new idea."

"Next, they meet the Pizons," said John. "What say you go next, Doc? Before you do, though, why don't you break out some of those donuts you brought along. I'm getting hungry."

"Sure thing." The man wearing the wire-rimmed spectacles got up and went to a sideboard, picking up a box of honey-glazed donuts. "Special mix tonight, folks. Atom smasher surprise."

"Sounds ominous!" said John. "Sit down, Demetrios. We'll deal you in. Sounds like you're doing a good job. You figure, what, about sixty more pages to go and we've got ourselves a serial for *Rip-Snorting Cosmic Tales*?"

"I figure I can whip out the last forty pages, John," said a dour, dark man (glasses again) who suddenly lit up with enthusiasms. "I did a whole *Captain Suture* serial last weekend, and I started to feel my oats."

"Hmmm. Well, if that's the case, Edmund, maybe we'd better put our heads together and figure out what's going to happen, eh? Any ideas?"

"Well, we're going to have to have at least a few worlds smash together," said the man they'd called "Doc," laying the donuts down on the table. A nearby meter started clicking ominously. "I'll handle that."

"Hmm. Here's a thought for you," said the hawk-faced man with the cigarette holder. "Suppose there was a world that had no bathrooms and then people woke up with a thousand Johnny-on-the-Spots landed from outer space. What would they do?"

"Relieve themselves?" said Rob.

"No . . . They'd go *nuts*."

"Ah . . . that one stinks," said Jack. "Give that

one to Isaac. He'll take every lousy idea you hand him!''

"Well that doesn't wrap up our book, though," mused John. "What do you say, Demetrios? You have any bright ideas."

Demetrios found himself with a honey-glazed donut stickily sitting in his hand, and the course of his future possibly hanging in the balance.

He looked around into the eyes of these writers, and all he saw was trouble.

How often could he take his own destiny in his hands? All he had to do was to tell them what he wanted . . . What should he say . . . Should he request a quick return to Earth? A nice cozy tenure with plenty of money to fund his researches? A nice little house on the beach where he could write obscure articles for scientific journals?

Somehow, it all just didn't appeal.

"Ah, I'm fried, guys," he said, popping the beer in front of him and taking a long, cool, satisfying sip. "Just wing it. You'll come up with something."

"That's the spirit!" cried A.E. "I know! The Pizons are really a part of a cosmic conspiracy to sell weapons to the interdimensional Nazis!"

"Wait a minute!" said the man who had been called "Ted." "Where's the *love*. Where's the *feeling*? Here you go. Try this one. The *Mudlark* runs into a planet of hermaphrodite rutabagas and the crew discovers the meaning of free sex."

Hmm, thought Demetrios. Now *that* had merit! He had a sudden and delicious image of himself rolling around naked with Vivian and Diane and root vegetables. However it burst with the growling bark of the next suggestion.

"No!" said the man called "Bob." "We'll have them all go through loops and hoops of time, meeting themselves in the past and then in the future when they've all become galaxy-class athletes. We'll call that section 'By Their Jockstraps'!"

"Wrong!" said the man called "Jack." "Where's the space patrol! Where's the law and order involved here!"

"Right!" said Edmund. "We need heaps and heaps of ludicrous, silly science!"

"Quiet! Quiet, you dopes!" yelled John, glaring at them all. "Now this is *supposed* to be a civil game of poker, and a round robin space-opera novel for publication in one of the lesser paying pulp magazines, to buy beer and whiskey and pretzels and donuts for our games—not a free-for-all!" He turned to the man wearing the wire-rimmed glasses. "Doc, just do what you want but please try and be grammatical for a change! And be sparing with the tractor beams. These things are *farming* science fiction!"

Chortles and guffaws all around.

"Yeah, Doc! And make sure all the women have got great big iron brassiers for their mammoth bazookas!" said Ted.

"Yeah, Doc!" growled Bob. "And how about inventing some inertialess cookware for the starship's scullery!"

"Yeah, Doc!" said A.E. "And make sure everybody wears spectacles so they all can be Lensmen!"

Dr. D. watched as the man they addressed stood, holding one of his donuts. The man's face grew redder with every comment and his fist closed around the honey-glazed donut, squeezing it through his fingers.

"You jerks! You just wait and see what I do! I'll take our heroes on adventures so mind-boggling and horrendous that readers will gasp with the thrills and wonder and danger!"

"Yeah, Doc," said Bob, pulling up his cards. "Just try to spell it all right, okay?"

Hurumphing, the man named "Doc" spun and

walked into the next room, slamming the door behind him.

Soon there came the sound of typewriter keys clattering away feverishly.

"Oh, boy, what have I done now," said Edmund. "And I get to finish the thing."

"I don't know, Ed," said John. "The way he's going now, we may have goaded him into finishing the whole goddamned serial. Wouldn't *that* be terrific! We can just keep on playing this game and I can just keep on winning."

"Course," said Ted, "you'd have to do a heck of a lot more editing on the thing."

John shrugged, examining the set of cards he'd just been dealt. "Ah. Take out some adjectives, throw in a few atomic bombs. That's all it takes. This editing business is easy!"

Dr. D. looked back at the door. From behind it came the sound of furious typing.

"C'mon, Demetrios. Let's play cards. It's draw. How many cards to you want."

Dr. D. picked up his hand, still feeling the hot and crazy breath of sci-fi destiny breathing down his neck.

All of the cards were queens of spades.

# Chapter Eighteen

"Doctor! Doctor! Wake up!"

Something about a yellow brick roadgrader, squashing munchkin donuts.

Donuts. Black donuts. Black hole donuts. Quantum wontons. Let's play poker, boys! What's the ante matter! Five parsecs, Doc. Game's seven-card stellar stud. Comets and quarks wild.

Are you in pall? Or would you rather go back and hack out some more pages?

"There's no place like home, there's no place like home!" said Dr. Demopoulos feverishly.

Someone slapped him, and the lights came on. He opened his eyes and he looked up. Staring down at him with concerned looks on their faces were the rest of the crew of the spacetime ship *Mudlark*.

"Doc! You okay?"

"That's a nasty bump on your head!" said Spon.

"Don't worry," said Diane. "That's just his nose. It's always big and red."

Dr. D. struggled up to a sitting position. "Oh, God. It was awful!"

"Gee, Doc. You look like you've seen a ghost," said Troy. "Usually you're always in control!"

"That's what the dream was about . . . who's really in control of our fates!" Dr. D. shook off his dizziness and stood up, albeit shakily. "I believe the appropriate term is 'nightmare.' " And yet, it seemed so *real*. He could almost feel those cards in his hands now! As soon as he'd seen them, he'd just blanked out . . .

And awoke on this cold hillside.

"Where *are* we?" he said, peering around. It didn't take much peering to get to the vu-plate, and what was there, if noticeably better than the interior of the Proons' ship, was nonetheless disconcerting.

*Stars.*

They were hanging in space again. Clear space, fortunately, not fuzzy quantum space. But, alas, about as far away from Earth as before.

"We escaped!" he said, looking on the sunny side of things. (And they were most certainly on a lot of sides of suns out here.) "Spon! Let me shake your hand . . . or whatever you use for a hand." He grabbed the end of the alien's limb and pumped enthusiastically. "That had to be a record rebuilding of a space drive!"

Spon looked profoundly distracted. "I changed my record collection to CDs years ago."

"Problem is," said Diane, going back to her chair on the navigational board. "At least we knew where we were when we were on the mother ship. Now we haven't got the faintest!"

"Don't worry, gang!" piped Troy, holding up an economy-sized can of dinner. "We've still got plenty of fuel. And plenty for dinner, too!"

"My ship," moped Spon. "I had to go without my ship. And here I am, out in the middle of nowhere with a bunch of crazies in a creaky ship."

"But with an astonishing space drive!" Dr. D., fully recovered, draped a friendly arm over what served the alien as shoulders. "Let's go have a look at this thing. I think there's a thing or two you can teach me . . . And maybe we can modify it so that next time we'll know where it's going to take us!"

"Unlikely," said Spon sourly.

"Diane, you keep on working on finding out where we are . . ." Dr. D. instructed.

"Roger," Diane said, swiveling back into position.

"Great, and I'll fix dinner!" Troy volunteered.

Dr. D. cringed a bit. "Great. But not too much. Remember, that's space-drive fuel we're eating."

He directed the alien back toward the engine to examine it.

Nothing like a bit of brass tacks engineering to take one's mind off one's troubles!

Errr . . . *onnnk*!

ERR . . . ONNNNK!

The Klaxon rang out loud, alerting Dr. D. to danger.

Which was all very well, but he didn't realize that the *Mudlark* even had a Klaxon, and he'd *built* the stupid thing.

He looked up from the spacetime drive, holding a grommet spanner in one hand and a pile of beans in the other.

"By the dip in the Big Dipper!" said Spon, holding his hands over his upper thorax (location of rather pendulous ears). "What is that terrible *noise*!"

"The alarm," said Dr. D., not wanting to admit that he didn't really know what it was, either.

A voice rang out on the loudspeakers. "Attention, Dr. Demopoulos. Attention, Dr. Demopoulos. Return to the Bridge immediately!"

Diane's voice, urgent, coming over the loudspeaker.

Wait a minute, though. He'd never installed loudspeakers on the ship? He'd meant to but had never gotten around to it.

Well, he could examine these technical surprises later on. Right now, he'd better see what was going on. "Spon, why don't you put all this back together again, just in case. I'll go up and see what the problem is."

Spon nodded. "If it's my brood-mate, tell her I stepped out to the bar."

Dr. D. chuckled and bounced away toward the bridge.

Diane Derry was in her usual seat, only the dials and needles in front of her were going absolutely bonkers. And it was pretty clear why.

Standing smack dab in the middle of the vu-plates, screening out most of the stars, was a spaceship.

It was a conical-looking thing, attached to a sphere, attached to a pyramid, attached to a football field. What looked like wings sprouting from its side at unlikely and certainly nonaerodynamic angles. Indeed, it looked rather like one of those ships from that incredible space battle before.

A long, wormlike tube extended from the unknown ship, snaking toward the *Mudlark*.

"Some sort of boarding device!" said Doc, awe creeping into his voice. "These must be the Pizons. Look at that ship! Why . . . it's absolutely."

"Ludicrous?"

"You took the words right out of my mouth, Diane. What kind of minds would build with that kind of contorted mess?"

"Something between the sublime and the ridiculous, a bit tilted, I think, toward the latter. But then again, these are alien minds we're dealing with here."

"Let's just hope they're not as weird as those Proons!" He turned around to see Troy wandering up behind him, holding a kettle with steam rising from it, aromatic of beans.

"Who—ee!" said Troy. "Company for dinner?"

A bell-like *clang* sounded from belowdecks.

"The hatch!" said Diane.

The sound of the hatch unscrewing rose up from below.

"Glad we invited them in!" said Diane, looking a little miffed. "Polite creatures!"

Spon waltzed in, a couple of eyestalks cocked toward the vu-plate, a couple of eyestalks canted down at the ladder and the hatchway.

"Pizons, huh? Rude bastards. 'Course, better than the Wart-Togas who tend to come in and eat your popcorn and watch your Three-Dee without even saying hello. And of course far, far preferable to the Proons."

"Still, they *are* the good guys! Right?"

The alien raised his eyebrows—a sight to behold. "I suppose you could say that."

"But if it's a battle between good and evil," said Diane. "Surely the Proons are the bad guys. Which logically implies that it's the Pizons that sport the white hats."

"I'll leave that for you to decide. Meantime, I'm afraid I owe them a *lot* of money!" He took a gun from his pocket, put it between his eyes, and pulled the trigger. Green ichor and gray matter splattered against the wall. Spon flopped over like a bag of alien potatoes.

"Spon!" cried Diane, who never cared much for splattering alien potatoes.

"Please, just don't toss me out into the vacuum!" rasped the alien with what appeared to be his final breaths. "Just stick me in the larder. Okeydoke!"

"Okeydoke, no problem!" Troy replied agreeably.

The alien flopped back onto the floor.

"Hmmm," said Dr. D. "This doesn't exactly bode well for our prospects, does it, gang?"

Even as he spoke, the hatch banged open. A creature stepped in, looking around imperiously as it did so.

The alien was humanoid, no question about that, but the actual nature of his body was difficult to ascertain, since it was covered by white robes. However, it was rather vaguely humanoid. But from the shoulders, there sprouted what appeared to be bird's wings.

The face, however, was far from angelic. Two dark

holes for eyes beneath a greasy cap of black hair. Long
sideburns and a pencil-thin mustache.

"An angel!" said Diane, quite awestruck by the
sight.

"Wid doity faces, ma'am. But t'anks for da compliment. Dese white robes are just our force-screen
spacesuits. Dey double as bulletproof vest, ya know?"

"No bullets here!"

"Looks like dat guy ran into one!" The alien lighted
on the floor and strolled toward what was left of Spon.
"Not much left of da face to recognize. Musta owed
us money! Well, we'll just take da gun and pawn it or
something." He pried the weapon from Spon's paw
and pocketed it beneath the folds of his bulletproof
robe. Then he strolled around, examining the facili-
ties. "Nice little joint you got here. Ever think about
doin' a little remodelin'?"

"Who *are* you?" said Diane, getting a little annoyed, and also upset that her fantasy creature appeared to have feet of pepperoni. (Come to think of
it, thought Dr. D., the guy *did* rather smell like a hero
sandwich, heavy on the oil, vinegar, and oregano.)

"A nice little card game in here, some slots on da
side!" The alien strolled casually over to Diane, his
wings flapping a bit with his motion. "Yeah! Stick you
in one of da bedrooms, we make a lotta money offa
you!" His eyes traveled lasciviously down her face and
figure. He reached out and pinched her cheek.
"Whatta babe!"

She slapped him, and he stepped back a bit. His
wings went up like shields for a moment, and a couple
stirred feathers drifted out of the batch onto the deck.

Without warning, he pulled something from beneath
his robes, something yellow, stepped forward, and
mashed it into Diane's astonished face.

It was half a sliced grapefruit.

Then he started laughing wildly. "Hey, boys. Come

on up. These folks . . . They're okay. They like to play da game!''

Diane's face was livid. She raised a fist, looking like she was going to clobber the alien, but Dr. D. stepped in before she was able to and caught ahold of her arm.

"Not a good idea, dear. Anyway, we all need some Vitamin C once in a while."

"Wow!" said Troy. "That was just like Jimmy Cagney in the movies! Keen! What a guy! Well, I guess I go and stick Spon in a cabinet like he wanted."

Dr. D. considered this. "You do that, Troy. We should abide by our expired friend's wishes. Too bad he can't stick around and tell me about spacetime drives, but I believe he imparted to me a significant amount of knowledge that I can concoct all sorts of new drives now."

"I thought these were the *good* guys," said Diane. "They're acting like *gangsters*!"

"Cosmically speaking, perhaps the gangsters *are* the good guys. Would you prefer to be back in the cold hands of the Proons?"

Diane shivered. "No."

"Well," said Dr. D., looking down at the grapefruit. "At least we know with these boys we won't get scurvy!"

Meanwhile, several other angelic gangsters stepped through the hatchway, landing inelegantly on the floor, sniffing and peering around like rodents. They were shorter and bulkier than the first, and a good deal grosser looking, with hair sprouting from ratty noses and ratty ears and the profound odor of garlic emanating from their robes. They all carried violin cases slung around their thick necks.

"Hey, boss!" said one with a bulbous cigar sticking out from thick lips. "Never seen a ship as rickety as this one!"

The head angel/gangster slapped the dumpy henchman upside the head. "Pizon! Have you no manners!

It's a good boat, this one. We must not be rude.'' He
turned and faced Dr. D. ''We are the Pizons. My name
is Bugsoid. We're just patrolling the area, shakin' some
action, collectin' protection money, ya know, and we
hear your distress call.''

Dr. D. turned to Diane. ''Distress call?''

''A little something I rigged up. I wasn't sure if it
worked or not.''

''It apparently worked quite well.'' He turned back
to the Pizon thug. ''My name is Dr. Demopoulos. My
companions are Diane Derry and Troy Talbot . . . and
until you showed up an alien named 'Spon.' ''

''Spon. Hmmm. Wouldn't know him,'' said Bugsy.
''Freydo, you wanna check on the list?''

The thug whipped out a flat computer screen connected by a wire to a plug-in unit in his belly. He
tapped a few buttons, the screen came alight, and
names unreeled. ''Ah, here we go, boss. Spon, from
the planet Squint-Thog. Two million three hundred and
twenty-two bucks in back interest and principle on an
Aquarius cruiser, plus a half mil on gambling debts.''

Bugsoid's face mashed in on itself ruminatively.
''Can't hardly take it out of his hide now. Guess we
gotta repo his ship.'' He looked at Dr. D. ''So where
is it?''

''I'm afraid we had to abandon it back on the Proon
mothership, where it was stranded and where we
picked up the fellow.''

''No kiddin'. You escaped those tight asses. Whad-
dya know. Youse guys must have somethin' good goin'
for ya!'' Bugsoid seemed honestly impressed.

''That's what I was rather hoping to chat with you
folks about. You see, we're a little bit lost and would
like to find our way home . . . Unfortunately, we've
really got to deal with a little bit of trouble some trai-
torous associates have stirred up!''

''You asking us for help?''

''I guess so.''

''We Pizons, we don't do somethin' for nothin'.''
Bugsoid snapped his fingers and was handed the cigar
butt, dripping with salivoid fluids. He dragged on it
and blew out a shredded plume of purplish smoke. His
thick eyebrows waggled. ''What's in it for *us*, Bud?''

''How about a nice Heinz bean dinner?'' said Dr. D.
''On spaghetti, with garlic bread if you like . . . but
I'm afraid you'll have to provide those.''

The Pizon hood grinned. ''Friends!''

# Chapter Nineteen

The interior of the Pizons' ship looked like nothing less than a space-faring casino.

As Dr. D. and his companions—Troy lugging the bean dinner that they'd promised—walked down the corridor after being ushered into the Pizon ship, Dr. D. was amazed at the number of slot machines that lined the halls. From greenly lit rooms came the spinning of roulette wheels, the hushed roll of craps dice, the slap of cards. Smoke hung everywhere, and waitresses in frilly costumes with high hems and low necklines carried cocktails with pink umbrellas sticking out of them to waiting customers, who gambled away like there was no tomorrow. Somewhere, crooning orchestras played and comedians joked, all under a tomatoey haze of garlic and excitement.

"We call dis place Lost Wages!" said Bugsoid. "Good joke, huh?"

Dr. D. didn't really get it, nor did Diane or Troy. However, they figured it was politic to laugh, and so they did.

Bugsy grinned happily and sailed on, feet a good foot from the ground, trailing foul cigar smoke.

"Say, babe," said one of the Pizons, who Bugsoid had previously addressed as Freydo or some such improbable name, to Diane. "You know, you'd look awfully good in one of those dancer's costumes, kicking those beautiful legs up in the air?"

He pointed to one of the side rooms, where a line

of spangled chorus girls were doing synchronized dancing to the sound of big band music.

"You mean, like this?" Diane stepped forward and kicked the Pizon directly in the juncture of his legs—a point clearly just as vulnerable in the Pizons as in humans, if the creature's yelp and changing of colors was any indication.

"Ah—we got ourselves a spirited filly!" crowed Bugsoid. "Da Big Fella—he likes 'em sassy."

The stricken hood merely whimpered, putting his snub-nosed blaster back into its violin case.

"Good," said Dr. D. "No violins!"

Diane groaned, both with the pun and from honest relief. These jerks looked like serious customers!

"Just mind your own linguine from now on," she scolded the hood, falling back into line.

The party continued along the plush carpeting, swishing past plush violet drapes, until they reached a set of double doors, done in fancy carved wood, or whatever it was.

"Nice woodwork," said Dr. D. "That's rococo designing, isn't it?"

"No," said Bugsy. "Rocco."

"Rocco?"

"Yeah, Rocco, the Big Guy's designer."

"Big Guy," Diane said. "Who exactly is this 'Big Guy' you've been talking about?"

"The Pizons you're about to meet," said Bugsy. "But come on in. Drinks on da house."

He pushed the double doors open and swept through into the room. Gently he lowered his bulky form onto the Oriental-looking rug upon the floor. It was all very homey-looking here, from the fire in the marble (?) hearth to the huge frame pictures of dour Pizon patriarchs brooding from the walls. Richly brocaded couches were arrayed around a walnut table, upon which perched a silver beverage service.

"Yum! Walnuts. My favorite!" Troy grabbed one,

cracked it against his head, and popped it into his mouth, crunching happily.

"Yeah. Help yerselves. Put those beans down there," commanded Bugsoid, who proceeded to divest himself of his bulletproof robe. The garments he wore underneath were nothing more nor nothing less than a striped, dark mobster suit, with a bright yellow silk tie. And spats. A white carnation rustled from his lapel. He snapped his fingers and a white hat dropped from the ceiling, settling down upon his head gently. He tapped it into place. "Associates, please remain here. Guests, please follow me. We'll take our drinks in the next room. Telepathic impulses tell me dat da master awaits. Away we go!"

He stepped lightly and daintily for a creature of his girth. Dr. D. ascribed it to the wings, fluttering now lightly above his shoulders. He gestured for the others to go first, and then, as he followed them, he leaned over and scooped up a couple of petit fours. Chopped chicken finger sandwiches, from the taste of them. Hardly his favorite, but then, he was getting a bit peckish and he was getting awfully sick of baked beans!

They were led into a long narrow room, in which was situated a long narrow table, highly polished and bracketed by high-backed wooden chairs. At the head of this long table was an older-looking Pizon, leaning, a jowly frown upon one hand, his wings settled and relaxed upon his shoulders. He had on a black tuxedo with a red carnation in one lapel. The man's hair was gray and he wore a mousetashe. The mouse wiggled as the old Pizon looked up at the guests, but couldn't get up, since it had been strapped in by some peculiar metallic device resembling teeth braces, attached by silver holders to an odd, plastic bubble rising from the Pizon's back like a hump on a hunchback.

"Don Dellamonte," said Bugsoid. "May I introduce our guests—" Quickly the Pizons ran down the roster. "Dis, guests, is our Godfodder . . . Don Dellamonte!"

A shining drop of grease dripped from the older man's head onto the top of one of his wings. "Welcome to my spaceship. Please sit and make yourselves comfortable."

The party arranged themselves in the chairs to which they were shown.

"Bring in the coffee and eats, Bugsoid! And make it snappy!"

"Yes, Godfodder," said the suddenly obsequious Pizon, scurrying off to do his master's bidding, a look of servitude and, yes, terror in his eye. This graying creature before him hardly seemed the sort to arouse such fear and devotion . . . but then, of course, Dr. D. realized that he was judging by human standards—and although humanoid (with a touch of wingoid as well) the Pizons were not human.

"What planet do you come from? I do not believe I am familiar with the genoatype our meters show."

"You mean genotype?" corrected Diane.

"No, genoatype. Like bolognatype, and milanotype." The Godfodder turned toward Dr. D. "Your women—dey not only got big gozangas, dey got bigga mouths. You can shut her up?"

"No, sorry."

"I was afraid of that. Oh, well, same wid my wife, only she don't sit with me in my chamber."

"You know," said Troy. "You remind me a lot of mobster folks I know. In fact, dollars to donuts I'd say that you *were* a mobster."

"Troy, that's nonsense. The mob is an Earth phenomenon. How could there be mobsters in space?"

Don Dellamonte fixed her with his dark penetrating chocolate eyes. "The mob is not a phenomenon . . . it is a metaphysical state of being. We Pizons . . . We're just more advanced in concept and practice. We run our empire according to the old ways. We get

things done. An' you know what . . . We're the good
guys!''

"Thank God," said Diane, but without much con-
viction.

"So, your organization pretty much runs the galaxy?" Dr. D. asked.

"Hey, we don't want to run everything. Just all the
gambling, sex, contraband substances . . . you know,
the stuff that intelligent beings everywhere in the universe like a lot! We're a business. And we do pretty
well, too.''

"Except for the problems with the Proons."

Don Dellamonte threw his hands up with disgust.
"Bafungool! Those bluenoses! We don't want none of
their action! They can keep their worlds. They're the
ones who come and bust up our operations—and open
up Sunday schools and tell us how to live our lives. We
*know* how to live our lives and we live good lives.
We have some fun, we have some action on da side,
sure . . . Maybe a few people get hurt, go into the
vacuum wid cement spacesuits from time to time . . .
Hey, dat's business. What's the hurt? People get to
gamble a little, play a little, drink a little, fool around
a little . . . But they all still go to worship on their
respective alien sabbath mornings, so the Big Guy up-
stairs''—the don made an appropriate gesture—"don't
mind!'' The alien seemed to get extremely exercised
suddenly, to the point where his wings started to un-
furl and flap about spasmodically. "But dese guys, dey
come and dey tell our people . . . naughty naughty!
Natural urges . . . dey dirty. Dey want our lives to be
*boring*. No vino, no action, no hoochie coochie . . .
know what I mean?'' Don Dellamonte's face grew red
as an alien beet. "So they try and push us around with
their big ships, and so we gotta push *them* around a
little . . . And *kabash*! We got titanic space battles!
We don't like titanic space battles! We like nice little
alley fights with knives and garrotes. Tradition. All

these power rays and beams and cosmic weaponry . . .
It make-a us sick! We just wanta them to leave us
alone!''

The poor guy seemed to be about to dissolve into
tears, but he recomposed himself as his flunkies
brought in the coffee and treats for the guests. When
all was poured and handed out and the serving folk
bowed and slunk away, Dr. D. gave the head Pizon a
moment to compose himself.

''I can certainly sympathize with you. We were stuck
on the mother ship.''

''That's what Bugsoid says! Nobody every leaves that
place with their *cajones*! How did you get away?''

''Beans!'' said Troy, grinning.

''No . . . not the sacred beans!''

Dr. D. nodded. ''That and a pretty advanced space
drive . . . but look, Mr. Dellamonte . . . You seem to
be an honest . . . well, let's just say reasonable fellow.
You've got some trouble, we've got some trouble . . .''

''Yeah! Like botha our asses . . . dey in a da crack!''

''And all because of these Proons!''

''Well, we've got a little more immediate problem,
but I think that if you help us, we can help you, eh?''
Ideas were flowing into Dr. D.'s noggin with gratifying speed and fertility. ''How about a little deal?''

''Deal? You speaka our language.'' He stared at
Dr. D. somberly. ''This deal, there's somethin' in it
for us?''

''Don Dellamonte,'' said Dr. D. happily, ''it's a deal
you can't refuse!''

''Letta me get this straight,'' said Don Dellamonte
as he strode down the passageway alongside Dr. D.
and companions. To either side of him slot machines
chinged and binged in rolling salute. ''You took a couple of your own with you who've turned stoolie. They
want to take the Proons to your planet and conquer
it.''

"That's right! Vivian Vernon and Geoffrey Wussman, the rotters!" said Diane, coloring at the very thought of them.

"What kinda people are these that would rat on their own race!" asked the Godfodder. "Especially to uptight scum like the Proons."

"Hard-core academics," said Dr. D. "Looking for scholastic power!"

"So what you want us to do is to help you stop the Proons by blowing da mother ship. How the hell we gonna do *that*?"

"Well, I figure you let me in to your super-science workshops and I'll whip some sort of power beam up and we'll whip the bastards!"

"Don't you think we'd have done that by now if we could?" huffed the don. "Don't you think we got our own scientists!"

"Yeah, but not like the doctor!" Troy enthused. "He can't handle a screwdriver worth beans, but he's an incredible whiz at the theory part of it."

"Exactly," said Diane. "As long as I've known him, he's always complained about the primitiveness of earthly technology. Why just last month he was saying, 'My goodness, Diane. If only I could use some advance *mobsteroid* technology! I'd have the whole universe at my feet. Right, Doc!"

"Exactly," Demetrios said, playing along. "And by the way, I'm very impressed indeed at the level of your engineering. Ours, as you can no doubt tell, is quite primitive. Perhaps you might take the *Mudlark* into your shops and do a little bit of refitting or what not?"

Don Dellamonte mulled this over a bit. "We could add a little chrome here and there. And the ugly thing could use a little bit of expansion, streamlining . . . Maybe some mag hubcaps. A fancy pair of dice to hang on the rearview mirror? Maybe a turret laser in the bag for those little police problems?"

"Just the thing, Don."

"Look. My question is, whadda we get? I mean, what's in it for da boys and me?"

"I know just the thing. You look like reasonable, rational souls. You don't want to conquer another planet, do you? No, of course not. All you want is a little action . . . So here's the deal. I'll put you in contact with the mobster folks on our planet . . . and they'll cut you a piece of the action!"

"Why should dey do that? They *stupid* or something?"

"No. 'Cause with those power rays you can turn them all into fried pizza if they don't!"

The don considered it. "Yeah! Yeah, I like the style of your reasoning. Meantime, we deal a painful blow against the Proons. Maybe teach them a thing or two about steppin' into our territory!"

"That's right. You see, we all win, Don. But first, let me fiddle a little bit in these workshops you mention."

"Yeah. No problem." Don Dellamonte halted them in front of a pair of steel doors. He hit a button and they squeaked open rustily. "Sometimes the civilizations we put our slots and games and stuff into, dey can't make their payments in time. So what they do, they give us what they can. We got heart. We don't like to knock heads or break kneecaps less we got to. So we take this junk, figurin' maybe sometime—hey, it might be useful or somethin'."

He swiveled and hit a switch. Naked light bulbs hanging from the ceiling turned on, illuminating rows of tables, overflowing with an odd metallic garden of unclassifiable junk. There were all kinds of machines and gizmos and what nots. Cut glass and weird alloys and alien gems gleamed and glittered in the harsh light. There was the smell of exotic desserts here, and the taste of cold minerals. Dr. D. could see pieces of robots and androids poking from the junk, as though somehow disinterred from a cemetery.

"It's all yours, Doc. It'll take us a couple a days to do a number of dat sad boat of yours. Think you can whip somethin' up by then."

"Tools. I'll need tools. Soldering irons, screwdrivers, wires . . ."

"No problem. I send in a couple of my hit men. Dat's why we call them *mechanics*. They'll fit you out good."

Dr. D. smiled for the first time in what seemed like a very long time indeed. "Excellent. And I have my trusty lab assistants."

"Gee, Doc!" said Troy happily. "That's us!"

"Well, I suppose *one* big problem doesn't bear mentioning . . . just kidding, Troy. We're all one big happy family, aren't we. And this one big happy family is about to roll up its sleeves and save the Earth!"

"Could we get some more of those canned oil desserts, Mr. Dellamonte? They were *great*!"

"I believe you are referring to the cannoli?"

"Uhhmmm! And canned ravioli, too. With lots of extra ketchup!"

The don was appalled. "This boy is sick! Dat's very nice. Well. I'll let you go on about your business, and you can be sure that I'll tend to your ship in a way that will make your mission back to the Proons effective as possible. Ciao!"

"Yeah," called Troy after him. "Chow. And send lots of it, too. I'm famished."

Dr. D. dropped a piece of cast iron onto Troy's foot.

"Yow!" said Troy.

"Sorry, dear boy. How clumsy of me." He looked around, pure glee shimmering in his eyes. "What a treasure trove. Let's do see what exactly we have here, eh?"

# Chapter Twenty

What they had there was the most astonishing amount of stuff that Dr. Demopoulos had ever seen in his life. There were mechanisms of such clearly alien nature that he didn't really have the faintest what they were or what they did.

Item by item he examined them. There were motors, odd weapons, and decidedly strange kitchen appliances by the score, but for the life of him, Dr. D. didn't have the faintest how they could be used singly or collectively against the Proons.

"Sure is a lot of *junk*!" said Troy, shaking his head. "I haven't seen such a lot of junk since I played baseball as a kid in the town junkyard. And you know what, though? Least I had an idea what that junk *was*!"

"Whatever it is, it certainly is colorful," said Diane, sifting through the mess. She pulled out what appeared to be a sun dial on a huge belt.

"Peculiar wristwatch, eh?" said Dr. D. "Now, though . . . this looks familiar. What have we got here?"

He reached down and pulled what appeared to be a pair of spectacles from a tangle of wires and Popsicle sticks. The eyeglasses were plastic, connected to a coil of spring, connected to fake bloodshot eyeballs. The thing appeared to be just something out of a novelty ad from a pulp magazine—the old eyeballs popping from the fake spectacles gag. A buck ninety-eight, plus postage and shipping.

What was it doing here on a Pizon ship?

Garbage! A wave of disappointment spread through him, and he tossed the thing away.

There had to be something better around here!

"Wow! Keen!" said Troy. "I've got one of these back home!"

"Oh, my God—that disgusting thing. What's it doing here?"

"Well, apparently there are indeed common threads through all civilizations in the galaxy. I mean, bluenoses. And these mobsteroids or whatever." Dr. D. began sifting through the mess again. There had to be some kind of makings of a field generator or a death ray or he'd even settle for some kind of super-science stink bomb, for God's sake.

"Hey, Diane! Look! I'm a bug-eyed monster!"

"Troy. Must you always clown? Take those ridiculous things off this instant!"

"Wow. These things are weird. It's like . . . Well, it's like I'm looking through a pair of kaleidoscopes!"

"Alien novelty items are bound to have alien novelty tricks!" muttered Dr. D., pushing aside what appeared to be a giant ashtray made of bottle caps.

"Gee—my head feels funny. All tingly. Doc—you know, I think I finally understand that theory of relativity thing! It's *not* about family!"

"No, you simpleton. It's not."

"Troy, take those ridiculous things off this instant."

"Hey, Doc. Look at that thing underneath that pile over there. *That* looks interesting, huh?"

"What?" All Dr. D. could see was a pile of old coat hangers and go-cups.

"That."

Suddenly the mess was lifted up by an invisible force. Beneath it was some sort of device, complete with a lever.

"Interesting. It looks like some kind of explosives plunger," said Dr. D. "But how did you do that,

Troy . . . No, that's impossible. It must have been some kind of static energy field, reacting as I approached.''

"I don't know, Doc, but these glasses are making me think really strange things.''

"Troy . . . take those asinine glasses off this instant. They bother me!''

"Gosh, Diane—'' said Troy. "I can see right through your sweater!''

Dr. D. spun around. Troy had put the eyeballs back into place and was staring all agoggle at Diane's chest.

"No kidding! Let *me* see!''

He grabbed the glasses, took his own off, and fitted them around his ears and on his nose.

The eyeballs fell out, dangling ridiculously in front of him. Everything was blurry now (as was always the case when he didn't have his glasses on) and he felt terribly stupid.

"Doctor!'' said Diane, hands across her chest. "What are those things! And please don't stare at me!''

Damn! He could have used a spurt of male hormones to get his thinker going. As it was, he was probably going to have to take a plunge back in the old fantasy factory, crunch some numbers, squeeze his fantasy babe.

He pushed the eyeballs back into place.

And almost instantly, something other than cheap metal and plastics *clicked*.

It was as though his brain were a car and he'd always driven in first or second gears, never realizing that there were other, higher gears. He looked at Diane a moment, finding he really wasn't interested in looking at her bare breasts (how odd) but was much more interested in more cerebral matters. He turned and stared out over the field of trashed artifacts.

Suddenly he *recognized* them.

Suddenly he understood the meaning and importance of each and every item!

"Geez!" he said. "What *garbage*!"

"Huh? Oh, yeah, Doc. I forgot to tell you, this stuff is mostly trash. But over there, under that pile of petrified automatic drier lint—there's something that appears to be a positronic particle-gooser gun!"

Dr. D. turned toward where Troy had pointed, and it was as though someone had turned on an entirely new and different kind of light over the entire room.

Everything seemed much *clearer, sharper,* with startlingly deep outlines. He could see things so clearly that he could almost make out their molecular structure. But what was unique about the device (and now he understood perfectly how a clod like Troy could recognize alien articles) were the little labeled red arrows in the air now, pointing toward things and labeling them in clear and legible English!

Yes, there was the pile of "Petrified Automatic Drier Lint."

And, underneath it as advertised, was a rifle-shaped thing labeled "Positronic Particle-Gooser Gun."

"Incredible!" said Dr. D., awed at this example of high-octane alien super-science.

The question was, what was this thing?

He looked around quickly, hoping to find a label hanging in the air, but saw nothing. He snapped his head upward, but there was no label dangling above him.

"Are you okay, Doctor?" said Diane.

"No use explaining, Diane. You'll have to see for yourself, eventually. Apparently these aren't simply novelty glasses!"

"I rather gather that. But please—no looking through my shirt."

"Of course not! Far more serious things to deal with . . . Like that Positronic Particle-Gooser gun. Now, we'll just have to heft that pile of Petrified Automatic Drier Lint off it—" He visualized the engineering problems involved. Yes, Troy would just have to lift it and—

Suddenly the pile of lint simply jumped off on its own accord, hovered for a moment above the floor, and then bounced off into a corner where it clanged and crashed into a suit of alien armor.

"My word . . . again . . . levitation. While I thought about it!" Quickly Dr. Dimension took off the glasses. "Psychokinesis!"

"Yeah, Doc. You can really lift some skirt up with those babies now!"

"Troy!" Diane hit him in his muscular upper arm.

"That's all well and good, Troy. I'm glad you've advanced somewhat in priorities . . . but at the moment, I'm a little more concerned about other matters!"

"Doctor! How encouraging!" said Diane.

Dr. D. took off the glasses and examined them. "Yes. Most marvelous. The lenses of these glasses somehow focus not only one's mental acuity and thought energy into an actual physical force—hence the levitation—and eyesight but are able to increase the levels of one's latent psi powers!"

"Gee, Doc. I thought Dr. Vernon was the spy!"

"Psi, Troy. *Psi*," said Diane. "You know, super powers of the mind. Like telepathy, dowsing, astral projection . . . Often considered occult in nature, but now discovered to actually be grounded in scientific fact."

"Oh, you mean like Claire Voit."

"Clairvoyance, Troy."

"No, I dated a Claire Voit once. She could read my mind."

"Oh, I bet she could."

Doc D. said, "Have to give it to the guy, he's the one who had the smarts to try them on first. Here you go, Diane. Care to test them out?"

"Maybe later, Doctor. Perhaps it's best if I continue to be a control."

"Good point. Just make sure there aren't alien intelligences about, seeking to take over our minds. Always a possibility.''

"So how about that gun, Doc. Let's have a peek!'' said Troy, hopping forward and grabbing it. "Wow, what a keen piece of artillery this is. I—''

He put his finger around a stud, inadvertently pressing it.

A burst of sizzling energy erupted, spraying coherent light in a ragged pattern along a pile of junk, tearing it apart explosively. Startled, Troy hung on to the rifle for all he was worth, spinning haphazardly on his quivering feet. Dr. D., fortunately for the continued narrative of this book, was able to keep his presence of mind sufficiently to jump forward and knock Troy's hand off the trigger grip.

"Wow!'' said Troy, clearly shaken. "This thing packs a wallop!''

"Yes,'' said Dr. D. "I would definitely have to say that quite a few positrons in that pile of stuff over there have been most obviously goosed. No real harm done, my boy. It was all junk, anyway. We've got the real McCoy here . . .''

Diane looked doubtful. "Are you entirely sure how to use it, though, Doctor? I mean, look at what happened when Troy picked up that gun! Exactly what *are* those spectacles? How can you be sure they won't backfire in the heat of battle? And most importantly, how can you shut off that peering through clothing business! It's horrid!''

"Maybe I can give that a try,'' said Troy, reaching for the alien spectacles.

"What? You? How!'' Diane was incensed.

"Well, the Doc says it focuses thoughts. I'll just stare at you, Diane, and *will* it to not look at your gorgeous naked body. It'll be hard, but I think I can do it!''

"Don't you *dare* give him those glasses, Doctor! Troy, I thought you were a clean-living young man.''

"Cripes, Diane. That ain't the question. You used to be a lot of fun," said Troy. "The question is, what have those Proons done to you." He turned to Dr. D. "Maybe it was breathing that air, huh, Doc?"

"Quite possibly. But I think there are more important things to consider, Troy, than examining Diane's extremely large nipples."

Diane flushed. "How—"

"Your point is quite well taken. It is best to thoroughly understand the tools, the weapons that one is using, lest they backfire on you."

He took up the glasses, donned them again, and surveyed the area, reading the labels.

Quite a lot of raw materials here. And with the tools that Don Dellamonte was providing.

"Moreover, I am not entirely satisfied with this as a weapon. We must realize that it was created with alien brains in mind."

"Gee—what are you going to do, Doc?"

"You'll see soon enough. Troy, hand me that hacksaw there! You are about to observe Dr. Demetrios Demopoulos at one of his finest moments!"

Diane's attention averted to Troy as he went to get the hacksaw, allowing Dr. D. the opportunity to test out the X-ray glasses on her clothing again.

# Chapter Twenty-one

Troy Talbot held the spectacles braced in his powerful hands.

It was but the work of a few strong back and forth movements of the hacksaw. The blade went through the frame with surprising ease. Not only was it plastic, it was apparently *cheap* plastic.

"There we go!" said Dr. D., taking one of the sections of the glasses up and examining it for any damage. "Now we have what you could truly call 'half frames.' "

One of the fake eyeballs sprang loose and dangled ludicrously.

Diane was aghast. "But, Doctor! You've ruined it!"

(She pronounced it "rooned," which Dr. D. found most amusing.)

"What? No, no! It works quite well, I assure you. I'm simply allowing science to do its work!" He put the eyeball back in, put the section of the cut eyeglasses up to his eye, and baldly stared at her chest. "Yes indeed. It works *splendidly*!"

She slapped his head. *"Doctor!"*

He averted his gaze, grinning. "Can't help but feel my oats, my dear. I've come up with a brilliant idea." He pointed around him in an expansive gesture. "Thanks to these glasses, we know what all of this stuff is here. Inner workings, right down to the molecular structure. These spectacles, however, were not able to analyze themselves . . . until now! Voilà!"

He placed one of the sawed-off sections to his eye.

"Incredible!" he said. "Astonishing! *Marvelous*!"

Diane shook her head. "Doctor, would you stop staring at my chest and get to work!"

"Oh. Sorry, Diane. Just staying in character. Here we go, this is my idea."

He directed his attention down to the other half of the spectacles, scrutinizing it carefully for what seemed like an eternity.

"Doctor, we haven't *got* forever!" Diane reminded him, and not gently.

"How fascinating!" said Dr. D. He looked up and this time utilizing both frames of the spectacles, he examined the environs. "Yes, yes—I think we have what we need . . . right here!"

"What are you talking about, Doctor?"

"My friends, roll up your sleeves! There's work to be done!"

Troy, who was wearing short sleeves, spent a full minute trying to roll them up his pronounced biceps before Diane could convince him that Dr. D. had simply been using a figure of speech.

Dr. D. hardly noticed.

He was too busy tackling his latest invention.


"Is that *all*?"

"What did you expect?"

Diane shook her head, clearly shocked at what Dr. Demopoulos was showing her.

"I don't know. Something big. Something nasty-looking. Something that has some panache and power to it."

"Gee, Doc. It looks like something you get in a Cracker Jack box!"

Troy had just gotten up, too, after being prodded awake by Dr. D. They'd worked for hours, going through most of the junk in the room. Diane had been shocked by the number of used alien condoms they'd found (to say nothing of the unusual *shapes* of those condoms). Troy had been shocked when he put his fingers in the wall socket.

With this and all they'd been through before, they were quite fried. (Troy extra crispy.)

So after their hosts had brought a particularly savory meal of spaghetti and beet sauce and gargle bread and Bean-O, a special wine that prevented bottom burps. (We said mobsteroid, not mobster, remember.) Troy and Diane, at Dr. D.'s suggestion, took a little snooze, rolled up like ravioli squares.

They woke up amid the sprawl and tangle of paper plates and the spaghetti that Troy had spilled, to the clanging and banging of Dr. D.'s work.

Excited, expecting some wonderful new death ray or something truly stupendous (Dr. D. did, after all, deal in largely outrageous inventions) they were surprised at what the Doc had concocted.

"Behold, assistants!" said Dr. Demopoulos, brandishing the thing before him proudly. "The Magnetic Monocle!"

He held in his hand what looked like nothing more than the sort of magnifying glasses utilized by Sherlock Holmes in silly stage versions of the Arthur Conan Doyle stories. As he stared at them, though, the lens was a chiaroscuro of color and movement—Walt Disney's *Fantasia* in fast forward.

The lens was wrapped in a frame much more complex than the plastic version that inspired it. There were all sorts of zigzags and doodads of electronic paraphernalia. Connecting the stem of the monocle to a power pack on the doctor's back was a long series of curlicued wire. On the power pack was a single vacuum tube, pulsing purple vibrantly.

"Doctor, are you *looking* at me again?" said Diane suspiciously.

"Hmmm? No, no, my dear. The X-ray characteristics of this particular device have been distinctly downplayed.''

''Doctor, sorry . . .'' said Troy. ''What exactly *is* a magnetic monocle?''

''Only the salvation of Earth, lad. Of course, we'll need more than a touch of luck, and maybe a few more megawatts of power for it to work properly—but I think I'm on the right track!''

''You really didn't answer Troy,'' said Diane imperiously. ''How is that silly-looking thing going to stop the Proons from conquering Earth?''

She *had* to ask that question!

''Not terribly sure, my dear. But it does some awfully keen things!''

''Like *what*?''

''Er—well, much the same kind of things as these alien spectacles do!''

''You mean, *parlor* tricks?''

She was getting red and it wasn't from the beet sauce. Maybe he'd peered at her bounteous curves once too many times through those trick glasses. He couldn't really blame her though—it was rather rude.

''No, of course not. Though I'm admit that—crude and lascivious fellow that I am, I was utilizing them for such.''

''Is that an apology?''

''As much as you'll get from this old goat, I suppose.''

''I'll take it. Now what does that contraption do?''

''It sure makes some neat squiggly colors,'' Troy said. ''Is this the kind of stuff that they do in that magazine, *Fantastic Tales of Super-Science,* Doc?''

''How observant of you, Troy. You've been paying attention. Yes. Well, as you remember, I utilized the analytic aspects of the spectacles upon themselves.''

''And lucky you were you didn't destroy the thing!''

''These are very special lenses, you see. Lenses are usually associated with light. Light, as you know, can't make up its mind whether it's a particle or a wave. A very wishy washy thing, light. That's why Einstein used it in his theory. Every thing is relative with light.''

"I always thought that area of physics was rather incestuous!" said Diane.

"However, if you think that light has problems making up its mind—and remember, there's a whole lot more light than we can perceive with the naked eye—"

"Something about a special rectum, right, Doc?"

"Troy, would you just let me lecture please? The word you mean is 'spectrum.' "

"Yeah, like I said . . ."

Dr. D. ignored him. "Anyway, the other waves in the universe are *much* more fickle!"

"Other waves. You mean like electromagnetic and radio waves, Doctor?"

"Yes, Diane . . . but there's a spectrum of those which we've only glimpsed . . . thought waves."

"Can you surf on those kinds of waves, Doc? I'm a pretty good surfer."

"A very good analogy, Troy. However, more to the point, what the alien spectacles do is to focus alien thoughts into other forms of energy. Thus, the levitation . . . The X-rays, etc. Very low grade, I'm afraid, and fairly incompatible with the unique and frankly baroque patterns of human thought."

"I understand!" Diane beamed, this time with admiration. "You just made something that would work with a human mind . . ."

"Well, *my* mind! Yes—the Magnetic Monocle! When placed up to my eye, like so—" Dr. D. adjusted it. "Not only do I look rather dashing, but my thought waves are channeled through it, locused into a vortex, channeled through the processors on my back, and then directed outward again by the lens of the glasses by the directional vector of my latent psi forces. I simply haven't done much of a test run with it, so I'm not sure exactly what it will *do*."

He turned around and faced the piles of junk, concentrating. He started to hum the "Russian Saber Dance" and the effect was immediate and most gratifying.

Pieces of junk not only levitated . . .

They formed rough simulacra of Cossacks and executed a spritely kick dance.

"You see," said Dr. D. "Psychic powers *can* be fun."

The moment he turned his attention away from them, the dancers collapsed back into heaps of junk.

"So you can toss things around. How's that going to deal with the incredible powers the Proons clearly have?"

"Let me show you something, my dear." He took a pocket flashlight out and turned it on, using its beam to illuminate a dark corner. He switched it off. "A simple ordinary light beam, correct?"

"So it would seem."

"Well, if my theory is correct—and soldering skill is accurate, then something interesting should happen here . . ."

He placed the light up to the lens, directed it—and clicked the power on. The small bulb shone brightly, and brighter still as it accumulated in the crystalline cache of the lens. Round and round it rolled through the glass, vortexing out and then streaming on the edges—up and up and up through the wires it shot, glowing, and the vacuum tube pulsed prismatically as though undergoing extreme sexual gratification with a rainbow.

Stillness. A pause as though for wave breath.

Then, in an instant exhaltation of exhalation, the light flamed out from the lens, in a coherent flash of concentrated energy.

It sounded like a god clearing his throat.

It laid waste to everything in its path, cutting a biting swathe through metal and plastic and glass.

"My *word*," said Diane. "Whatever was *that*!"

"I shall call it a 'laser,' " stated Dr. D.

"Keen," said Troy. "Why?"

"Sounds like an anagram," said Diane. "Let's see. Light Amplified through Stimulated Emission of Radiation?"

"Good guess. Actually, I was thinking more along the lines of 'Let's Attack the Sucking Extraterrestrial Rats!' "

"Ya *hoo*!" Troy cried. "Geronimo!"

"That's the spirit," said Dr. D. "Now, let's see what it does with simple thought upon another creature!"

He turned and directed it upon Troy.

"Hey, Doc . . . What—"

"Don't worry, dear boy. I'm not going to harm you."

Dr. D. concentrated.

Troy suddenly became ramrod-straight, zombie eyes staring out vapidly.

"How interesting," said Troy, only his voice now sounded a great deal like Dr. D.'s. "I seem to have complete control of his mind!"

Troy suddenly started barking like a dog. He meowed like a cat and grunted like a pig. He got down on all fours and began to crawl around, snapping at the air.

He rolled over, played dead, and was about to take a leak on a bit of junk that looked like a fireplug, but was stopped by a simple mind command from Dr. D.

"Now," said the doctor. "I shall try it on *intelligent* life!" He rolled the lens away from Troy and toward Diane.

"Doctor, please!"

"All in the interest of science, Diane! To say nothing of the welfare of Earth."

"I don't care. I don't want you crawling around in my mind. Besides, how's it going to resemble trying to control Proon minds?"

"Hmm. Good point. Nonetheless, you surely are impressed with what I've achieved."

"Why do you think I hang around with you? I never said you weren't brilliant. You've just got a few problems that we haven't ironed out yet. Little did I know when I signed on that I'd end up out in the middle of space with you, with only Troy to fend off your advances!" There was a saucy insouciance in her voice, a touch of flirtation. Most curious, thought Dr. D. She really is starting to appreciate my virility and my charm, as well as my genius.

"Oh, come now, you know you can trust me, Diane. On that subject I'm actually just a shy little boy."

"Right. Now you're playing innocent, you randy old goat." She smiled at him tauntingly.

Inside, he could feel the old juices flowing. Ah, the tingle of testosterone! The prickly hot goose up his cerebral cortex! More than anything now he just wanted to jump on Diane and ravish her with hot kisses, Troy Talbot be damned. God, the way she was batting those baby blues was driving him absolutely out of his gourd.

"Troy, would you be so kind as to go and get us a couple of slices of pizza. Cooked from scratch. Hydroponically grown black olives are a must."

"Uh—sure, Doc." Troy, oblivious to what was going on, clomped out of the room on his mission.

"Doctor," said Diane. "You know, it's getting so hot in here. Would you mind terribly if I just take off my shirt for a while."

All the liquid left Dr. D.'s mouth immediately at the very thought. "Why no, of course not, my dear!" he said through desert dryness.

Diane shed her blouse, revealing a startlingly white, startlingly filled bra.

"Ooooh," she said. "I've got this terrible itch right in the small of my back. Would you please scratch it?"

Dr. D. advanced and, tentatively, reached up to touch her creamy white skin near the base of her back, nearly those wonderful rounded hips. Contact! Ignition! Soft, so wonderfully soft. Dr. D. thought his head was going to explode with desire. Could this be true. Was he finally going to have his way with this delectable morsel? Would all his work and showboating finally bear fruit . . . way out in the middle of space?

"Doctor?"

"Yes, Diane."

Pant pant.

"Do you like me?"

"I adore you, my dear."

Pantless pantless.

"Do you really think I'm beautiful?"

"Beauty incarnate."

"You are rather a bad boy."

"How can I help myself. I've always desired you, my dear."

"But do you love me?"

"As only a genius can love his assistant."

"Doctor, that Magnetic Monocle—it seems rather incomplete."

"It is I who am incomplete, Diane. Without your soft body against me!" He lunged for her, but somehow Diane Derry lithely sidestepped his advance.

"I don't know, Doctor. You know, it seems to me that if something happened to you . . . well, then where would we be. I mean, don't you think that the Magnetic Monocle should be adjusted to *my* thought patterns as well?"

"Of course. Wonderful idea. First though, let me get out of these trousers. It is rather hot, you know . . ."

"Of course, my big stallion. But maybe you should just have a look at the thing . . . Just one quick look, maybe an adjustment, before I grant you any of my favors!''

Dr. D. could feel the lust streaming through his system now like pounding locomotives. He was flushed, he was breathing hard, and his heart was going haywire. The bald invitation from Diane was almost enough to send him straight to propulsive ecstasy without even touching her—

One little peek at the Magnetic Monocle, then, surely would do no harm.

''Okay.''

Thus, brimming with spermatozoa, the little critters wiggling and tickling his neurons, he turned and picked up the Magnetic Monocle again.

Inspiration struck like a thunderbolt.

''Of course! How could I be so *stupid*!''

He'd been thinking entirely too micro. When dealing with macro enemies like the Proons, you had to think *macro* or lose.

He immediately set to work, quickly and feverishly, absorbed with cathartic glandular inspiration.

Diane Derry, smiling slyly to herself, stepped lightly to the side, donned her shirt again, and began making helpful suggestions.

# Chapter Twenty-two

"You know, Geoffrey," said Vivian Vernon, bilious in her new robe, her hair pulled back into a stern bun behind her ears. "I think that since you've become the mystic of the two of us, we should adjust accordingly in our plans toward Earth."

She gave him a good sound *whack* across the fleshy part of his buttocks as he knelt in the Proons' version of the Lotus . . . the Bum Mantra. His posterior sticking out like that was simply too much of a temptation for poor Vivian. Besides, it seemed entirely appropriate for the Proonian mystical path that Geoffrey was taking, anyway, and it allowed her to vent her natural sadistic tendencies.

"Mom," said Geoffrey. "Mooooommmmmmmmmm!"

She whacked him again, this time a touch harder. "Aren't you listening to me?"

"Oh. Sorry. I was lost in blissful chant."

"Exactly. You've gotten mystical, Geoffrey, and I'm not entirely sure if that's going to sit well with the duties and responsibilities necessary in running centers for the pursuit of excellence in academic applications. By the way, I thought the proper chant was 'Om.' "

"Freudian slip."

In fact, Dr. Wussman seemed entirely oblivious to everything around him, even the smacking with the belt. He'd been this way the whole time since he'd had that vision of his, and while on some levels Vivian found it enjoyable to take advantage of his distraction, a zoned-out Geoffrey was admittedly getting a tad *boring*.

Ever since that nasty little scene with old Demetrios and his odious companions escaping somehow (they'd just kind of shivered off into nothingness, leaving the Proons all befuddled . . . it had taken a great deal of verbal tap dancing to convince the old Grand Proon that she and Geoffrey had not been conspirators in that escape!), Geoffrey had just sort of withdrawn, leaving everything to her.

He just sort of knelt there in that kneeling position, spouting off all manner of religious gibberish of an incoherent Proonian cast. Sermonish stuff like "Sinners in the Hands of a Breakfast Cereal-Hating God" and talk of the damned of the universe writhing in lakes of hot oatmeal with no milk or sugar. It was positively *weird*. No *way* did she want him to be in charge of anything important in any of *her* universities!

"At any rate, Geoffrey, I thought that rather than split up colleges and such among us, you can head up all the departments of religion and philosophy, and I can relieve you of all those awful duties and responsibilities attendant to dealing with the rest of that nonsense. You'll get a nice little salary, a nice cold cloister to pray and meditate in, the promise of at least one scouring a week by Yours Truly—and all the bread and water you can eat and drink. Rich rewards for a man who's clearly become a matchless ascetic."

"Yes, dear. Sounds delightful. And did I tell you about the Proon OverDeity, Ex-Lax, and the punishment that will meet those who do not swallow his holy message!"

"Indeed, Geoffrey—'For behold, those wretched souls shall slide down the Holy Lower Intestines and be defecated down the tubes of Eternal Despair.' Cheerful stuff, Geoffrey. The masses will eat it up.

You'll have a wonderful time upon the planet Earth with this delightful message.''

"I trust, Vivian, that you are heeding my words sufficiently to take the appropriate spiritual action!''

"Indeed. Aren't you happy with the purging qualities of the purging I'm giving you?''

"I have great concern for your soul, Vivian. For you know, we used to sin greatly! I especially I admit, for I had great amounts of lust for you!''

Vivian frowned. "*Used* to?'' Was she doing something wrong. Admittedly, she didn't exactly have her killer perfume around, and this thing she wore now was worse than a potato sack . . . but surely her sheer *presence* was enough yet to send men into a tizzy of desire.

"I have given up the baser elements of my nature. Sacrificed them on the altar of decency and prudence. Thank you for the departments of philosophy and religion. Thus will I disseminate the wisdom and vision of total sexual abstinence upon the whole of Earth!''

Vivian was somewhat bothered by this, and not just because she felt rather spurned. "Come on now, Geoffrey. Surely you don't buy that stuff. I mean, how do the Proons reproduce if they don't fool around once in a while?''

"None of my business!''

"All well and good, but you're a scientist, man. Don't you have any curiosity on the subject?''

"I am borne upon the wings of uplifting spirituality!'' proclaimed Geoffrey. "I am swallowed up by the blissful All-ness of Self-Denial!''

"Come, come, Geoffrey, don't hand me that manure. You're still dying to get inside my pants . . . I mean my robe.''

"I want no part of sinful decadent body fluid exchange!'' said Geoffrey, turning away from her adamantly.

Hmm. This was serious. Maybe she should show

him some thigh or something . . . flash him some flesh. That would get his pot cooking. Still, in any event he wasn't complaining about her getting the top spot in the universities they were going to control once the Proons conquered Earth . . .

She never got a chance to implement any bid for sexual attention, however, because the Grand Proon chose that moment to make his entrance, along with his royal train.

The train looked like an old-fashioned steam variety, and it tooted along the tracks, merrily gusting up puffs of smoke, Proon situated in a seat in one of the cars, scowling powerfully at his/her/whatsits allies in the bid to conquer the promised terrestrial climes.

"All hail, honorary Proons!" he called. "All hail, newly sexless ones."

"Ah, hell," muttered Vivian, never exactly thrilled to see her new boss. As soon as Earth was divvied up according to plan, the first item on her agenda was to make sure she had thorough autonomy with the universities . . . with limited visits from Proons.

"And what visionary triumph have you enjoyed today, newly anointed one?" the Grand Proon inquired, raising an eyebrow Wussman-ward.

Geoffrey Wussman proclaimed, "I went unto the mountain peak, and there I saw Tampax, the angel of uprightness, and he saith, 'Heedeth the words of Proon, for they run like delicious from the dried plum and they maketh the bowels run fast and quick!' "

"Excellent. I'm glad I'm appreciated on the higher strata of being. Although I have less lofty matters to deal with at the moment."

"Why don't you two commune, and I'll just go and use the Neuter's Room!"

"No, Vivian human. We must discuss certain necessary matters. It is becoming more and more obvious to us that while your pulmonary organ seems in the correct place, you haven't got the faintest idea where this home planet of yours is.''

"What? Earth? I gave you *specific* instructions!''

"As I explicitly recall, when showed a model of what of the galaxy you titled the 'Milky Way'—''

"Right. *This* galaxy, true?''

"We call *our* galaxy by its *correct* name.'' Proon sniffed. "The *Chastity Belt*. Now, as I was saying, when showed the Chastity Belt, you simply pointed one of your extensor digits toward a cluster containing thousands of suns, to say nothing of planets, and said, 'Somewhere in there.' ''

"Look, I'm a physicist, not a goddamned astronomer.''

"Your description of your system lacks somewhat as well. The Earth, you say, is right by the 'Moon' and the third planet from the 'Sun.' By the way, may I applaud your most original names for your planetary bodies,'' said Proon dryly. "And the location of your home . . . Nebraska? Now, tell me, Vivian-human. What are we to make of that?''

"Nebraska, Grand Proon! Everybody knows where Nebraska is! It's right by Iowa!''

" 'For behold,' saith Ex-Lax,'' quoted the newly be-monked Geoffrey. " 'I shall create the center of the universe and it shall be called Omaha!' ''

"Well, you can quote all you like,'' said the Grand Proon testily. "But that won't help us find the blasted place. And need I remind you, Vivian-human—if we do not find the Earth, you cannot have your universities.''

Yes, there was the rub.

If only they'd been able to capture Dr. Demopoulos. He'd know . . . And they'd be able to torture the information out of him easy enough. Hell, she would have shown them his most sensitive spots . . .

And she knew that she wouldn't be able to put up with this barren hellhole much longer. It was so boring here that she was afraid that she'd fall asleep sometime and simply not care to wake up anymore.

Which wasn't like Dr. Vivian Vernon at all.

"Well, you're the ones with the super-science. Haven't you found a number of possibilities."

"A mere five hundred and ten."

"Well, you should have said something. That's an easy enough number to handle. I'll just go on up to your map room and have a look."

Besides, she thought to herself, it would be a sight more interesting than hanging around here, listening to Geoffrey drone on and on with his mystical nonsense.

"That *would* be extremely helpful," said the Grand Proon, voice adrip with the nastiest of sarcasm.

"Why do I get the feeling that you don't believe me?"

"What proof have you offered us to even the existence of this planet you call Earth? For all we know, this is all part of a plot! Yes, a complex and sinister Pizon plot to undermine our holy domination of the galaxy!"

"You're *paranoid*!"

"Perhaps. But we had better find the location of Earth soon—Or you both will suffer dire consequences!"

"Look, pal. I don't care *who* you are. Nobody talks to me like that!"

"Get back, foolish creature! Or meet the wrath of the mighty Proon!" The little creature got up, his scrawny muscles quivering.

"Yeah, you and who else!"

Although Vivian was plenty peeved, she was still under control. She knew it wasn't exactly wise to commit violence upon the person of the Proon leader. Nonetheless, it was her understanding that a stance of defiance, albeit mild, was always considered a stance of strength. It was best that the Grand Proon and the other Proons *never* consider her weak-willed—or how long would they allow her to hang on to her precious universities?

So she stepped up to the Grand Proon, squared her shoulders proudly, extended her hand, and flicked a finger at the tip of the Groucho Marx mask the creature wore.

The rubber band that held it on snapped.

The mask fell off.

"Oh, my God," said Dr. Vivian Vernon, quite astonished to see what was beneath the mask.

Its color a ghastly blue, it was possibly the longest, most obscene generative organ in the known universe!

# Chapter Twenty-three

When Troy Talbot wandered in holding a cardboard box filled with steaming pizza pie, he stopped in full astonishment. The pizza almost toppled from his hands, but Diane stepped in and dexteriously salvaged it.

"Hmmm!" she said. "Lots of parmesan cheese! Yum!"

"What . . . what is that, Doctor?"

Dr. Demetrios, lost in frantic creation, looked up from his project. Somewhere in the back of his mind he was making love to Diane Derry—in actual physical reality, however, he had cobbled together something quite incredible.

He blinked, and looked at it, his conscious mind not quite knowing what to make of the thing and certainly unable to label it properly.

"Let's just call it the Magnetic Monocle, Mark II," said Diane, through a mouthful of crisp crust, squishy tomato sauce, and chewy mozzarella cheese.

"It's awfully . . . well, *big*, Doc!"

"That's why we've got you along, love. Your wonderful muscle!" Diane chuckled. She was in a good mood. There was hope yet for them, it would seem.

"Why, yes, the Magnetic Monocle, Mark II," said Dr. D., stepping back and regarding his handiwork.

In fact, that's obviously what it was. The thing was a metallic circle, connected by snaking wires to a power pack.

The difference was there was no glass inside it.

"How can it be a monocle, Doc," said Troy. "When there's no monocle?"

Coming out of his fugue, Dr. D. found that he was starving. He leapt upon the pizza, tore a slice off, and devoured it ravenously.

"What?" he said, looking up, blinking, olive oil leaking down his chin.

"The monocle, Doctor. Troy wants to know why there's no glass inside."

"Oh. New and improved. I'm simply utilizing field mechanics for the same effect. Greater pliability. And if there were glass inside, you'd probably break it, Troy."

Troy nodded solemnly. "Good point. So what does *this* do, Doctor?"

"Haven't totally explored the possibilities yet, m'boy. But we'll test it thoroughly against those war-mongering Proons, eh?" He tapped the rim with great satisfaction. "What we've got here, my boy, is nothing less than room temperature super-conductor metal."

"Where'd you get that, Doc—whatever it is."

"It was lying around here in starship conductor badges. I just hammered them all together. Nice job, huh? At any rate, it focuses the wearer's thought waves just like the other one . . . only much more macro."

Dr. D. pulled a large coiled rod from his trousers.

"This however is the significant innovation. Thought waves can be very tricky things and often we don't have proper control of them. Observe."

He turned the ring around and pointed it toward the piles of junk. "Diane, would you kindly hum 'The Blue Danube'?"

Diane obliged.

Almost immediately, as Dr. D. focused the ring toward the junk pile and concentrated, the bits and pieces formed themselves into rough stick figures that waltzed around the room.

"But watch. I can *focus* the ring now—and my thoughts—by penetrating the force field with this coil!"

Dr. D. stuck the rod inside the Magnetic Monocle. The effect was startling. Bits and pieces of paper and junk flew together, and suddenly the dancing figures were no longer sticks, but distinctly resembled Ginger Rogers and Fred Astaire!

"Now observe! To induce fluctuations in field strength, I merely move this coil in and out of the monocle!"

As he did so, the dancing humanoid forms not only danced . . . they danced very well indeed, fluidly and with grace.

Dr. D. turned the power off, and the figures sank back into heaps of junk.

"So what do you think, Troy?"

"Gee, Diane. I didn't think you could hum so well!"

Dr. D. brushed it all off with a wave. "It doesn't make any difference what he thinks, just as long as he can carry it around."

"Oh, sure. No problem, Doc. I can lug that thing for miles!"

"That won't be necessary. Here, you'd better eat the rest of the pizza, Troy. For energy. This adventure isn't over yet!"

After Diane selected a petite section for herself, Troy happily chomped down the rest of the pizza, while Dr. D. tinkered with and fine-tuned his latest invention.

You know, he thought to himself with great pride, where have these intergalactic picaresque jaunts *been* all my life. Worthy stuff for my memoirs!

If, that is, he survived them.

Less than an hour later, Don Dellamonte sauntered in, filing his nails nonchalantly.

"Youse guys will be happy to know dat—" he

started, and then made a face. He stuck his hand in his mouth, probed around the sides, and pulled out several wads of Kleenex. He tossed these away onto the junk heap, cleared his throat, and spoke again. "There. *That's* much better! I can actually speak properly now! Anyway, as I was attempting to say, Dr. Demopoulos, we have successfully modifed your ship and—my goodness—whatever is *that*?"

"The Magnetic Monocle, Mark II," Dr. D. proclaimed happily.

Swiftly, he described and then demonstrated its workings.

"With this," he concluded. "I believe that we might beat the Proons!"

"Well, bravo! Do it by all means, and bring that beautiful thing back. I have a few worlds I'd like you to blow up!"

"Sorry, Don. We don't do that sort of thing."

"Ah, well, just a thought. Defeating the Proons will be sufficient. Walk this way, please!" said Don Dellamonte, turning and leaving the room.

"Gosh, Doc, I can't walk that way," said Troy. "I haven't got wings! And even if I did, I've got to carry this heavy thing."

"Just follow him, Troy," said Diane, fingering the super-conductor metal of the Magnetic Monocle contemplatively. "And, Doctor, you say that I can use this if I have to?"

"Oh, indeed, Diane. I've adapted it especially to work with you. We can test it in the *Mudlark*."

Diane nodded cannily, her thoughts unreadable.

No matter, thought Dr. D. as they followed Don Dellamonte. At least I know she's loyal . . . and certainly inspirational!

They followed Don Dellamonte and his hatted goons down to the shuttle bay where their engineering confederates had been working on the ship.

The *Mudlark* proved quite a surprise.

"You like?" said Don Dellamonte.

Troy almost dropped the Magnetic Monocle, Mark II, on Dr. D.'s toes. "Wow! Oh, *wow!* Keen! Spiffy! It's *great!*" Fortunately, Dr. D. still wore the Magnetic Monocle, Mark I, and he caught it in time, lowering it psychokinetically. (In truth, of course, he could have carried it all the way in that manner—but when you had muscle, why not utilize it?)

"Have a care, fellow!" said Dr. D.

However, he did have to admit that he, too, was quite impressed with what had been done with the *Mudlark*.

Where before it had been merely a huge, glowering globby hunk, squatting stolidly on thick supports, it was now oblong and snazzy, chrome flashing everywhere.

"It looks like something from a Flash Gordon serial!" said Diane. "My God, how *garish*. I thought you mobsteroids had good taste?"

With mingled gratification and misgiving, Dr. D. had to agree. It looked like an art deco car designer's idea of what a spaceship should be. It had filigreed silver and gold fins, and mag hubcaps on wheels . . . Wheels? Why did you need wheels in space?

The wheels had mud flaps with engraved rhinestone wings.

It even had a winged hood ornament sprouting from its nose.

"Garish, of course, is the ultimate compliment from Earth people," said Dr. D., kicking his assistant gently in the shin. "And of course mobsteroids don't have good taste . . . they have *great* taste!"

"I *love* it!" cried Troy, capering around the vessel. "I bet it's got horsepower galore!"

"There are no animals inside, I assure you!" said Don Dellamonte.

"A figure of speech," said Diane.

"And you're a fine figure of a human!" said Dellamonte admiringly. "All you need are a pair of wings and you'd be a real angel. Care to stick around here for some surgery?''

"No. I don't care for the injections that would certainly be involved."

"Oh, well . . . Doctor, perhaps I should point out a few features of your new vessel."

They were ushered into the *Mudlark* (Mark II), and Dr. D. was suitably impressed. The place had not only been rebuilt with superior alloys (looking distinctly stronger than the rickety structure that preceded it), but it had been refurnished and refurbished with elegant and plush fittings similar to those inside the Aerie ship.

"Wow!" said Troy, putting the Magnetic Monocle, Mark Two, down in a safely padded spot. "It hurts my eyes."

Indeed, all the chrome fittings gleamed, and the gemlike studs on the controls sparkled magnificently. Velvet curtains hung sumptuously, purple and red wallpaper glowed with unearthly effulgence.

"My God," said Diane. "It looks like a *whorehouse*!"

"Hmm. No wonder I feel so comfortable here," said the doctor, full of brio. Now *this* was a spaceship! He'd been operating on an extreme budget in the construction of the *Mudlark,* and thus had to scrimp on interior decoration. But even if he'd been able to go whole hog, he could *never* have come up with anything so absolutely *opulent,* so wonderfully *scrumptuous* as this delightful mélange of plush color and comfort.

He turned to Don Dellamonte. "Nice. Very nice indeed. Thank you."

"Ah, but you can thank me by kicking Proon *butts*! You can thank me by scuttling the mother ship as you have promised to do. Toward those ends, let me show you the other more strategic innovations we have accomplished with your vessel."

Don Dellamonte pulled aside a curtain and there

was the control room, lambently metallic in the soft glow of its dashboard lights. Levers and switches glistened gold with silver highlights. Shiny black buttons and verniers were spread out on a panel field, fronted by two turret-mounted control chairs.

Hanging from a rearview mirror was a pair of dice.

"Just like the old control board—only much prettier," said Diane, finally conceding that there had been some improvement.

"And much more functional, I assure you," said Don Dellamonte. "Also, we have installed a subspace radio, with which to keep in contact with us . . . and monitor space waves."

"Radio!" said Troy. "Great, I *love* radios. Can we listen to *The Jack Benny Show*?"

"You are armed with the usual Pizon panoply of power beams, tractor beams, and such—but we *have* made a bit of an innovation upon your star drive."

"Oh, good," said Diane. "Like some kind of *control* over it?"

"Yes. It turns out that your Quantum Fuzzy Drive was quite similar in principle to one of our drives—the Garlic and Onions Drive. And so we simply tacked on similar features. This Garlic and Onions Drive, though, creates a field so ripe with the essence of—well—garlic and onions around the ship that the universe rebels, sending it into a parallel universe. A patina of olive oil judiciously spread over the ship allows the vessel to slip frictionless and inertialess through this so-called Sub-Space—or Cold Cut Space—toward the location logged onto the computers."

"Wow. Garlic. Onions." Troy's face scrunched up with disgust. "Those can be pretty rank. How do you shut down the field and get back into bland old normal space?"

"I'm glad you asked that. A damper field—the Pasta field wraps around the Garlic and Onions field at the appropriate time and pops you out at your destination.

254 John DeChancie and David Bischoff

And by the by—we have taken the liberty of programming the location of the Proon mother ship into your ship's computer, so all you need to do is sit back, relax, have some prosciutto and melon, enjoy the ride, and it won't be very long until you're back where you started . . . Armed, of course, with this excellent ship and your excellent new device . . . And your mission, of course.''

"Aren't you going to help us?" said Diane. "You know, back us up with your fleet or something?"

"That is why we are sending you back to the mother ship. Although you need not actually destroy it, the Proons *do* have a field generator on board that must be shut down if we are to defeat them. It has been their most effective tool in their insane war against us!"

"What field generator is *that*?" said Troy.

"Don't ask . . ." said Diane, flinching.

For the first time, they saw the Godfodder look forlorn. He sighed heavily.

"The Anti-Pasto Device."

"And once that happens?"

"Once that happens we will finally be able to contain the advance of the Proons through the universe—and thus prevent them from conquering your planet!"

"This thing sounds pretty nasty," said Dr. D. "But if we're going to shut down this Anti-Pasto Device, we're going to have to know where it is."

"There are two ways of dealing with it. You may either destroy it—or destroy the mother ship itself. Either way will be sufficient. *Capisce?*"

"That's a pretty tall order."

"You have your world at stake. You must do your best, eh? Now, if there are any more questions, you can look it up in that nice thick manual in the glove box there. Or, and by the way, if you get hungry— there's some nice stuffed shells with meat sauce in the galley fridge.''

Diane looked at him suspiciously. "You're being terribly helpful. Why?"

Don Dellamonte shrugged. "We want the Proons off our back. You can help. Simple enough. It's a win-win situation!"

"There's gotta be something else going on . . ."

"Well, true. That offer for a gambling franchise on Earth . . . that does get the old macaroni boiling."

"I thought so." She turned to Dr. D. "Doctor, this is really beyond the pale. Selling out the morals of America for a souped-up speedster of a spaceship!"

"Diane, let's put it this way. Would you rather have those incredibly dull bluenoses in charge?"

"Well, there would have to be an adjustment, but I daresay they would stop all those ridiculous and wasteful wars that go on there!"

"Very well. Would you like to have Vivian Vernon as your boss?"

Diane blinked. Exactly once.

"Well, I suppose I could learn to play a little cards," she said in a low voice.

"That'sa girl! All we ask is just a small amount of juice. Hey!" said Don Dellamonte, throwing up his hands. "A little business never hurt anybody. And look, sweetheart. We throw in a fur coat, maybe some diamonds for you. Eh?"

"No thanks. I just want to do what's best for humanity."

"Altruistic lass, eh?" said Dr. D. "I taught her everything she knows."

"Yeah, right," said Diane.

"I'll take a football field," volunteered Troy. "And a car, and a pizza joint and—"

Don Dellamonte turned and walked away. "Ciao. Good luck. Be talking to you on the radio."

Troy was left with his big jaw hanging low.

"Sorry, Troy. I think they've got enough muscle," said Diane, patting his head in a consoling fashion.

"And brains! Glad you're still with us, first mate."

"Gee, Doc. Thanks for the compliment!" He went off to batten down the hatches, or whatever it was that first mates do.

"Isn't that a mobster delicacy . . . bull brains?" said Diane.

"With olive oil and oregano and garlic. Yes, as a matter of fact I think it is. How about a kiss for luck, Diane."

"I'll tell you what you can kiss, Doctor!"

Diane pecked him on the cheek.

"That was a kiss?"

"Behave yourself, Professor Demopoulòs."

"I'm not a Behaviorist."

They strapped in and readied for takeoff

# Chapter Twenty-four

Dr. D. found it a wholly glorious experience, caroming through space. Where the *Mudlark* previously had been the Earth equivalent of Ford's Model T with worn and wobbly tires and a cranky engine, it was now a Cadillac with all the trimmings. He was actually able to enjoy the views provided, instead of worrying about things like navigation, a clunky motor, and keeping out the ether.

And spectacular views they were!

Roaring suns! Blossoming planets! Milky moons! Creamy comets!

Together he and his companions piloted the *Mudlark* toward their date with destiny. Dr. D. hadn't had a date for a long time, and he was looking forward to it.

"You are doing fine, Doctor!" said Don Dellamonte's voice through the radio speaker. "You already seem to have the hang of space travel!"

"That would be my copilots," Dr. D. explained. "Especially Troy here. Troy can fly anything he can tinker with. Right, m'boy?"

"You bet, Doc!" said Troy. "And gosh, this here ship was a treat to work on, you bet!"

The *Mudlark* flashed through the thronging stars like a darting fish through an awesome ocean. What strange beings lived upon all those planets? Dr. D. wondered. What fabulous females? However, he reined in his curiosity, setting his attention upon the duty that was before him.

Saving Earth.

The bedraggled place wasn't worth much, he supposed, but it was home. Already he was getting rather homesick. He frankly doubted that there was any other planet in the universe that had banana splits and ice cream sodas as good as Hardtack's Pharmacy on Main Street.

And so far as he could tell, Earth certainly grew the best women.

"Good working with you, Troy," said the don. "You came up with lots of innovations that we're going to use on our own fleet. Meantime, friends, we trust you're enjoying your journey. Enjoy it while you can—you shall have to engage the enemy shortly."

"Ready and willing for that, Don," said Dr. D. "Got the Magnetic Monocle all set up."

He'd had Troy place it in the clear gunner's turret on the bottom of the newly reshaped ship.

"Excellent," said Don Dellamonte. "You are indeed an interesting genus of genius, Doctor. We are fortunate to have found you!"

"Trouble is," said Diane. "If anyone gets blown up, we'll be first!"

"Don't worry. Those big chartreuse buttons on the right of the panel? Force fields! You got lots of protection! This should be a wonderful space battle. I can smell victory in the ether! The Proon forces are less than a light-year away! Over and out!"

"Gee . . . and I thought it was just the beans!" said Troy. "Oh, well, lots of grommets to tighten."

"Fine. Diane? You've got the hang of the main controls?"

"You bet, Doctor."

"Good. Troy, you tighten those grommets and deal with whatever incidental repairs and work that must be done. Diane, you pilot. I'll man the Magnetic

Monocle! Communications via intercom. Right." He patted them both on their shoulders. "Proons, here we come!"

The funny thing was that the Pizon engineers had fitted the new and improved *Mudlark* in such a way that even though it was upside down on the bottom, the gravity was such that Dr. D. felt as though he were climbing *up*.

He situated himself in the bubble and strapped himself in. He inspected the Magnetic Monocle. Yes, there it was in all its wonderful glory—a bright and shiny testament to his brilliance. He pushed it, making sure it could swivel properly, then made the necessary adjustments.

Then he fitted the thought-conducting apparatus in place.

Excellent. He could feel a frisson of power pass through his system . . . Like electricity goosing him.

He fired off a burst of energy into the ether, just to test the device. The air around him crackled with excited particles. It reeked of positive ions. His hair stood on end. Ah, the thrill! Perhaps he'd found his true and romantic calling. Turret gunner in a spaceship.

Only the breathless black of the ether, and the shiny eyes of the majestic stars, watching and awaiting the outcome!

"You all hooked up, Doc?" asked Diane through the speaker.

"You bet! Troy! How are those grommets!"

"All tightened, Doc. We're about as ready as we're ever going to be."

"That's good. Because I'm getting signals from the Proon fleet! And that mother ship we were on is right in the middle of the whole thing."

"Do they detect us yet?"

"Not that I can tell."

"Good. We'll dive in straight for the mother ship then. We deal with that, and they won't be able to invade Earth."

"That's one *big* mother ship," said Troy.

"We can do it, right, Doc?"

"You bet, Diane. Who would have guessed it last year when the *Mudlark* was just a gleam in my eye that we'd be fighting space battles today! Well, just goes to show you—science is a wonderful thing!"

"Hip hip hooray!" yelled Troy.

Diane laughed. "I guess you're what they call an example of celestial mechanics, Troy!"

There was a clonking noise. "Ouch!" said Troy. "Damned grommet! Not tight enough."

Dr. D. chuckled. "Batten down the hatches, Troy. Because I've got the feeling they'll be shaking loose soon."

Diane's readings soon became visual fact. Dr. D. could see spread before them a vast armada of Proon ships.

And in the very midst, like a bullfrog amid a horde of tadpoles, was a most ferocious and lumpy sight against the blazing field of stars.

The Proon mother ship!


"There it is!" Dr. Vivian Vernon tapped the thing in the holo-tank triumphantly. The thing in the holo-tank was a planet and a single pale moon sailed around it. It was also transparent, so Vivian's finger went right through it and into some kind of alien sludge at the bottom of the tank. Vivian nonchalantly wiped it off on Geoffrey Wussman's robe. "That's what we're looking for!'

"Your home planet, eh?" said Proon. He kept a good distance from the pair. Ever since he'd lost his glasses and noseguard, he'd kept a healthy distance away.

"Earth," Geoffrey Wussman said, peering down at

the globe of green, a trace of white clouds covering the oceans and the continents. "And right down there . . . that's Nebraska."

The Grand Proon glanced over the solar system, nodded, and then pushed aside a lesser Proon to get at a computer console. He tapped a few keys. A readout monitor lifted from the side table, and Proon perused the alien language messages that scrawled there.

"Hmm," he said finally. "Most surprising."

"You've got *records* of Earth?" said Wussman, snapping out of his mystical fugue.

"Sure. Hey, folks. We go back a *long* way!"

"But if you already *knew* about Earth . . . why did you need us to tell you?"

Wussman received a sharp jab in the shin for that one.

"Simple enough. Hadn't the faintest that it had *life* on it, let alone *intelligent* life." The Grand Proon emitted a muffled sniff. "Well, semi-intelligent, anyway."

"But you have the information stored on your computer . . . why?" said Vivian, unable to conceal her curiosity.

"We've got *millions* of solar systems recorded in our computers," said the Grand Proon. "And we know of your planet because . . ." One of his fingers drifted across the face of the computer screen. "According to our records, our ancestors utilized it as a toxic biological experiments dump!" He drifted narrowed eyes over to his allies. "That would explain a great deal."

"You mean you're not interested in it anymore?" said Vivian in a challenging way, even though she felt unnerved.

"No, actually on the contrary. Actually, I believe, it gives us not only moral but property rights to the planet. Being able to discipline entire races is merely frosting on the cake. If anything, it interests us extremely—since, although it is a loathsome thought, your human race is apparently our little mutated accident.''

''There's a disquieting thought,'' said Wussman.

Indeed, thought Vivian Vernon.

Well, they'd still get the universities. Heh-heh.

It had been touch and go ever since that little . . . accident.

When she'd unfortunately knocked off those Groucho Marx glasses, there'd been quite the shock.

Apparently, the Proons had their male procreative features where humans had their noses. It was a most startling and disconcerting sight.

In a fit of anger, the Grand Proon had thrown them into a cell, occupied by a solitary Proon tax evader and sex offender who'd explained that all Proons were hermaphrodites (the necessary female aspect of their plumbing in the more traditional humanoid spot) but were allowed to mate with themselves only at predetermined times—and then supervised to make sure that no pleasure whatsoever was involved. Those Proons (heaven forfend) caught in the closet being naughty with themselves were neutered and placed in the Proon Choir where they sang the high parts.

The imprisoned Proon reported that this was to be his fate the very next day, and wondered if perhaps Vivian and Geoffrey would like to see this verboten act in the raw, as it were, in return for an illustration of how their species mated.

They politely refused the offer.

''Well then!'' the head Proon said now with great satisfaction, briskly rubbing his spidery alien hands together. ''Coordinates are fed into the navigational system. How long before we can hit Manic Drive, Lieutenant?''

''Manic Drive?'' asked Vivian.

''A big step up from HyperDrive!'' explained the chief Proon. ''We're very anxious to get there.''

''Departure for destination can be accomplished at

any time," the lieutenant piped. "The fleet, as per orders, is already in formation. And, by the by, we're pointed in just the right direction."

"How fortunate. Well then, I must admit," said the boss of all Proon bosses. "You've been of great help to us, Drs. Vernon and Wussman. And these universities of yours will be under your control very, very soon!"

"You hear that, Geoffrey! We won't simply control a single department. We'll have departments galore. Colleges! Whole universities! And my theories will achieve the true recognition they deserve!"

"Theories?" said the head Proon, making a face. "There are no theories in Proonian science, philosophy, ethics, religion—or, for that matter, Proonian tiddledywinks. It's all *fact fact fact*! And that fact is what you will be allowed to teach at your schools . . . and that is all!"

"That violates academic freedom!"

"Perhaps you would like to be thrown back into the sex offender's cell?"

"Threaten me with taking off that mask again and you'll have me frightened!"

Vivian was about to jump on the Proon leader and claw his beady little eyes out; however, she was fortunately restrained by the more moderate Geoffrey.

"Now, now, dear," he whispered. "Who knows what will come to pass. You have your ways . . . And besides, take it from me, the Proon Way is a most righteous path!"

"Who asked you?" Nonetheless Vivian calmed down. She smoothed her hands down her side, as though rearranging ruffled feathers. She was loath to admit it, but Geoffrey for once was right. Now was not the time to object.

"You are accepting then?" said the Grand Proon, after he had made the necessary orders to send his incredibly large and powerful military fleet against the comparatively puny and feeble (and hardly super-scientific or even high-tech) forces of Earth.

"Yes. You seem to be the boss, O boss of the Proon."

The head Proon nodded with great self-satisfaction.

"Very well! Ready the engines." He raised a pointed finger. "We will enter ManicSpace at—"

Suddenly, however, the whole room lurched. Again, it jumped, as though struck by an earthquake. But of course there were no earthquakes in space . . .

"This normal procedure for jumping into Manic-Space?" Vivian asked.

"No!" said Proon, swiftly moving to a control technician. "What is happening?"

"The Pizons are firing upon us, sir!" said the Proon by the screens.

"We will crush them! They are fools!"

"But, sir . . . there appears to be a new kind of Pizon ship . . . right out in front!"

"On screen."

As soon as the image flashed upon the projection screen, as soon as they saw the chrome and the odd shape of it, both Vivian and Geoffrey knew who it was.

"Dr. Demopoulos!" they exclaimed.

It was an awfully big mother ship, and Dr. D. was hardly in the habit of fighting huge space battles, so at first he was a bit daunted.

However, as soon as he got the thing within his sights, his target fever returned, and he felt as though he'd been living in this cockpit for a very long time.

The Magnetic Monocle was something else again. On the one hand, it was so alien to his sense of proportion and reality—and yet, on the other, it was a *part* of him. Even now as it warmed up, veins of light streaming through it like hot rich blood, he also felt his own excitement rise.

The primeval lust for battle overwhelmed his rational self.

The points of light on the starfield around the massive mother were now almost discernible as ships.

"We have visual!" came Diane's voice from the intercom.

"Remember the Alamo!" Dr. D. cried, losing himself in the excitement.

"Geronimo!" whooped Troy.

Dr. D. wanted to test the range of the Magnetic Monocle, so he aimed the thing at the biggest target—the Proon mother ship—inserted the coil control, and concentrated.

The thing, hooked into place on the bubble so that it rotated all around, let loose a blast of energy like nothing that Dr. D. had ever seen—let along *produced*—before. The energy slid in a straight shot to the mother ship, clipping it on the side in a fiery explosion.

Even at this distance, Dr. D. could see it *rock*.

"Good shot, Doc!"

"Lucky. We're going to have to get closer!"

"I suggest you get those force screens ready—we're going to need them."

"Right. They're going up now!"

Dr. D. could see the vibrant, colorful wash of sparkling energy as the force field erected itself. It seemed to shimmer with excitement, as though it wanted to pierce the enemy defenses itself.

The small Proon ships—each bigger than the *Mudlark*—were coming at them, letting loose rays of every color and description. Disintegrator rays, disruptor rays, manta rays, Man rays, Ray Bans—the whole catalogue of super-scientific energy beams were let loose upon the *Mudlark*.

Dr. D. swept them with his brain ray, cutting a huge swath in their numbers.

The Proon ships whirled and crashed and flared.

They sank and fell and crumbled, crashing into one another in silent brilliant wrecks.

It was all like a spectacular Fourth of July in hell.

However, the first foray had been lucky—Diane had been able to avoid the larger rays beamed at them.

But then a particle beam struck them full on, turning the force fields bright scarlet and shaking the whole vessel up considerably. Dr. D. was flung back and away—a good thing he'd buckled in, or he'd have crashed straight through the canopy!

The time before he could get the Magnetic Monocle ready and aimed again was just seconds, but it gave the Proons time to regroup and swoop in above them.

"Doc! They're coming from the other side!" cried Diane.

"Veer! Veer!"

"I can't! Not fast enough!"

If all those myriad ships concentrated their beams on their force shields, it would crack like an eggshell, and they'd be disintegrated by the whorling torrent of energy.

It seemed hopeless.

However, just at the very last moment, a volley of multicolored rays erupted from another part of the ether, blasting the first advance of Proons into sparks and glowing dust.

"Hey, hey! We told you we'd not be far behind!" Don Dellamonte boomed through to them, jubilant. "That Magnetic Monocle of yours is something, Doctor. There's the mother ship—go get it. We'll divert the smaller ships!"

"Thanks!" said Diane.

"Damn. This thing is shaking apart!" cried Troy. "I'm fixing and tightening as fast as I can!"

"Okay. Diane . . . head for the mother ship! I'm okay, and I'm ready to blast!"

Dr. D. aimed.

The mother ship, however, was not without its defenses. Although it had been caught unawares before, it had already strengthened its shields. They'd have to crack those before they could even hope to get at even the main body of the ship.

However, Don Dellamonte had equipped them with a secret weapon.

Dr. D. concentrated, using the other as yet untapped resources of the great mind-focuser. Its projection abilities!

A mighty, diffuse beam of light originating from the magnificent lens of the Magnetic Monocle and modulated by rapid in and out penetrations of the special power coil spread out a gigantic projection of a holographic image.

It was based upon a film that Don Dellamonte had shown him.

The image was that of a miles long, miles wide luminous Proon, face bereft of Groucho Marx mask, rest of body bereft of clothing, performing a remarkable and unmentionable act upon itself.

"Show this to the critters. *That* will get their goat."

Sure enough, all beams from the mother ship ceased.

"We've got weakening of the force screens!" yelled Diane. "Get 'em, Doctor."

Dr. D. ceased visualizing, and the gigantic image faded away like swamp gas. He channeled every bit of concentration, every bit of energy into the Magnetic Monocle, and started thumping away with the coil, a series of in-and-out jerkings at a remarkable rate for someone of his years.

This time the beam produced was truly thick and powerful. And well aimed. It slammed with instantaneous and unspeakable velocity into the very center of the mother ship.

An explosion of crimson, purple, and yellow flowered out of the center. Dr. D. kept concentrating. He dipped down into the remote reaches of his psyche, to the very heart of his secret world of computation and

268 John DeChancie and David Bischoff

cogitation. There, his fantasy sweetheart was wearing a bright red and white and blue cheerleader's outfit, with bouncing pom-poms.

"Go, Doc, go!" she proclaimed, her hair and teeth sparkling delightfully. She winked, and the doctor's hormone level rose significantly.

The beam intensified, boring into the dark metal hide of the vessel.

The explosions ignited were magnificent. They cracked the mother ship, spewing out threads of flames and garbage. Clearly, the doctor's efforts had initiated a chain reaction!

"It's gonna really blow, Doc!" said Diane. "We'd better get—"

However, she did not finish her sentence. The Proon mother ship shattered like a pulverized cue ball. The energy waves were so tremendous that it took only seconds for them to reach the *Mudlark*, which was thrown back, tail over bow, like a little rubber duck in a storm-tossed bathtub.

Dr. D. shut off the Magnetic Monocle and clung to consciousness. But only barely. When the *Mudlark* finally drifted to a halt, under Diane Derry's excellent piloting, he took a relieved breath. "Status report!"

"Everything's shaky, Doc," said Troy. "But it's still holding together."

"Thank God for those grommets!" said Dr. D. "Diane?"

"Still under control, Doctor. Good job. You're wonderful!"

"I did nail them, didn't I. Too bad about Vivian and Geoffrey, though. However, it was Earth or them!"

"Wait a minute, Doctor. I'm getting some sort of reading on the sensors."

"Good God. Another battleship. My mind waves are just about fried!"

"No, Doctor," said Diane, voice terse with disbelief. "It's some kind of *lifeboat*!"

# Chapter Twenty-five

"Good job, Doctor!" proclaimed Vivian Vernon, giving Dr. D. an impassioned hug and kiss as soon as she passed through the airlock (another nifty Pizon addition to the ship).

Dr. Demopoulos was so nonplussed, he didn't even try to cop a feel.

Dr. Geoffrey Wussman, however, was not quite so happy. "You've ruined the chances for Earth's peace and happiness, damn your eyes!" He was promptly rewarded by a whack across the back of his head, courtesy of Vivian Vernon.

"Sorry about him, folks. You can tell by his new clothing he's not the same old lovable Geoffrey. You see, the Proons got hold of him and scrubbed out that puny brain of his."

"Gosh—" said Troy. "Maybe we'd better stick him in the bathroom!"

Arms folded across her chest, Diane Derry squinted suspiciously at the new arrivals. "Well, I'm not sure I trust you—but I'm glad you're still alive. How did you escape that incredible cataclysm?"

"It wasn't easy, believe me," said Vivian. "In the first place we were being held prisoners—under mental control of the Proons. Working for them certainly wasn't our idea."

"But, Vivian!" said Wussman. He was rewarded for his efforts by a swift shin kick. "Ow!"

Vivian covered with a forced grin. "Got any straitjackets around here? I believe poor dear Geoffrey's still under the sway! Some sort of gag wouldn't be a bad idea."

"I was just going to comment on your willpower in resisting Proon mind control!" woofed Wussman.

"Ah! Misinterpretation. Sorry. Belay that strait-jacket thing! Dear Geoff's still with us!" She bussed him on the cheek. "Now, where was I? Oh, right— well, fortunately, we were not incarcerated when your rays hit. We were being *forced* to identify our home planetary system. The Proons were set into such a tizzy by that first unexpected assault that they didn't notice us slipping out. So by the time you finally gave that last, mighty blast, we'd already gotten to one of their lifeboats. We only had to cast off to get away. Luck and Providence guided us away . . . and Fate led us back to the good old *Mudlark*."

"Mind control, eh?" said Dr. D. "I suppose that's plausible enough. They would have that technology. Well, whatever . . . In the end, we're all human and we'll have to give you the human benefit of the doubt."

Vivian stepped over and kissed him. "You're a *wonderful* man!"

"Maybe a fool. Maybe I should make you walk the plank! Control of all the universities in the world indeed!" He scrutinized them. "And if you suffered from Proonian mind control, who's to say you are not still 'under the influence' as it were. No, my professional friends . . . we won't abandon you. However, I think we're going to have to confine you under observation for a while."

Vivian's eyes shot wide open. "But . . . but you *can't*. If I get cooped up with this loon anymore . . . I'll go absolutely nuts myself!"

"Calm yourself, my love. We're at least safe here," said Wussman. "And I'll have time to teach you the nine hundred and ninety-nine basic tenets of the Enlightened Way philosophy!"

"Gahh! You've got to help me, Doctor! I *beg* of you!" Vivian grabbed him by the collar, crushing herself provocatively against him. "Please! Please, I'll do anything!"

Dr. D. gently pushed her away, resisting her temptations, considerable and evident though they may be. "Sorry, Viv. We'll deal with this whole matter again, once we get the physics department back in order. Under my command! Now if you'll just follow Troy, he'll take you back and show you your quarters."

Vivian composed herself, somehow managing to regain her dignity. She stood erect, straightened her shoulders, and eyed Dr. Demopoulos haughtily. "Very well, Doctor. Truce. And thank you for your taking us back on board." Her small nostrils flared. "However, I think you will come to regret the rejection!" She winked at Troy. "Show us to the room, Troy. Come along, Geoffrey. I'll show them that I can take my medicine like a trooper!"

Vivian Vernon trooped out haughtily, head high.

A shudder passed through the ship. A squeaking of the seams sounded. Diane Derry looked around, clearly alarmed, but Dr. D. calmed her down.

"A few loose grommets. Troy will see to them. Now let's see if we can't persuade the Pizons to take us back home!"

However, they had a hard time getting hold of their erstwhile battle companions. Clearly they were doing some kind of mopping up after the battle. Or perhaps, after their victory, Dr. D. suggested, they may be negotiating with the Proons on setting up slot machines on neutral worlds. Whatever it was, he figured there had to be some pushy economics involved somewhere.

Troy returned. However, he did not return alone.

Spon, the alien, was with him.

"Hi there," said the wiggly-eyed creature, looking little the worse for having a hole blasted through his head. "Nice job with the Proons. Too bad about my ship, but *c'est la guerre* and all that."

"Spon! You're alive!" Diane Derry said.

"The rumors of my demise were entirely exaggerated. I just had a hole in my head and stopped breathing. A little ploy to distract those to whom I owe vast sums. It worked, didn't it? There's still a matter of this hole, but it will mend soon enough. Fortunately, my brain is located in my nether regions rather than my head!"

"Hey!" said Troy. "That's where the doc says mine is!"

"Only occasionally, Troy," said Dr. D. "Well, Spon . . . there does seem to be a bit of a problem . . . We're going to get the Pizons to scoot us on back to Earth, and it's going to take quite a bit of work to conceal a spaceship, let alone an alien creature!"

"Don't worry about me. I see you've got a nice little example of a Proon lifeboat by your airlock. Just loan me some tools and supplies and I'll cobble up a quick sporty little warp drive and I'll just be on my way."

"Give him some tools, Troy. And some of that bean pizza. That should do him."

"Sure thing, Doc. C'mon, Spon. We'll fix you up right. And maybe you can give me a quick course in drive mechanics."

They rambled out like long-lost brothers.

"I still can't get hold of the Pizons," said Diane, looking up from her control chair. "I'm beaming out a call, but there's no response."

"Give them a little while, my dear. I'd better take a look at how well we're holding togther and then—"

He was interrupted by a blazing flash of light, and the sudden materialization of a quite bemused-looking being.

Krillman.

Krillman, from the Triple-A.

"Good grief," said the celestial-looking being. "What's been going on here?"

Diane Derry leapt up from her chair and placed her hands indignantly upon her hips. "You were supposed to send us home! Instead you dropped us straight into the Proon mother ship!" she scolded.

"Yeah, sorry about that. Little miscalculation." He pulled out a compact device, opened it, fiddled with some knobs, and examined the screen. "And in doing so, it appears I've futzed things up quite awfully in the balance of power here. I'm going to have hell to answer for to the Elders! They'll demote me for sure. Oh—what am I going to do?"

"Well, for starters you can get us back to Earth like you promised!" said Diane, wagging a finger under the man's nose.

"Now, now, things really aren't that bad," said Dr. D. "I'd say, all in all, if anything the Proons were due for a setback. They were out to conquer our part of the galaxy . . . including Earth, and set up a most tyrannical system. You might mention that to your leaders."

"You tell it to them!"

Such a forlorn and fearful look passed over those previously self-assured features that, Dr. D. could tell, Diane Derry's stern attitude softened somewhat.

"Well, do you think that you really should be running about the galaxy with this proclivity for error, Krillman," said Dr. D.

"I know I can do better! If I only could get a chance!"

"Well, I'll tell you what. We'll make a deal. You get this ship back to Earth and we won't report you!"

"Really?"

"I'm a man of my word. This whole incident will be just a little blip on your Elders' bureaucratic system. You play your cards right, they won't even notice.

And we've got another fellow here by the name of Spon.''

"Oh, dear. I remember him. Don't tell me I did the same . . .''

"You've really got to get your coordinates straight, you poor thing,'' said Diane.

"Well, I suppose a little numeric housecleaning *is* in order. Thank you. I'll do that.''

"Good. You'll find Spon in the lifeship. Make whatever arrangements are necessary. And by the way send back our friend Troy. I don't think Spon needs him anymore.''

"Certainly. Thanks, Doc. You two really are really swell people. I'll get to work on this whole thing immediately.'' He toddled off, shaking his head, staring at his compact computer module. "Now, how in heaven's name did I go wrong?''

"Who says that God doesn't throw dice,'' said Dr. D. "Clearly he does and bonked that fellow right on the noggin.''

"Do you think we can trust him this time?''

"We're going to have to, if we can't get ahold of those Pizons. I don't understand it. Where *are* those guys . . . ?''

Krillman looked very concerned. "Well, actually, I'm not entirely sure that—''

A voice emerged from the speaker, that of the boss of all Pizon bosses.

"Hey. We're back. Say, Doctor. Congratulations again. You did a good job.''

Dr. D. stepped over to the speaker. "Thank you. Now you'll help us get back to our home?''

"I was meaning to talk to you about that, Doctor. We've been having some trouble collectin' from a couple of worlds. Nothin' serious, but we thought maybe you'd waggle that Magnetic Monocle at them a little, make 'em think twice about not coughin' up!''

Dr. D. blinked, becoming most disconcerted. "That *wasn't* what it was created for!"

"Ah, come on, Doctor. You can give us a little of your time. Nobody'll get hurt. Be a sport. You *owe* us!"

Dr. D. whispered to Diane. "Turn it off. Make it look like there's interference." As Diane accommodated him, rubbing her hand over the microphone, he turned to Krillman. "I don't care to do this, and I don't want any violence here. Can you get us back to Earth . . . *right* this time?"

Krillman looked up from his work on his portable unit. "I think I see what the problem was before . . . and I believe I can help you."

"Fine. And the alien, Spon?"

"Tell him to push off in his lifeboat and I can help him as well."

"You can tell him that yourself when you get the chance. Diane, go get Troy out of that boat and in here. Preferably strapped into a chair somewhere, both of you!"

"You got it, Doc." Diane scurried off.

"Krillman, how long will it take you to do your cosmological magic?"

"About ninety seconds."

"Fine. You make sure that Diane and Troy are back, and you do it. Understand. And this time, make sure it's Earth, USA, Nebraska, Flitheimer University. Got it?"

"No problem, Doctor."

"I certainly hope not!" Dr. D. swiveled back to the microphone and switched it on. "Don Dellamonte. Are you there?"

"Sure, Doctor. Little problem with communications. Look, I can make this deal even sweeter for you. Make your life easy back on Earth when we connect with our counterparts there. Little money on the side never hurt anybody, eh?"

"Hmm. That sounds most interesting. But I'm confused, Don. You never mentioned this aspect of your business before. Threatening worlds? I thought you all were the good guys?"

"We are, we are! We stand for a little fun in life, a little joy. A little vino, some song . . . a nice game of craps. What more can one want? These people who don't play with the rules, though . . . They need to be reminded. No harm intended, eh?"

"Oh, of course not. I suppose that I could accommodate you. Besides, I rather enjoyed using my new invention. And after all, if it weren't for you, I wouldn't even have invented it."

"That's the kind of thinking I like, Doctor!"

"What's the plan then?"

"Let me get some information from my navigation people, and we'll get right back with you. And, Doctor . . ."

"Yes?"

"You're not going to regret this!"

"Over and out, Don. I'll talk to you later."

Dr. D. cut off the comm switch. "Later than you think, my friend."

Diane and Troy hurried in and strapped themselves into chairs. "Oh, boy," said Troy. "Maybe I'll get back in time for the Saturday football game!"

"Spon is set?"

"Yes," said Diane. "He's got provisions and some tools. He's already working on a drive . . . He's apparently not as confident in Krillman here as you seem to be."

"We haven't got much choice, have we?"

"No, I suppose not."

"Krillman, are we anywhere near getting out of here?"

The celestial alien's fingers were working like lightning over the tiny keyboard. "Hold your horses. Just a matter of seconds."

However, a mere split second later, Don Dellamonte's voice boomed out from the speakers.

"Doctor. You wouldn't be thinking of double-crossing us, would you? Because if you are, you should know—the Pizons do not like double crosses!"

"Nor does anyone, I shouldn't think."

"But not just anyone gets revenge—or has the wherewithal to accomplish it."

"Very well. Understood, Don." He looked over to Krillman, who signaled ten seconds to go. He buckled himself in. "Now then, we're going to be needing directions to wherever it is in the universe that you want to go."

"Yes. We'll get back to you on that."

Five seconds.

"Oh—and Don!" said Dr. Demopoulos. "I just want to thank you for giving me that Proon projection business. You were quite correct. It distracted the Proons marvelously. I never asked you—where did you get that information?"

"We have our ways," Don Dellamonte said, chuckling. "We have our ways!"

The transmission ended.

"Gee, Doc," said Troy, looking slightly white. "That guy sounded like he meant what he said. We're not going to double-cross him."

"Sorry about that, Troy," said Dr. D., nodding to Krillman. "But I believe we are!"

Krillman hit the final button, and everything got very strange again.

# Chapter Twenty-six

"We've gone quantum fuzzy again!" Dr. D. screamed.

"Not quite," Krillman said. "It's a modification. Call it the Uncertainty Drive."

"What the hell is that?"

"We're not quite certain."

"Where are we going?"

"Not certain of that either," Krillman said, "but there are a number of possible destinations."

Everything in the ship took on a colorful, prismatic blurriness. Spectra danced, rainbows did the jitterbug. But the effects seemed more controlled this time.

Soon, the blurriness disappeared and Krillman rose from the control panel. Resuming his persona as a Catskill comedian, he put his violin to his chin and played a few scratchy notes.

"Well, folks, closing time."

Everyone had rushed to the viewport. Hanging against a starry backdrop was a khaki-colored planet mottled with darker areas that might once have been oceans. It looked a little like Earth's moon, minus the craters (or at least no craters were visible from this distance). Streaks of white banded the world here and there: clouds, presumably, so there was an atmosphere.

"That doesn't look like Earth," Diane said.

"It's not!" Vivian turned and snarled at Krillman, "You miserable, rotten, no-good—"

"Rough crowd, rough crowd," Krillman said.

"Whew! I've played some tough rooms before, but this is the worst!"

"You haven't seen anything yet," Vivian said.

"Take it easy, Viv," Dr. Demopoulos told her. "Krillman, what's the meaning of this?"

"Well, I guess it's time I leveled with you people."

"Yes, it certainly is. You're not what you say you are, are you?"

"You mean I'm not a construct? Sure I am. But I wasn't constructed by any race called the Krill. That was just gas."

"You're a tool of one of the godlike races. What are you, an Asperan or a Dharvan?"

"Ain't sayin'. But we've been helping you all along."

"Helping us?" Vivian scoffed. "You nearly got us killed, dumping us off on the Proons like that!"

"Oh? And who do you think sent you all the nifty equipment and parts and stuff so you could get your silly toy spaceship to work right in the first place?"

"You did?" Dr. D. asked.

"Natch," Krillman said.

"But which race do you represent?"

"I'll let you figure it out."

"Okay, but why are you dumping us here? Why won't you get us back to Earth? You know its location. That stuff about taking years to find it was all bilge."

"Yeah, we were pulling the old sheep fuzz over your eyes. We had to stall you some way. We can't let you go back to Earth with all this fancy technology. Not just yet anyway."

"Why not?"

"We have our reasons," Krillman said, playing a soft tune on his ersatz Stradivarius.

"And you won't tell us whether you're an Asperan or a Dharvan?"

Krillman thought about it as he played. "Nah."

"Great. Well, what do we do now?"

"That's up to you guys," Krillman said. "You got a planet down there that's not a lot different from Earth. Got air, water. Well, not a lot of water. Most of it dried up. But there's food and everything." Krillman took the violin from his chin. "Well, not really food. There's animals you can hunt, and that sort of thing."

"So, let me get this straight," Dr. Demopoulos said. "You're ditching us here, abandoning us."

"You'll still have your ship."

"But we have absolutely no idea of how to get home."

"If you can figure out a way to get there, you're free to go. But we ain't gonna help ya. You've helped us advance our interests in the universe. You've been a handy tool. But we got no further use for you at the moment. Maybe later on."

"He must be a Dharvan," Diane said. "The Asperans wouldn't ditch us like this."

"But we still have a working spacetime ship," Dr. Demopoulos said. "We don't have to stay here."

"Right," Krillman said. "But you got no way of navigatin' your way around. You're lost. You better stay put for the time being. You could go bopping around the universe forever without ever finding another planet as good as this one."

"You call that a planet?" Dr. D. said. "That's a wasteland down there!"

"It's the best we could do on short notice," Krillman said apologetically. "Well, folks, for my last number, I'd like to—"

*"Let's get him!"* Vivian screamed.

Diane, Troy, and Wussman followed Dr. Vernon's lead. They lunged as one, trying to get their hands on Krillman's pudgy body.

"Whoa! I gotta talk to my agent!"

Krillman promptly disappeared, leaving the humans grasping at air.

"That *rat*!" Diane said.

Vivian picked herself off the floor. "He's not a rat. He's a mouse going to rat night school."

"Forget him, kids," Dr. D. said, returning to the control panel and seating himself. "What should we do now? Try another random jump? Keep spinning the wheel until we come up winners?"

"You mean find Earth that way?" Diane asked. "It'd take forever."

"Very possibly. Well, let's take a vote. All in favor of landing on this dirtball—this 'planet,' if you can call it that—say 'Aye.' "

No one said a thing.

"Okay, it's unanimous," Dr. D. said, his finger poised above a button. "We spin the wheel again . . ."

"Uh-oh," Troy said.

Red lights were blinking all over the control panels.

"Massive systems failure," Dr. D. said calmly. "Looks like we have no choice but to try a landing."

"How?" Vivian Vernon said fearfully. "Have you ever landed anything in your life?"

"A ten-pound bass, once."

"Oh, my God."

"Not to worry, Viv. The ship's antigravity functions still seem, uh, functional. I think."

"But you've never had any experience piloting this crate as a spaceship, or an aircraft, or . . . or anything!"

"There's much to be said for on-the-job training," the physics professor said.

"We're all going to die."

"Eventually."


The dun-colored planet loomed ever larger in the viewport. All hands had strapped into their seats, Demopoulos and Diane in the pilot's and copilot's seats, respectively.

The planet became a world as the craft approached,

its curvature flattening. Above, the stars were washing out, growing dim and milky.

"Trim the electrostatic stabilizers," Dr. D. commanded.

"Where?"

"Those thingees."

"Oh."

"You're the copilot! You should know every single control and instrument on this board."

"Hull temperature rising," Diane said.

"Huh? Where?"

"Right there," Diane said, pointing. "Don't you know where the hull temperature gauge is?"

"No, I never looked at it before. Why is the temperature going up?"

"We must have entered the atmosphere," Diane said.

"Of course! What's our speed?"

"Terrific," Diane said. "Something like Mach 15."

"Yeow!" Dr. D. began snapping switches all over. "We'll burn up, just like a meteor! We gotta slow down."

"Speed decreasing," Diane said. "Mach 14, Mach 13, Mach 12 . . ."

"More, gotta slow down more."

"We're all doing to die," Vivian moaned.

"It's been my fervent hope that we could one day die together, my darling," Geoffrey Wussman said, taking Vivian's hand.

*"Bugger off and die by yourself, you little toad!"*

"Don't reject me now, darling, at a time like this," Wussman pleaded.

*"Screw you, weasel!"*

"Charming couple," Dr. Demopoulos commented.

"Antigravity malfunctioning!" Diane shouted.

"Uh-oh," Troy Talbot said.

Dr. D. turned to Talbot and snapped, "Is that all you have to contribute? 'Uh-oh'? You know, we're pretty much okay in the uh-oh department. Everyone here can uh-oh just about as good as you can.''

"Doc, I'm sorry, but I think it's curtains for us.''

Vivian Vernon screamed, "I'm too young to die!''

"I'm with you, my love!''

*"Shut the hell up, you odious little worm!"*

"Vivian, you know you love me.''

*"Yuck! Ptooey! Pttttthhhhhhhhhh! I loathe you, I despise you, you make me sick!"*

"Denial, just denial.''

"What's our altitude?''

Diane reported, "Forty thousand feet now. Dr. D., we're slowing down, but we're dropping like a rock.''

Demopoulos continued frantically trying to control the craft, which had now begun to buffet. A high-pitched howling sounded through the hull.

The planet's surface came up fast. The terrain was arid, bleak, and mostly flat, barring the odd range of craggy mountains or the stub of an eroded butte or two.

"Brace yourselves!'' Demopoulos cried.

"Demopoulos, if we die, I'll kill you!'' Dr. Vernon howled.

"Uh-oh,'' Dr. D. said.

Every light on the instrument panel began flashing red.

"Did he say uh-oh?'' Vivian asked Wussman.

"He did. He said, 'Uh-oh.' ''

"Twenty thousand feet . . . fifteen . . . twelve . . . ten . . . nine thousand . . .''

"Folks, I'm sorry, but it looks like we're going to crash,'' said Dr. Delmore Demetrios Dunhill Demopoulos.

"AIEEEEEEEEEEEEEEEEEEEEEEEEEEEEEEEE-EE!!!!'' said Dr. Vivian Vernon, Ph.D., late of Flitheimer University.

"AIEEEEEEEEEEEEEEEEEEEEEEEEEEEEEEEEE-

EE!!!!'' said the curvaceous and toothsome Diane Derry.

''AIEEEEEEEEEEEEEEEEEEEEEEEEEEEEEEEE-EEEEEEEEEEEEEEEEEEEEEEEEEEEEEEEEEEEEE-EEEEEEEEEEEEEEEEEEEEEEEEEEEEEEEEEEEEE-EEEEEE!!!!!!!!'' said Troy Talbot and Dr. Geoffrey Wussman, Ph.D., in unison. (They were *very* afraid.)

''I hope that was cathartic for all of you,'' said Dr. D. ''Actually, we're going to hit the ground at a mere one hundred feet per second. It will be a calculated, controlled crash. Whoops. Make that two hundred feet per second. No, two-fifty. Oh, hell . . .''

''We'll make it!'' Troy Talbot yelled. ''Don't give up hope, Dr. Demopoulos!!!''

The professor turned to his assistant with a strange look. Something dim and distant was in his eye. ''Don't call me that anymore. From now on, I will be known as . . .''

''What?'' everyone chorused.

''Dr. Universe! No. Dr. . . . Quantum! No, that's no good.''

*''What the hell does it matter, you insane fool?!!''* (This from the nearly psychotic Vivian Vernon.)

Dr. D. thumped the control panel with his fist. ''I know! I will be called . . . Dr. Dimension!!!!!''

Troy asked, ''Why?''

At that moment, the impact came.

## TO BE CONTINUED
## IN OUR NEXT
## THRILLING INSTALLMENT!!!!!

**ROC** ∅ (0451)

# FANTASY AND SCIENCE FICTION FROM SIGNET AND ROC

☐ **SURFING SAMURAI ROBOTS by Mel Gilden.** This first case of Zoot Marlowe's Earthly career would see him taking on everything from the Malibu cops to Samurai robots, motorcycle madmen to talking gorillas, and a misplaced mistress of genetic manipulation. (451007—$4.50)

☐ **TUBULAR ANDROID SUPERHEROES by Mel Gilden.** Nothing can throw Zoot Marlowe off the trail of his kidnapped surfer buddies....

(451163—$4.50)

☐ **THE MAGIC BOOKS by Andre Norton.** Three magical excursions into spells cast and enchantments broken, by a wizard of science fiction and fantasy: *Steel Magic, Octagon Magic,* and *Fur Magic.*

(166388—$4.95)

☐ **BLUE MOON RISING by Simon Green.** The dragon that Prince Rupert was sent out to slay turned out to be a better friend than anyone at the castle. And with the Darkwood suddenly spreading its evil, with the blue moon rising and the Wild Magic along with it, Rupert was going to need all the friends he could get.... (450957—$4.99)

Prices slightly higher in Canada.

---

Buy them at your local bookstore or use this convenient coupon for ordering.

**NEW AMERICAN LIBRARY**
P.O. Box 999 – Dept. #17109
Bergenfield, New Jersey 07621

Please send me the books I have checked above.
I am enclosing $_____ (please add $2.00 to cover postage and handling).
Send check or money order (no cash or C.O.D.'s) or charge by Mastercard or
VISA (with a $15.00 minimum). Prices and numbers are subject to change without
notice.

Card #_____ Exp. Date _____
Signature_____
Name_____
Address_____
City _____ State _____ Zip Code _____

For faster service when ordering by credit card call **1-800-253-6476**

Allow a minimum of 4-6 weeks for delivery. This offer is subject to change without notice.

If you and/or a friend would like to receive the *ROC Advance*, a bimonthly newsletter featuring all the newest and hottest ROC books and authors, on a complimentary basis, please fill out this form and return it to:

**ROC Books/Penguin USA**
375 Hudson Street
New York, NY 10014

Your Address
Name _____
Street _____ Apt. # _____
City _____ State _____ Zip _____

Friend's Address
Name _____
Street _____ Apt. # _____
City _____ State _____ Zip _____